Waves

by Bei Dao

POETRY

The August Sleepwalker, 1990

translated by Bonnie S. McDougall

SHORT STORIES

Waves, 1990

translated by Bonnie S. McDougall
and Susette Ternent Cooke

Waves

Stories by

Bei Dao

Edited with an introduction by
Bonnie S. McDougall

Translated by
Bonnie S. McDougall and Susette Ternent Cooke

A New Directions Book

Copyright © The Chinese University of Hong Kong, 1985, 1986

All rights reserved. Except for brief passages quoted in a newspaper, magazine, radio, or television review, no part of this book may be reproduced in any form or by any means, electronic or mechanical, including photocopying and recording, or by any information storage or retrieval system, without permission in writing from the Publisher.

Translators' Note: "Waves" is translated by Susette Ternent Cooke and Bonnie S. McDougall; "In the Ruins" and "The Homecoming Stranger" are translated by Susette Ternent Cooke with the assistance of Bonnie S. McDougall; "Melody," "Moon on the Manuscript," "Intersection," and "13 Happiness Street" are translated by Bonnie S. McDougall. The translators gratefully acknowledge the assistance of Chen Maiping, Leonella Liu, John Minford, and Zhu Zhiyu.

Published by arrangement with William Heinemann Ltd. London
Manufactured in the United States of America
New Directions Books are published on acid-free paper.
First published clothbound and as New Directions Paperbook 693 in 1990
Published simultaneously in Canada by Penguin Books Canada Limited

Library of Congress Cataloging-in-Publication Data
Pei-tao, 1949– [Po tung. English]
Waves : stories / by Bei Dao ; edited with an introduction by Bonnie S. McDougall and Susette Ternent Cooke.
p. cm.
Translation of: Po tung.
Includes bibliographical references (p.)
ISBN 0-8112-1133-9 (hard : alk. paper).—ISBN 0-8112-1134-7(pbk. : alk. paper)
I. McDougall, Bonnie S., 1941– . II. Cooke, Susette Ternent. III. Title.
PL2892.E525P45 1990
895.1'.352—dc20 89-13346
CIP

New Directions Books are published for James Laughlin
by New Directions Publishing Corporation,
80 Eighth Avenue, New York 10011

Contents

"Poets should establish through their works a world of their own, a genuine and independent world, an upright world, a world of justice and humanity."

Bei Dao

Introduction

Love, Truth, and Communication in Contemporary Chinese Fiction: The Case of Bei Dao

Undistorted by propaganda or self-righteousness, the stories in this collection offer an unusually honest depiction of contemporary Chinese society by a native-born writer, and at the same time represent some of the finest writing to come out of China since the '40s. Products of a democratic movement which challenged both the misrule of the Cultural Revolution and the reformist government that followed, they are critical studies of a society where ordinary human needs and wants are thwarted by design or neglect. Through the lives of intellectuals, factory workers, drifters, and criminals, the author shows the distortion of human feelings and relationships under the stress of such an environment. The cynicism and despair that characterize his protagonists, especially the women, are nevertheless not seen as an inevitable feature of the human condition: instincts for love, friendship, courage, and creativity persist. The existential anguish that marks his characters off from the orthodox ensures their loneliness but also their unique identities.

Bei Dao is the pen name of the author Zhao Zhenkai, born in Beijing in 1949 to a family originally from the south. Educated at one of the country's best schools, he seemed destined to take his place among the bureaucrats and intellectuals that ran the New China in the '50s and early '60s, leading comfortable lives and duly grateful for it. The Cultural Revolution, which broke out when he was only sixteen, seemed to put an end to such a future. Interrupting his schooling, it cut short the education in orthodoxy that had been the primary influence on the previous generation. Exposing the corruption and special privileges of politicians, bureaucrats, and senior intellectuals, it awakened a new sense of idealism among the young, a desire for greater social justice in a postrevolutionary society. Hauling down aging rulers and their protégés from their ruling positions, it promised also rapid access to freedom and power for the new generation. But before too long, it became apparent that the violent upheavals of the late '60s were leading only to new kinds of tyranny in the early '70s, where intermittent campaigns in the struggle between Leninists and populists perhaps put an even greater pressure on society than the open brutality of the earlier period.

Disillusioned by the violence and factionalism of the political struggle, Bei Dao turned to literature to express his desires and frustrations. His most personal thoughts were cast into verse, creating poems which made him a nationally known figure by the end of the decade. Embodying his search for meaning in life, they spoke for a whole generation of young readers, his first, largest, and most faithful audience. His poetry also won the respect of an older group of writers and academics candid enough to admit their artistic achievement. Not wholly satisfied with his early lyric verse, Bei Dao also tried his hand at a more objective medium. His first major work of fiction was the novella "Waves," of which the first draft was completed in November 1974. Written at a particularly confused period in the late Cultural Revolution, it was one of the first works to portray the complex new world of disillusion, betrayal, and despair. Given the clandestine nature of its origins and the youth and inexperience of its author, "Waves" is a remarkably mature work of considerable philosophic depth and artistic inventiveness. Instead of seeking refuge in dreams or seclusion as in his poetry, the author here confronts the society around him with cool sympathy. Avoiding autobiography but basing himself on the lives of the people he knew, the author analyzes the moods and impulses of a group of drifters who represent China's "lost generation." (Critics have commented on the parallels between Hemingway's postwar generation and Bei Dao's Cultural Revolution youth.) Embittered but still half-unconsciously searching for communication through truth and for regeneration through love, the characters in "Waves" nevertheless fail to break through the constraints imposed on them by the forces of orthodoxy and its victims.

Despite the achievement of "Waves," Bei Dao did not immediately follow up with more fiction. Working as a laborer for a Beijing construction company and living in a workers' dormitory in the western suburbs of Beijing, he had little time or privacy for sustained periods of concentration. Dramatic changes in the political situation also claimed his attention. After the death of Premier Zhou Enlai in January 1976, the factional struggles among the top leadership became more intense, and the populists headed by Jiang Qing were gaining ground. In a show of anger and dissatisfaction, Beijing residents turned out in vast numbers at Tiananmen Square on the days leading up to Qingming ("pure and bright"), the traditional time of mourning in China. That year, Qingming fell on April 5, and the protest movement that culminated on that day was subsequently dubbed the April Fifth movement. The mourners were brutally dispersed by the police and militia, and the commemorative poems, speeches, and gathering itself were declared counterrevolutionary acts. Bei Dao was among the participants, and his most famous poem dates from this event:

> I don't believe the sky is blue,
> I don't believe in the sound of thunder,
> I don't believe that dreams are false,
> I don't believe that death has no revenge . . .

He also made substantial revisions to "Waves" that June, but afterward, in part because of a sudden family tragedy and in part also because of the increased political repression, he temporarily stopped writing.

Mao Zedong's death in September that year signaled the end of the populists. Jiang Qing and her supporters, execrated throughout the country as the "gang of four," were arrested and incarcerated. Normality, in fits and starts, was gradually restored to political, social, and family life. People were released from jail or allowed to return from banishment, and the old leaders from the '50s and '60s returned to office. In an almost universal reaction to the repression exercised over all realms of the intellect by the "gang of four," even the old Leninists and Stalinists of the '50s endorsed the new slogan, "Emancipate the mind!" The April Fifth activists, with renewed courage and hope, demanded fundamental changes in the country's basic polity, taking their case to the streets in Beijing and other big cities. Manifestoes and magazines calling for a variety of political and social reforms were published unofficially but openly in the second half of 1978. Short stories exposing the horrors of the recent past and poems in praise of liberty and democracy were also prominently featured in the publications of the Democratic Movement (as it was popularly known), but most exhibited the same stridency and melodrama as the official product. An exception was the work in *Today*, edited by Bei Dao and his friend and fellow-poet, Mang Ke. *Today* was part of the Democratic Movement and supported its aims, but its own role was to publish a significantly new kind of literature.

The chance to publish openly brought forth a new burst of writing from Bei Dao. His first stories after "Waves"—"In the Ruins" and "The Homecoming Stranger"—were written expressly for the first and second issues of *Today*, and "Waves" itself was revised again for publication. "In the Ruins" and "The Homecoming Stranger" are set during the Cultural Revolution and in the period of adjustment that followed. Unlike most unofficial writing, they are not so much concerned with exposing the past as exploring the problems of the present: the search for truth in human relationships and in personal identities that had been twisted almost out of recognition.

The Democratic Movement and its publications were permitted by the new authorities to flourish only briefly. The first arrests of the movement's leading activists took place at the beginning of 1979. By mid-1979, many of the unofficial publications had been forced to close down, and Democracy Wall, the center of the movement in Beijing, was declared out of bounds in November. *Today*, as a literary magazine, managed to survive until September 1980. Although the proscription of *Today* was a severe blow to the newly emergent writers, it was not a fatal one. Some of the new literature had already found its way into the multitude of new periodicals that were springing up all over the country. Bei Dao's next two stories, "Melody" and "Moon on the Manuscript," made the transition from unofficial to official in a matter of months, and a third, "Intersection," made its first appearance in the official press.

"Melody" is set at a time when memories of the Cultural Revolution and its overthrow were receding into the past, and its main characters are preoccupied by problems that dated back much earlier: the neglect of basic living conditions and the indifference of bureaucrats. The heroine of "Melody" resembles one of the characters in "Waves," now older, married and working, but although her social environment is more stable, the human problems remain. She is still an individual in crisis, dimly conscious that life should be more honest, natural, and fulfilling than it is, but unable to express or even formulate to herself a truth so much at variance with present reality. All of Bei Dao's stories are about communication and its difficulties, but in "Moon on the Manuscript" and "Intersection" this theme takes on an even sharper focus. "Moon on the Manuscript" tackles the problem of writer's block, the first story ever in Chinese literature to do so; "Intersection" is one of the first attempts since 1949 to treat class antagonism in a realistic fashion. The people in these short stories are not confronted with major disasters that threaten basic safety or survival. It is a question of the quality of their lives as they face the daily routine hemmed in by forces that seem to block them at every turn. Even more, it is a question of their ability to sustain their insights, imperfect and incommunicable as they are, into the truths of their lonely existence.

As the distance from the Cultural Revolution grew, China's new leaders, especially at the middle levels, began to turn toward a new orthodoxy as a means of bringing stability and order to the chaos around them. They also came to resent the disaffection and disillusion that possessed creative writers and young people. From late 1981 to early 1984, the Democratic Movement writers were increasingly denied access to the mainstream national press. Bei Dao's stories voice no stronger criticism of the society around him than does the Party now in the media under its control. But because Bei Dao does not automatically express faith in the Party's ability to lead China toward a better future, but rather places his faith in art and in ordinary human instincts, his stories implicitly assert an autonomy both for literature and the individual. Since the end of the 1983–1984 campaign against "spiritual pollution," the call for the emancipation of the mind has been heard again. Bei Dao, granted the recognition he deserves as a writer of international stature, may yet become a symbol of national pride and unity.

Bonnie S. McDougall
Beijing, July 1984

Preface

To most observers, China in the 1980s promised a new future of economic progress, political reform, and cultural enlightenment. The brutal suppression of the students' democratic movement in 1989 showed the promise to be an illusion. Bei Dao was one of the very small group of Chinese writers and artists who did not believe in the promise, who did not trust in the illusion.

The stories in this collection, written in the late '70s and early '80s, show how little had changed in the quality of people's inner lives since the Cultural Revolution of 1966–76, despite the tremendous surface improvements in Chinese society. Material prosperity, though not to be despised, highlighted the barrenness of an alienated existence; relaxation of political controls, welcome as it was, did not disguise the ultimately repressive nature of the régime. "13 Happiness Street," with its grimly sardonic title, relates the reality behind the illusion: disturb even accidentally the centers of power, and you too will end up behind the anonymous walls of a lunatic asylum.

In February 1989, Bei Dao and an associate organized a petition of thirty-three prominent Chinese literary intellectuals to protest against the continued incarceration of one of the leaders of the 1978 Democratic Movement, Wei Jingsheng. Some of those who signed the petition are now believed to be under detention; several of them, including Bei Dao himself, are in involuntary exile abroad. But the hope and courage of the

Tiananmen students and their supporters will not be forgotten. Bei Dao and his fellow-editors are reviving *Today*, their literary magazine from the Democracy Wall of '78. A new age of Chinese culture in exile is about to begin.

Bonnie S. McDougall
Oslo, October 1989

In the Ruins

Two hours had passed.

It was autumn, but the fields were a picture of bleak desolation. A few sparrows perched on the overhead lines, crying endlessly from an old abandoned shed; the sound seemed unduly loud and clear under the cloudless sky.

He looked at his watch again. He really did not understand what he was expecting himself. It was as if he still hadn't freed himself from the mechanical concept of time that professors had; the empty echo, the dust on the bookshelves, and the mist-wrapped lamplight were still waiting for him. Yes, past time had slipped by in his hands like an old monk's rosary beads, rubbed bright and shiny. And now, what meaning had time for him?

"Wang Qi, old-line British spy and reactionary authority, report to the organ of mass dictatorship tomorrow morning at eight o'clock, pending criticism and denunciation. This order must be promptly obeyed!"

In fact, when he saw the order, he was extremely calm, as calm as a bystander, horribly calm. At the time, digging out a bit of broken brick with the tip of his shoe, his arms folded together, he had stood firmly before the red paper, reading it carefully several times over. The handwriting was not bad, but one could tell it had been written by a young man. Over his name was a yellow cross. He inwardly congratulated himself that the characters of his name had not been written upside down—as far as he was concerned, that was the most extreme form of insulting behavior.

He groped for a cigarette, and again his hand touched the photograph of his daughter as a child which he had hurriedly taken from the photo album just as he was leaving home. His daughter had left home almost two months ago; after formally denouncing her relationship with her father, she had moved to live at school in the city. At mealtimes, he laid bowl and chopsticks as usual in the empty place; he would not allow anyone to sweep his daughter's room, but would shut himself inside and stare blankly . . . he did not know why, but since his daughter left, he could not recall the likeness of her laughing face. It troubled him so much that he would spend the whole night lost in unhappy thought, often getting up during the night to open the photo album. But as soon as he closed it, the impression would disappear immediately. And trivial events from her childhood spun in his brain throughout the night. Some of the details were so distinct, he even wondered whether they were not the result of his own fabrication. Look, the smile that filled her slight dimples was offset by the puzzled frown between her eyebrows, as if she already had a premonition of misfortune in her young soul.

"Papa, I won't have my picture taken with a doll."

"Why not?"

"I'm grown-up now."

"Then have one with Papa."

"No, your mustache prickles me, I want one by myself."

He put the photograph back in his pocket, lit a cigarette, and sat down on a dry bank at the side of the road. The irrigation water and time had flowed past here together, carrying mayflies, grass and leaves, perhaps even a few carefree little fish. Everything would pass. Sometimes, people's choices could be terribly simple; there could be no regrets because of haste or avoidance because of fear.

He closed his eyes: a strong light focused on the balding crown of his head, the coldly gleaming lead wire engraved itself into his neck, the black dumbell at the end of the wire rocked back and forth. Behind were rows of faces shining with excitement and a crimson curtain as bright as if it were dripping with blood. . . . At the time he saw everything too clearly, never moving his eyes away although his whole body was trembling; he thought he saw his own end in the body of this old friend. Yes, he understood too well his old fellow-student from Cambridge. The death that night of this hefty six-footer, who had once been a sensation as a university softball star, was not because of physical torture, but because of shame, grief, and indignation. It was then he learned to understand everything completely, it was only through learning to understand that one truly experienced things personally. The light roasted the top of his own head, the lead wire was engraved in his own throat, the large beads of sweat streaked with blood dripped down his own face. . . . He had already died once, ten times, a hundred times! He believed that if he could choose to live again, his old friend would die with dignity, without compromise.

For two weeks the spotlight kept pursuing him. He hid, he ran, until he was completely exhausted. What was the use? The light fell on his head in the end. He looked up, gazing at the sun, gazing in that dazzling direction until his eyes, smarting with pain, shed tears.

He wrapped his windbreaker tightly around him and walked on again. This time, he felt a sudden pity for that boy who'd written the order. He couldn't have been more than twenty. Ah, so young, his life had just begun. He would regret it. Perhaps, waking in the dark from a nightmare, the shifting lights and shadows on the ceiling would arouse associations with the past; perhaps it would come from an individual's unhappiness, his eyes blurred by tears beside a friend's coffin; perhaps after he kisses his girlfriend for the first time, the passionate, meaningless low murmuring would suddenly break off, and the emptiness that follows needs certain genuine sentiments to fill it . . . what would the boy say then? Lord, even if such a time would come, he could console himself and the girl by his side: "At that time, I was still young."

"When Papa gets old, you should get married too."

"Stop it, I won't, I'll stay with you for the rest of my life."

"What if Papa dies?"

"You're just saying silly things!"

"Dear girl, Papa's only teasing."

His eyes were moist with tears. Already, at this very moment, he couldn't distinguish the limits of imagination and reality clearly, nor did he care about the reliability of memory. He only hoped that her tender expression and voice would reappear, allowing him to savor a certain kind of delight amidst the numbness.

On a secluded little path in the university grounds just now he had bumped into Wu Mengran, the head of the history department, sweeping up fallen leaves. This time he didn't make a detour but walked straight on. Wu Mengran hung his head, strenuously wielding the big broom. Two deep, intersecting furrows had been shaven through the white hair he had once been so proud of, and now it was uncombed and full of dust, like a handful of withered grass covered with hoarfrost. Seeing him coming, Wu Mengran hesitated a moment, pulling his eyes away from the toes of his shoes.

"You?" Wu Mengran looked up and down nervously. "You'd better keep away!"

"You and I will be the same tomorrow."

"That's impossible, you've been earmarked as a key object for protection."

"Protection? You're a Harvard Ph.D."

Wu Mengran forced a smile. As in the past he brought up his hand majestically to smooth his white hair, but as soon as he touched the furrows on the top of his head he involuntarily withdrew his hand.

"Our problem will be clarified eventually," Wu Mengran said.

"Perhaps."

"Where are you going?"

"Going?" he responded like an echo and walked off. After walking some distance, he turned his head and saw Wu Mengran still standing there, holding the broom like an old soldier dragging a gun.

He climbed a slope, not thinking about where he was going. The side of the slope facing the sun was warm and sunny, tall straight little poplars clustered around him. Climbing to the top of the slope, he felt a little tired. He felt in his pocket for his handkerchief, but drew out a piece of rope. What, had he come to hang himself? Death: he repeated the unfamiliar and well-known word in several different ways until it lost all meaning, leaving only an empty sound. A blue mist wavered before his eyes, the whole sky wavered for a moment and he clutched at a small sapling beside him.

. . . The first time he met Jie was at the school reunion dance. The dim wall-lights spun round, casting long shadows; the brass instruments in the orchestra-pit gleamed, the conductor's slender shadow alternating on the wall, the waving baton extending to the ceiling. He felt Jie's breath brush his face, and under her half-closed eyelids gleamed an elusive light.

A sound of wings beating the treetops. In the twinkling of an eye twenty years passed, and his daughter had grown up, as pretty as her mother in those years. He couldn't help his fist touching the photograph in his coat pocket.

"Papa, do you like Mama?"

"Yes."

"Mama likes crying."

"We all have our weak moments."

"I don't like crying."

"You haven't reached the time for crying yet."

"Even then I won't cry."

No, child, you will cry. Tears will soak a person's conscience, tears will ease the weight of suffering and let one's life become a little more relaxed.

A light breeze drifted past, and he breathed in a deep mouthful. Blending all the flavors of autumn, it dispelled some of the painful bitterness in his breast. He raised his head and stared in surprise: opposite, on the hillock opposite, was a group of stone ruins—the Yuanmingyuan. He didn't understand how he had got here. It had been a completely unconscious act. No, he remembered someone saying that consciousness existed in the midst of unconsciousness. Probably it was true that a kind of summons from the unseen world had drawn him there in spite of himself.

He walked toward the ruins.

The sun, which had lost its warmth, had already sunk behind the jagged edge of the distant hills. In no time, it would disappear to finish the other half of its journey. Amidst the rubble, an ancient Roman-style archway stood tall and upright, its huge shadow lost in the rustling weeds.

Standing before him was China's history, the history of the last decades, or even of the last centuries or millennia. The endless arrogance and revolt, dissipation and vice; the rivers of blood and mountains of bones; the sumptuous yet desolate cities, palaces, and tombs; the thousands upon thousands of horses and soldiers mirrored against the huge canopy of the heavens; the ax on the execution block, dripping with blood; the sundial with its shadow revolving around the glossy stone slab; the thread-bound hand-copied books piled in dusty secret rooms; the long, mournful sound of the night watchman beating his wooden rattle . . . all these together formed these desolate ruins. However, history would not stop at this scene of ruin, no, it would not, it would proceed from here, and go on into the wide world.

He touched the cooling stone pillar. Finished, he thought, this once-illustrious palace, which had been the celebration of an age, had collapsed, and once it had collapsed, it was no more than so many pieces of stone. And he himself was just a little stone among them. There was nothing to be lamented; in the midst of a people's deep suffering, individuals were negligible.

He gazed sentimentally at the distant hills. Goodbye, sun, but I hope that tomorrow you shine on a different world. A pity I won't see it, it doesn't matter, I'll die, but my books will live, they haven't paled into insignificance through years of criticism; on the contrary, they have proved even more that they are worth surviving. As long as one's thoughts are spoken and written down, they'll form another life, they won't perish with the flesh.

He thought again of the autumns of those years, the autumn of his prime, the autumn of richly blossoming chrysanthemums on his desk, the autumn of the bowknot dancing in his daughter's pretty hair.

"Papa, some people say you're bad, is it true?"

"Yes."

"Why?"

"Because I speak the truth."

"You can't tell lies?"

"No."

"Suppose you don't speak?"

"Only when I'm dead, silly child."

He walked down the hillside. In a clearing, a red-gold smoke tree soughed in the wind. A little pool of rainwater reflected his changed shadow and the azure sky. He lit a cigarette. His hand, a hand covered with blue veins, calmly shielded the flame, then this movement suddenly seemed to stop, come to a standstill. Time congealed, and everything around him lay still on the glassy smooth water. The wind dropped, the leaves made no sound, and even the birds' wings came to rest in the air. At length, the match fell into the pool, giving off a little stream of white smoke. Time began to flow again, and everything returned to its original state. He now felt a kind of calmness he had never experienced before.

He drew the rope from his pocket, skillfully tied a sailor's knot (he had learned this the year he went to London, when he had been a temporary deckhand on the packet-boat *Victoria*) and threw one end of the rope toward the fork of the tree. His action was as deft as if he had been doing this all his life.

Everything was set. He breathed a sigh of relief, walked to one side, and lit his extinguished cigarette again. Suddenly he gave a start, almost dropping his cigarette. Not far away, in the clump of trees opposite, stood a little peasant girl, staring at him curiously. Beside her was a wicker basket filled with grass.

"Hello," he said tentatively.

The little girl didn't move, but stood there unflinchingly.

"What are you doing here?"

"Cutting grass."

He walked a little closer. "What's your name?"

"Erya."

"How old are you?"

"Eight."

"Do you go to school?"

"No, Ma says that it's all a mess now, maybe next year."

"Your home's near here?"

"Over there," she pointed a grubby finger in the direction east of the woods. "Across the vegetable patch."

"You're cutting grass for the goats?"

"For the rabbits. They're so crafty, they prefer this grass here." She rubbed her nose with her little fist, raised her head and gazed at the noose. "Uncle, what are you catching?"

He smiled grimly.

"Are you catching birds?"

"Yes, I'm catching an old bird."

"Old—bird—" she repeated in a singsong. "There are owls near here, their call makes my flesh creep."

"Hurry back home, your Papa's waiting for you."

"My Pa's dead," she said expressionlessly. "Last month, on the sixth, he was tied up and beaten to death by Erleng, Shuanzhu, and the others from the north end of the village."

"Why?"

"My Pa stole some of the brigade's watermelons."

He went over, clasped the child in his arms, and impulsively pressed his face against the little girl's startled face, big teardrops starting from his eyes. This was the first time in many years that he'd shed tears. The little girl gave a cry of alarm, kicked and struggled to free herself, and plunged deep into the woods.

Night fell. In the darkness, the outline of the ruins could still be distinguished clearly. He sat on a piece of stone for a long time, then stood up and silently went away.

The noose swayed in the wind.

The Homecoming Stranger

1

Papa was back.

After exactly twenty years of reform through labor, which took him from the Northeast to Shanxi, and then from Shanxi to Gansu, he was just like a sailor swept overboard by a wave, struggling blindly against the undertow until miraculously he is tossed by another wave back onto the same deck.

The verdict was: it was entirely a misjudgment, and he has been granted complete rehabilitation. That day, when the leaders of the Theater Association honored our humble home to announce the decision, I almost jumped up: when did you become so clever? Didn't the announcement that he was an offender against the people come out of your mouths too? It was Mama's eyes, those calm yet suffering eyes, that stopped me.

Next came the dress rehearsal for the celebration: we moved from a tiny pigeon loft into a three-bedroom apartment in a big building; sofas, bookcases, desks, and chrome folding chairs appeared as if by magic (I kept saying half-jokingly to Mama that these were the troupe's props); relatives and friends came running in and out all day, until the lacquer doorknob was rubbed shiny by their hands, and even those uncles and aunts who hadn't shown up all those years rushed to offer congratulations . . . all right, cheer, sing, but what does all this have to do with me? My Papa died a long time ago, he died twenty years ago, just when a little four- or five-year old girl needed a father's love—that's what Mama, the school, kindhearted souls, and the whole social upbringing that starts at birth told me. Not only this, you even wanted me to hate him, curse him, it's even possible you'd have given me a whip so I could lash him viciously! Now it's the other way round, you're wearing a different face. What do you want me to do? Cry or laugh?

Yesterday at dinner time, Mama was even more considerate than usual, endlessly filling my bowl with food. After the meal, she drew a telegram from the drawer and handed it to me, showing not the slightest sign of any emotion.

"Him?"

"He arrives tomorrow, at 4:50 in the afternoon."

I crumpled the telegram, staring numbly into Mama's eyes.

"Go and meet him, Lanlan." She avoided my gaze.

"I have a class tomorrow afternoon."

"Get someone to take it for you."

I turned toward my room. "I won't go."

"Lanlan." Mama raised her voice. "He is your father, after all!"

"Father?" I muttered, turning away fiercely, as if overcome with fear at the meaning of this word. From an irregular spasm in my heart, I realized it was stitches from the old wound splitting open one by one.

I closed the composition book spread in front of me: Zhang Xiaoxia, 2nd Class, 5th Year. A spirited girl, her head always slightly to one side in a challenging way, just like me as a child. Oh yes, childhood. For all of us life begins with those pale blue copybooks, with those words, sentences, and punctuation marks smudged by erasers; or, to put it more precisely, it begins with a certain degree of deception. The teachers delineated life with halos, but which of them does not turn into a smoke ring or an iron hoop?

Shadows flowed in from the long old-fashioned windows, dulling the bright light on the glass desktop. The entire staffroom was steeped in drowsy tranquillity. I sighed, tidied my things, locked the door, and crossing the deserted school grounds walked toward home.

The apartment block with its glittering lights was like a huge television screen, the unlit windows composing an elusive image. After a little while some of the windows lit up, and some went dark again. But the three windows on the seventh floor remained as they were: one bright, two dark. I paced up and down for a long time in the vacant lot piled with white lime and fir poles. On a crooked, broken signboard were the words: "Safety First."

Strange, why is it that in all the world's languages, this particular meaning comes out as the same sound: Papa. Fathers of different colors, temperaments, and status all derive the same satisfaction from this sound. Yet I still can't say it. What do I know about him? Except for a few surviving old photographs retaining a childhood dream (perhaps every little girl would have such dreams): him, sitting on an elephant like an Arab sheik, a white cloth wound round his head, a resplendent mat on the elephant's back, golden tassels dangling to the ground . . . there were only some plays that once created a sensation and a thick book on dramatic theory which I happened to see at the wastepaper salvage station. What else was there? Yes, add those unlucky letters, as punctual and drab as a clock; stuck in those brown paper envelopes with their red frames, they were just like death notices, suffocating me. I never wrote back, and afterward, I threw them into the fire without even looking at them. Once, a dear little duckling was printed on a snow-white envelope, but when I tore it open and looked, I was utterly crushed. I was so upset I cursed all ugly ducklings, counting up their vices one by one: greed, pettiness, slovenliness . . . because they hadn't brought me good luck. But what luck did I deserve?

The elevator had already closed for the day, and I had to climb all the way up. I stopped outside the door to our place and listened, holding my breath. From inside came the sounds of the television hum and the clichés of an old film. God, give me courage!

As soon as I opened the door, I heard my younger brother's gruff voice: "Sis's back." He rushed up as if making an assault on the enemy, helping me take off my coat. He was almost twenty, but still full of a childish attachment to me, probably because I had given him the maternal love which had seemed too heavy a burden for Mama in those years.

The corridor was very dark and the light from the kitchen split the darkness in two. He was standing in the doorway of the room opposite, standing in the other half of darkness, and next to him was Mama. The reflection from the television screen flickered behind their shoulders.

A moment of dead silence.

Finally, he walked over, across the river of light. The light, the deathly white light, slipped swiftly over his wrinkled and mottled neck and face. I was struck dumb: was this shriveled little old man him? Father. I leaned weakly against the door.

He hesitated a moment and put out his hand. My small hand disappeared in his stiff, big-jointed hand. These hands didn't match his body at all.

"Lanlan." His voice was very low, and trembled a little.

Silence.

"Lanlan," he said again, his voice becoming a little more positive, as if he were waiting eagerly for something.

But what could I say?

"You're back very late. Have you had dinner?" said Mama.

"Mm." My voice was so weak.

"Why is everyone standing? Come inside," said Mama.

He took me by the hand. I followed obediently. Mama turned on the light and switched off the television with a click. We sat down on the sofa. He was still clutching my hand tightly, staring at me intently. I evaded his eyes and let my gaze fall on the blowup plastic doll on the windowsill.

An unbearable silence.

"Lanlan," he called once again.

I was really afraid the doll might explode, sending brightly colored fragments flying all over the room.

"Have you had your dinner?"

I nodded vigorously.

"Is it cold outside?"

"No." Everything was so normal, the doll wouldn't burst. Perhaps it would fly away suddenly like a hydrogen balloon, out the window, above the houses full of voices, light, and warmth, and go off to search for the stars and moon.

"Lanlan." His voice was full of compassion and pleading.

All of a sudden, my just-established confidence swiftly collapsed. I felt a spasm of alarm. Blood pounded at my temples. Fiercely I pulled back my hand, rushed out the door into my own room, and flung myself headfirst onto the bed. I really felt like bursting into tears.

The door opened softly; it was Mama. She came up to the bed, sat down in the darkness and stroked my head, neck, and shoulders. Involuntarily, my whole body began to tremble as if with cold.

"Don't cry, Lanlan."

Cry? Mama, if I could still cry the tears would surely be red, they'd be blood.

She patted me on the back. "Go to sleep, Lanlan, everything will pass."

Mama left.

Everything will pass. Huh, it's so easily said, but can twenty years be written off at one stroke? People are not reeds, or leeches, but oysters, and the sands of memory will flow with time to change into a part of the body itself, teardrops will never run dry.

. . . a basement. Mosquitoes thudded against the searing light bulb. An old man covered with cuts and bruises was tied up on the pommel horse, his head bowed, moaning hoarsely. I lay in the corner sobbing. My knees were cut to ribbons by the broken glass; blood and mud mixed together . . .

I was then only about twelve years old. One night, when Mama couldn't sleep, she suddenly hugged me and told me that Papa was a good man who had been wrongly accused. At these words hope flared up in the child's heart: for the first time she might be able to enjoy the same rights as other children. So I ran all around, to the school, the Theater Association, the neighborhood committee, and the Red Guard headquarters, to prove Papa's innocence to them. Disaster was upon us, and those louts took me home savagely for investigation. I didn't know what was wrong with Mama, but she repudiated all her words in front of her daughter. All the blame fell on my small shoulders. Mama repented, begged, wished herself dead, but what was the use? I was struggled against, given heavy labor, and punished by being made to kneel on broken glass.

... the old man raised his bloody face: "Give me some water, water, water!" Staring with frightened eyes, I forgot the pain, huddling tightly into the corner. When dawn came and the old man breathed his last, I fainted with fright too. The blood congealed on my knees ...

Can I blame Mama for this?

2

The sky was so blue it dazzled the eyes, its intense reflections shining on the ground. My hair tied up in a ribbon, I was holding a small empty bamboo basket and standing amidst the dense waist-high grass. Suddenly, from the jungle opposite appeared an elephant, the tassels of the mat on its back dangling to the ground; Papa sat proudly on top, a white turban on his head. The elephant's trunk waved to and fro, and with a snort it curled round me and placed me up in front of Papa. We marched forward, across the coconut grove streaked with leaping sunlight, across the hills and gullies gurgling with springs. I suddenly turned my head and cried out in alarm. A little old man was sitting behind me, his face blurred with blood; he was wearing convict clothes and on his chest were printed the words "Reform Through Labor." He was moaning hoarsely, "Give me some water, water, water ..."

I woke up in fright.

It was five o'clock, and outside it was still dark. I stretched out my hand and pulled out the drawer of the bedside cupboard, fumbled for cigarettes, and lit one. I drew back fiercely and felt more relaxed. The white cloud of smoke spread through the darkness and finally floated out through the small open-shuttered window. The glow from the cigarette alternately brightened and dimmed as I strained to see clearly into the depths of my heart, but other than the ubiquitous silence, the relaxation induced by the cigarette, and the vague emptiness left by the nightmare, there was nothing.

I switched on the desk lamp, put on my clothes, and opened the door quietly. There was a light on in the kitchen and a rustling noise. Who was up so early? Who?

Under the light, wearing a black cotton-padded vest, he was crouching over the wastepaper basket with his back toward me, meticulously picking through everything; spread out beside him were such spoils as vegetable leaves, trimmings, and fish heads.

I coughed.

He jumped and looked round in alarm, his face deathly white, gazing in panic toward me.

The fluorescent light hummed.

He stood up slowly, one hand behind his back, making an effort to smile. "Lanlan, I woke you up."

"What are you doing?"

"Oh, nothing, nothing." He was flustered and kept wiping his trousers with his free hand.

I put out my hand. "Let me see."

After some hesitation he handed the thing over. It was just an ordinary cigarette pack, with nothing odd about it except that it was soiled in one corner.

I lifted my head, staring at him in bewilderment.

"Oh, Lanlan," beads of sweat started from his balding head, "yesterday I forgot to examine this cigarette pack when I threw it away, just in case I wrote something on it; it would be terrible if the team leader saw it."

"Team leader?" I was even more baffled. "Who's the team leader?"

"The people who oversee us prisoners are called team leaders." He fished out a handkerchief and wiped the sweat away. "Of course, I know, it's beyond their reach, but better to find it just in case . . ."

My head began to buzz. "All right, that's enough."

He closed his mouth tightly, as if he had even bitten out his tongue. I really hadn't expected our conversation would begin like this. For the first time I looked carefully at him. He seemed even older and paler than yesterday, with a short grayish stubble over his sunken cheeks, wrinkles that seemed to have been carved by a knife around his lackluster eyes, and an ugly sarcoma on the tip of his right ear. I could not help feeling some compassion for him.

"Was it very hard there?"

"It was all right, you get used to it."

Get used to it! A cold shiver passed through me. Dignity. Wire netting. Guns. Hurried footsteps. Dejected ranks. Death. I crumpled up the cigarette pack and tossed it into the wastepaper basket. "Go back to sleep, it's still early."

"I've had enough sleep, reveille's at 5:30." He turned to tidy up the scattered rubbish.

Back in my room, I pressed my face against the ice-cold wall. It was quite unbearable to begin like this, what should I do next? Wasn't he a man of great integrity before? Ah, Hand of Time, you're so cruel and indifferent, to knead a man like putty, you destroyed him before his daughter could remember her father's real face clearly . . . eventually I calmed down, packed my things into my bag, and put on my overcoat.

Passing through the kitchen, I came to a standstill. He was at the sink, scrubbing his big hands with a small brush, the green soap froth dripping down like sap.

"I'm going to work."

"So early?" He was so absorbed he did not even raise his head.

"I'm used to it."

I did not turn on the light, going down along the darkness, along each flight of stairs.

3

For several days in a row I came home very late. When Mama asked why, I always offered the excuse that I was busy at school. As soon as I got home, I would dodge into the kitchen and hurriedly rake up a few leftovers, then bore straight into my own little nest. I seldom ran into him, and even when we did meet I would hardly say a word. Yet it seemed his silence contained enormous compunction, as if to apologize for that morning, for his unexpected arrival, for my unhappy childhood, these twenty years and my whole life.

My brother was always running in like a spy to report on the situation, saying things like: "He's planted a pot of peculiar dried-up herbs," "All afternoon he stared at the fish in the tank," "He's burned a note again" . . . I would listen without any reaction. As far as I was concerned, it was all just a continuation of that morning, not worth making a fuss about. What was strange was my brother, talking about such things so flatly, not tinged by any emotion at all, not feeling any heavy burden on his mind. It was no wonder; since the day he was born Papa had already flown far away, and besides, in those years he was brought up in his Grandma's home, and with Mama's wings and mine in turn hanging over Grandma's little window as well, he never saw the ominous sky.

One evening, as I was lying on the bed smoking, someone knocked at the door. I hurriedly stuffed the cigarette butt in a small tin box as Mama came in.

"Smoking again, Lanlan?"

As if nothing had happened I turned over the pages of a novel beside my pillow.

"The place smells of smoke, open a window."

Thank heavens, she hadn't come to nag. But then I realized that there was something strange in her manner. She sat down beside the small desk, absently picked up the ceramic camel pen-rack and examined it for a moment before returning it to its original place. How would one put it in diplomatic language? Talks, yes, formal talks . . .

"Lanlan, you're not a child anymore." Mama was weighing her words.

It had started; I listened with respectful attention.

"I know you've resented me since you were little, and you've also resented him and resented everyone else in the world, because you've had enough suffering . . . but Lanlan, it isn't only you who's suffered."

"Yes, Mama."

"When you marry Jianping, and have children, you'll understand a mother's suffering . . ."

"We don't want children if we can't be responsible for their future."

"You're blaming us, Lanlan," Mama said painfully.

"No, not blaming. I'm grateful to you, Mama, it wasn't easy for you in those years . . ."

"Do you think it was easy for him?"

"Him?" I paused. "I don't know, and I don't want to know either. As a person, I respect his past . . ."

"Don't you respect his present? You should realize, Lanlan, his staying alive required great courage!"

"That's not the problem, Mama. You say this because you lived together for many years, but I, I can't make a false display of affection . . ."

"What are you saying!" Mama grew angry and raised her voice. "At least one should fulfill one's own duties and obligations!"

"Duties? Obligations?" I started to laugh, but it was more painful than crying. "I heard a lot about them during those years. I don't want to lose any more, Mama."

"But what have you gained?"

"The truth."

"It's a cold and unfeeling truth!"

"I can't help it," I spread out my hands, "that's how life is."

"You're too selfish!" Mama struck the desk with her hand and got up, the loose flesh on her face trembling. She stared furiously at me for a moment, then left, shutting the door heavily.

Selfish, I admit it. In those years, selfishness was a kind of instinct, a means of self-defense. What could I rely on except this? Perhaps I shouldn't have provoked Mama's anger, perhaps I should really be a good girl and love Papa, Mama, my brother, life, and myself.

4

During the break between classes, I went into the reception office and rang Jianping.

"Hello, Jianping, come over this evening."

"What's up? Lanlan?" he was shouting, over the clatter of the machines his voice sounding hoarse and weary.

"He's back."

"Who? Your father?"

"Clever one, come over and help; it's an absolutely awful situation."

He started to laugh.

"Huh, if you laugh, just watch out!" I clenched my fists and banged down the receiver.

It's true, Jianping has the ability to head off disaster. The year when the production brigade chief withheld the grain ration from us educated youth, it was he who led the whole bunch of us to snatch it all back. Although I normally appear to be quite sharp-witted, I always have to hide behind his broad shoulders whenever there's a crisis.

That afternoon I had no classes and hurried home early. Mama had left a note on the table, saying that she and Papa had gone to call on some old friends and would eat when they returned. I kneaded some dough, minced the meat filling, and got everything ready to wrap the dumplings.

Jianping arrived. He brought with him a breath of freshness and cold, his cheeks flushed red, brimming with healthy vitality. I snuggled up against him at once, my cheek pressed against the cold buttons on his chest, like a child who feels wronged but has nowhere to pour out her woes. I didn't say anything, what could I say?

We kissed and hugged for a while, then sat down and wrapped dumplings, talking and joking as we worked. From gratitude, relaxation, and the vast sleepiness that follows affection, I was almost on the verge of tears.

When my brother returned, he threw off his work clothes, drank a mouthful of water, and flew off like a whirlwind.

It was nearly eight when they got home. As they came in, it gave them quite a shock to see us. Mama could not then conceal a conciliatory and motherly smile of victory; Papa's expression was much more complicated. Apart from the apologetic look of the last few days, he also seemed to feel an irrepressible pleasure at this surprise, as well as a precautionary fear.

"This is Jianping, this is . . ." My face was suffocated with red.

"This is Lanlan's father," Mama filled in.

Jianping held out his hand and boomed, "How do you do, Uncle!"

Papa grasped Jianping's hand, his lips trembling for a long time. "So you're, so you're Jianping, fine, fine . . ."

Delivering the appropriate courtesies, Jianping gave the old man such happiness he was at a loss what to do. It was quite clear to me that his happiness had nothing to do with these remarks, but was because he felt that at last he'd found a bridge between him and me, a strong and reliable bridge.

At dinner, everyone seemed to be on very friendly terms, or at least that's how it appeared on the surface. Several awkward silences were covered over by Jianping's jokes. His conversation was so witty and lively that it even took me by surprise.

After dinner, Papa took out his Zhonghua* cigarettes from a tin cigarette case to offer to Jianping. This set them talking about the English method of drying tobacco and moving on to

*Zhonghua: a trademark of one of the best cigarettes in China.

soil salinization, insect pests among peanuts and vine-grafting. I sat bolt upright beside them, smiling like a mannequin in a shop window.

Suddenly, my smile began to vanish. Surely this was a scene from a play? Jianping was the protagonist—a clever son-in-law, while I, I was the meek and mild new bride. For reasons only the devil could tell, everyone was acting to the hilt, striving to forget something in this scene. Acting happiness, acting calmness, acting glossed-over suffering. I suddenly felt that Jianping was an outsider to the fragmented, shattered suffering of this family.

I began to consider Jianping in a different light. His tone, his gestures, even his appearance, all had an unfamiliar flavor. This wasn't real, this wasn't the old him. Could strangeness be contagious? How frightening.

Jianping hastily threw me an inquiring glance, as if expecting me to repay the role he was playing with a commending smile. This made me feel even more disgusted. I was disgusted with him, and with myself, disgusted with everything the world is made of, happiness and sorrow, reality and sham, good and evil.

Guessing this, he wound up the conversation. He looked at his watch, said a few thoroughly polite bits of nonsense, and got to his feet.

As usual, I accompanied him to the bus stop. But along the way, I said not a single word, keeping a fair distance from him. He dejectedly thrust his hands in his pockets, kicking a stone.

An apartment block ahead hid the night. I felt alone. I longed to know how human beings survive behind these countless containers of suffering, broken families. Yet in these containers, memory is too frightening. It can only deepen the suffering and divide every family until everything turns to powder.

When we reached the bus stop, he stood with his back to me, gazing at the distant lights. "Lanlan, do I still need to explain?"

"There's no need."

He leaped onto the bus. Its red taillights flickering, it disappeared round the corner.

5

Today there was a sports meet at the school, but I didn't feel like it at all. Yesterday afternoon, Zhang Xiaoxia kept pestering me to come and watch her in the 100 meter race. I just smiled, without promising anything. She pursed her little mouth and, fanning her cheeks, which were streaming with sweat, with her handkerchief, stared out the window in a huff. I put my hands on her shoulders and turned her round. "I'll go then, all right?" Her face broadening into dimples, she struggled free of me in embarrassment and ran off. How easy it is to deceive a child.

I stretched, and started to get dressed. The winter sunlight seeped through the fogged-up window, making everything seem dim and quiet, like an extension of sleep and dreams. When I came out of my room, it was quiet and still; evidently everyone had gone out. I washed my hair and put my washing to soak, dashing busily to and fro. When everything was done, I sat down to eat breakfast. Suddenly I sensed that someone was standing behind me, and when I looked round it was Papa, standing stiffly in the kitchen doorway and staring at me blankly.

"Didn't you go out?" I asked.

"Oh, no, no, I was on the balcony. You're not going to school today?"

"No. What is it?"

"I thought," he hesitated, "we might go for a walk in the park, what do you think?" There was an imploring note in his voice.

"All right." Although I didn't turn round, I could feel that his eyes had brightened.

It was a warm day, but the morning mist had still not faded altogether, lingering around eaves and treetops. Along the way, we said almost nothing. But when we entered the park, he pointed at the tall white poplars by the side of the road. "The last time I brought you here, they'd just been planted." But I didn't remember it at all.

After walking along the avenue for a while, we sat down on a bench beside the lake. On the cement platform in front of us, several old wooden boats, corroded by wind and rain, were lying upside down, dirt and dry leaves forming a layer over them. The ice on the surface of the water crackled from time to time.

He lit a cigarette.

"Those same boats," he said pensively.

"Oh?"

"There're still the same boats. You used to like sitting in the stern, splashing with your bare feet and shouting, 'Motorboat! Motorboat!'" The shred of a smile of memory appeared on his face. "Everyone said you were like a boy . . ."

"Really?"

"You liked swords and guns; whenever you went into a toy shop you'd always want to come out with a whole array of weapons."

"Because I didn't know what they were used for."

All at once, a shadow covered his face and his eyes darkened. "You were still a child then . . ."

Silence, a long silence. The boats lying on the bank were turned upside down here. They were covering a little girl's silly cries, a father's carefree smile, soft-drink bottle-tops, a blue satin ribbon, children's books and toy guns, the taste of earth in the four seasons, the passage of twenty years . . .

"Lanlan," he said suddenly, his voice very low and trembling, "I, I beg your pardon."

My whole body began to quiver.

"When your mother spoke of your life in these years, it was as if my heart was cut with a knife. What is a child guilty of?" His hand clutched at the air and came to rest against his chest.

"Don't talk about these things," I said quietly.

"To tell you the truth, it was for you that I lived in those years. I thought if I paid for my crime myself, perhaps life would be a bit better for my child, but . . ." he choked with sobs, "you can blame me, Lanlan, I didn't have the ability to protect you, I'm not worthy to be your father . . ."

"No, don't don't . . ." I was trembling, my whole body went weak, all I could do was wave my hands. How selfish I was! I thought only of myself, immersed myself only in my own sufferings, even making suffering a kind of pleasure and a wall of defense against others. But how did he live? For you, for your selfishness, for your heartlessness! Can the call of blood be so feeble? Can what is called human nature have completely died out in my heart?

". . . twenty years ago, the day I left the house, it was a Sunday. I took an afternoon train, but I left at dawn; I didn't want you to remember this scene. Standing by your little bed, the tears streaming down, I thought to myself: 'Little Lanlan, shall we ever meet again?' You were sleeping so soundly and sweetly, with your little round dimples . . . the evening before as you were going to bed, you hugged my neck and said in a soft voice, 'Papa, will you take me out tomorrow?' 'Papa's busy tomorrow.' You went into a sulk and pouted unhappily. I had to promise. Then you asked again, 'Can we go rowing?' 'Yes, we'll go rowing.' And so you went to sleep quite satisfied. But I deceived you, Lanlan, when you woke up the next day, what could you think . . ."

"Papa!" I blurted out, flinging myself on his shoulder and crying bitterly.

With trembling hands he stroked my head. "Lanlan, my child."

"Forgive me, Papa," I said, choked with sobs. "I'm still your little Lanlan, always . . ."

"My little Lanlan, always."

A bird whose name I don't know hovered over the lake, crying strangely, adding an even deeper layer of desolation to this bleak winter scene.

I lay crying against Papa's shoulder for a long time. My

tears seeped drop by drop into the coarse wool of his overcoat. I seemed to smell the pungent scent of tobacco mingling with the smell of mud and sweat. I seemed to see him in the breaks between heavy labor, leaning wearily against the pile of dirt and rolling a cigarette staring into the distance through the fork between the guard's legs. He was pulling a cart, struggling forward on the miry road, the cartwheels screeching, churning up black mud sods. The guard's legs. He was digging the earth shovelful after shovelful, straining himself to fling it toward the pit side. The guard's legs. He was carrying his bowl, greedily draining the last mouthful of vegetable soup. The guard's legs ... I dared not think anymore, I dared not. My powers of imagining suffering were limited after all. But he actually lived in a place beyond the powers of human imagination. Minute after minute, day after day, oh God, a full twenty years ... no, amidst suffering, people should be in communication with one another, suffering can link people's souls even more than happiness, even if the soul is already numb, already exhausted ...

"Lanlan, look," he drew a beautiful necklace from his pocket, "I made this just before I left there from old toothbrush handles. I wanted to give you a kind of present, but then I was afraid you wouldn't want this crude toy ..."

"No, I like it." I took the necklace, moving the beads lightly to and fro with my finger, each of these wounded hearts ...

On the way back, Papa suddenly bent over and picked up a piece of paper, turning it over and over in his hand. Impulsively I pulled up his arm and laid my head on his shoulder. In my heart I understood that this was because of a new strangeness, and an attempt to resist this strangeness.

Here on this avenue, I seemed to see a scene from twenty years earlier. A little girl with a blue ribbon in her hair, both fists outstretched, totters along the edge of the concrete road. Beside her walks a middle-aged man relaxed and at ease. A row of little newly planted poplars separates them. And these little trees, as they swiftly swell and spread, change into a row of huge insurmountable bars. Symbolizing this are twenty years of irregular growth rings.

"Papa, let's go."

He tossed away the piece of paper and wiped his hand carefully on his handkerchief. We walked on again.

Suddenly I thought of Zhang Xiaoxia. At this moment, she'll actually be in the race. Behind rises a puff of white smoke from the starting gun, and amid countless faces and shrill cries falling away behind her, she dashes against the white finishing tape.

Melody

Standing in front of the five-drawer bureau holding a long-necked bottle of lemon toilet water, Yin Jie felt the palms of her hands sweating. She would really have liked to turn around and laugh, putting an end to the quarrel that had barely begun. It was really quite stupid, they were all over such piddling little things, what did it matter if the meat was burnt, it could be heated up again with a bit of this and that over a low flame. Put aside the foreign pictorial from the reference room . . . She ought to laugh, turn her head around, and use that special smile she had; several clashes had been averted like that in the past. The crucial thing was the timing. Right now was an excellent opportunity, the quarrel had not yet gone beyond bounds, only a few sarcastic remarks had gone back and forth; smiling implied neither the humiliation of defeat nor the magnanimity of a victor. Yin Jie twisted hard at the cap of the bottle, but the harder she twisted the tighter it got. When was the last time they quarreled? Good heavens, won't there ever be an end to this vicious circle? Lemon toilet water is made out of the highest grade perfume essence. Where do lemons come from? The south. Are people a little better tempered there? With their sunshine, flowers, and the fragrance of lemons as well? She should smile and turn her head around.

"I've had enough!" were the words that finally escaped her lips.

"Enough? There's a long time to go yet—" He deliberately dragged out the sound of the word "long."

"What do you mean?"

"I'm saying you have to look at it in the long term."

The cap broke under her twisting, and a subtle fragrance drifted out. "All right, let's get divorced."

"Back to the same subject." He gave a cold laugh. "You're welcome to notify the administration tomorrow morning and pack your bags."

Yin Jie turned around abruptly. "And where should I go? You tell me where I should go!"

He leaned on the bed, arms crossed in front of his chest, his glasses flashing. "It's none of my business."

"You know full well it was for your sake I broke off with my family . . ."

"It was for your own sake."

Ping! The bottle of toilet water fell to the floor and broke into fragments. "You, you're disgusting!"

"If that's not loud enough, there's a thermos back there," he said.

Shaking with rage, Yin Jie grabbed the thermos and threw it down. Next, the teacups, the tray, the vase, the sugar bowl . . . everything that came to hand went flying. Who needs them, who needs anything! Don't give a damn then, we'll see who's sorry when everything's smashed! Telling me to pack my bags, it's not that easy. Hah! Every time I get stuck at this point. Those filthy regulations, drawn up by God knows who, were still solemnly pasted up at the entrance: "Married employees resident in factory accommodation who wish to divorce should go on their own initiative to the administration and start proceedings to move out." As for the old patricians in the administration section, especially that bastard of a section director with his mean little eyes, however, you can sit back and relax, there's nothing you need worry about. Swish, an accommodation voucher, swish, a furniture inventory. Pah!

Dazhi slipped out, she didn't notice when.

Yin Jie let her hands fall, and burying her face, she broke into heavy choking sobs. The tears rolled along the cracks between her fingers down her wrists, making them itch. She had acted like a vicious harpy, would she be standing in the courtyard screaming at everybody in another two years? She thought of her family, of her own room, of the glass eyes of the little woolly dog that sat on the table. A fair amount of dust must have formed over it by now. She had always been fond of talking to it, in murmurs, pressing her nose against its nose and gazing into its eyes. This little dog would never betray her secrets, it understood everything. But Mama, you understood nothing, you thought all I was asking for then was permission to be married. No, it was not so much a wild passion as a desire for the dignity of an independent life and becoming an adult. You poured a stream of abuse over me, and when I resisted, you couldn't bear it, weeping and shouting, and you wouldn't have anything more to do with me. You should know, Mama, this is a doctor's occupational disease: arbitrary decisions and ruthless emotions. But at the light industry exhibition last month, you were incapable of disguising your feelings, the corners of your mouth twitched. I strode past, but I was longing for you to call me. I would have stopped even for a little cough . . . Yin Jie began to calm down. Crunching the broken glass beneath her feet, she walked over to the washstand at the side of the door and wiped her face. She wouldn't think about anything, she wouldn't even think, there was no use in thinking. All she sought was to sleep in peace, to dream about something nice and forget for a while everything that lay before her.

She felt a little cold. As the icy quilt lining touched her body she gave a slight shiver. Reminded of the frozen chickens in the white porcelain sinks in the food market, she couldn't help smiling. She often smiled like that in these last two years, smiling at herself, at her innermost thoughts. She stretched out her arm and lowered the volume on the transistor radio on the bed headboard. They were broadcasting some piano music by Chopin, and the quick, lively melody and the light from the green table lamp spilled on to her pillow, blending into her curly hair. She seemed to relax a little, and the day's agitation, worries, and fatigue were banished beyond the lampshade, dispersing into the pitch-black emptiness. The heavy scent of the toilet water pervaded the room. I'm not going to let anything bother me, who cares about him, let him wander about outside, best if he froze on the street. When she was small there was a time when she loathed the piano, sitting on the piano stool every morning; the shadow of the window lattice slid across the black lines of the staves; behind her was her grandmother's stern gaze and even sterner cough; and the pendulum of an old-fashioned wall clock swayed to and fro above her head like a metronome ... Sometimes she couldn't help feeling secret amazement at how such wonderful melodies were produced, listen—remote, mysterious, seemingly running parallel with life, forever unable to merge with it. But life, on the other hand, consists only of fragmented notes, which often bear certain omens of misfortune. One day before they were married, after a row with Mama, she went back to her own room in a rage, opened the piano lid, and randomly struck a few keys. Papa followed her in and laid his hand on her shoulder, but she struck a dissonant chord, brushed off Papa's hand, turned and went out; she had never been back home since. This dissonant chord still lingered in her ears. It now occurred to her that it had actually been an omen of sorts: of her inner guilt at the break with her parents, and the consequent resentment not knowing who to blame; the immense void brought on by the southern nights at the time of their wedding trip, and her secret pain and distress after their first quarrel...

"Mama, look at Xiaosan, he's squeezing me so hard I can't breathe!"

"I can see you're looking for another hiding, now go to sleep! First thing tomorrow morning I damn well have to run myself silly for you."

The noise came from the driver's family opposite.

Housing, Yin Jie sighed, is simply a curse, a curse that makes people clutch at their heads in pain. But what can you do? Even if you've just had a quarrel, you can't go and sleep in the street. It was already eleven o'clock, and the news in brief was on. The odd thing was that even if the sky was falling and the earth collapsing, the announcer's voice never changed. She clicked off the transistor and turned over; why get married? But everyone does it, it's just a stage in life, that's all. Well then, no matter how high it is, now's the time to pay the price: for the first passion, for having beautiful longings, and for being stubborn. Do all women ask themselves these questions after they're married? Ah, that would be too awful.

The sound of heavy footsteps came from the passageway, followed by the sound of someone banging at the door. Yin Jie sat up with a start, switched on the light, and hastily put on some clothes. A sound of keys jingling, a flash of light from the mirror on the back of the door, and the door opened. Dazhi was leaning against the shoulder of a strange man, his head hanging in front of his chest and a lock of hair dangling down his face.

"No need to hold me up now, I'm not done for yet." Dazhi tried to push the man away, but his legs buckled and he fell sprawling on the floor, knocking his glasses off.

"What's the matter with him?" Yin Jie asked, coming a step closer.

"He's had a bit too much to drink. Come on, help me lift him over to the bed," the visitor said.

"I'm not drunk . . . let me introduce you, my drinking pal, ah, this is the missus . . . here's to friendship!" Dazhi stretched a hand into the air, as if he wanted to grasp something, then limply fell back.

Yin Jie went over after a moment's hesitation, and with a great deal of effort she and the visitor dragged him over to the bed. Face toward the floor, he retched without managing to bring anything up. Yin Jie picked his glasses up from the floor. It was really nauseating, the retching, the broken fragments, the stranger and the smell of perfume mixed in with the smell of liquor. Hah, usually he looked at the world and at you through these round bits of glass, all feelings cut off by this damn inanimate object.

"He'll feel better once he vomits." So saying the visitor drew out a lighter and lit a cigarette. "We've just got acquainted, he drinks too hard . . . What's the matter, you two just had a quarrel?" He glanced around at the floor and blew out a dense mouthful of smoke, his gaze coming to rest on Yin Jie's figure.

Realizing suddenly that she was wearing only a nylon blouse, Yin Jie became flustered and clasped her arms together in front of her breast, nodding her head.

"Oh, you shouldn't worry about it, it's just one of those things. Married life is like a spittoon, it's there to spit into. Me and my missus broke up a good six months ago . . ."

"Why?" As soon as the words left her mouth Yin Jie realized that she had really gone too far.

He bit his lip. "In a word, I wasn't willing to be a damn cuckold. Getting divorced is worse than arranging a funeral, they tell you you've to wait your turn on the roster . . ." He blew on the white ash at the tip of his cigarette.

"I'm off. Take good care of him."

"Thank you."

"Don't mention it." At the passageway, which was dark and cluttered with stoves and other miscellaneous objects, he asked, "I'd say you were educated folks, why do you fly off the handle like this?"

Yin Jie gave a wry smile but did not answer.

"Don't bother to see me out. Luckily he'll forget the whole thing once he sobers up tomorrow."

Yin Jie nodded, looking at the slightly puffy face that gave no hint of the man's age. But no one would forget, nothing would be forgotten. Tomorrow would be the same as today. Morning was the same as night. There wouldn't be any change.

She went back into the room and leaned against the door. Dazhi was still retching but had only brought up a little yellow liquid.

"Get me some water to drink," he said thickly, forcing his head up.

"The thermos is broken."

"I'm thirsty!"

Yin Jie stood there. Her heart was filled with disgust, disgust at him and at herself.

"I'm thirsty, Jie." His voice had weakened, sounding as if he were begging.

Yin Jie turned and went out, lit the kerosene stove in the passageway, put the kettle on to boil, and returned to the room. She wetted a towel in the washbasin, wrung it out, and passed it over to him. Dazhi took the towel with a shaky hand, about to wipe his forehead, but his hand went loose and the towel slid onto the pillow. Suddenly he clutched at his head convulsively and uttered a low groan.

"What's the matter?" Yin Jie couldn't help asking.

"It hurts, it's my head . . ."

"Do you want a painkiller?"

He only had enough strength left to wave his hand. Sweat trickled down the bumps on his forehead; his face was pale, making very evident the dent his glasses left on the bridge of his nose.

Yin Jie sat down beside the bed, wiping away the sweat from his forehead with the moist towel. Suddenly she remembered their wedding night, when Dazhi had also been this drunk. But then she had clasped his head close to her, wanting desperately to share his pain, and had not closed her eyes almost the whole night. At the present moment, from pity, from giving, from a recollection of love, she felt a touch of sweet contentment. That night, even though her clothes were fouled with vomit, she had still been very happy. The flowers on the table, a present from their friends, were in bloom. Following the clearly audible sweep of the second hand, the buds slowly unfolded, petal by petal, scattering a golden pollen . . . she did not know that flowers when they bloom are also fading. Another stab of pain. Bending over, Yin Jie clasped his head and pressed it tightly against her breast. She felt her own heart beating, steadily and powerfully, never again as urgent and flurried as when she was newly wed. She remembered each time after they were intimate then, she could not fall asleep for a long time. She would press her ear against the pillow, listening carefully to the beat of her heart. Everything changed, except the voice of the announcer, a voice like a platinum ruler telling you the distance between you and the past . . .

The water boiled. She mixed a cup of sugar water, propped up his pillow, and fed it to him spoonful by spoonful. He became calmer and swallowed it slowly, and soon fell asleep. Probably because he wasn't wearing his glasses, his face softened, as if long years of smiling had left their mark. Over the last two years she had rarely heard him laugh; his bluntness had got him into rows with almost all the factory leadership. Perhaps it would be better if they had a child, that's how it was in quite a few families. She felt a slight swelling in her breast, as if it were filled with white fluid. Yes, she was always waiting for something. Waiting, but no hope; without a purpose, realistic, patience . . . the wind singing . . . far away, they didn't have any ice or snow there . . .

In a drowsy haze she felt herself changing into a lemon tree.

The next morning, Yin Jie was woken up by the bustle in the passageway. She could distinguish several sounds: the wail of a baby that had just woken up, slippers shuffling to and fro, the usual exchanges of greetings, the clinking of tooth mugs, water gurgling out from the tap . . . the bed moved slightly; Dazhi was apparently already awake.

"Is your head still aching?" asked Yin Jie.

He grunted and turned over. Yin Jie stared at the ceiling. The morning light leaked in along the top of the window curtain, forming a moiré pattern. Entirely forgotten? Hah, no one had forgotten and would never forget. It was just a nightmare she'd been waiting for. A nightmare without a beginning or an end, a nightmare that was made up of all their days.

"My glasses?" he asked.

Yin Jie turned over, her back toward him.

"Where are they?"

"On the bureau." Yin Jie gave an unfriendly snort.

Dazhi started getting dressed, the metal buckle on his belt jangling. Ping! He kicked away a piece of broken glass and moved across the room crunching the glass underfoot. Yin Jie hoped he would hurry up and leave; she didn't want to get dressed in front of him, letting him see her half naked. He seemed to be dawdling deliberately, first shaving and then clinking his cup. Finally, his footsteps stopped at the doorway, as if he were hesitating for some reason. Yin Jie's heart lurched.

"I won't be coming back to eat tonight." The door banged shut.

Yin Jie would have loved to jump up and follow him out, yelling in his ear: Why don't you starve to death! Don't ever come back! Roam around and get drunk with your drinking pals! Just don't come crawling back here crying that your head aches and you want some water! A spittoon, it's absolutely true; it's for people to spit in, so go on and spit in it, and vomit while you're about it.

It was misty in the street. Gradually the number of people increased. A trolley bus rumbled past, its loudspeaker crackling as the conductor's voice announced the stop. Buying a roll at a mobile vendor's cart, Yin Jie ran into the old couple, almost as punctual as a clock. The old man taught language and literature at a nearby high school. Almost every morning and evening Yin Jie would see him take his old wife to and from the bus stop in person, and usually they would nod at each other and exchange greetings. But today she felt a revulsion in her heart against them, almost hatred, seeing how oblivious they seemed of everyone besides themselves, so intimate, like sweethearts in love for the first time, supporting each other as they walked along, occasionally exchanging a wordless smile. They walked along the cold, dark street as if flaunting the happiness they had managed to preserve and hinting at others' estrangement and disputes. Hah, this pair of ancient living specimens was like the announcer's voice, yet another disgusting constant. Pretending not to see them, Yin Jie turned her head away.

"The road's slippery, be careful not to fall over," instructed the old man.

"You want to mind that high blood pressure of yours . . . you can heat up the beef in the small pot for lunch, it's not too overdone."

"That's the third time you've told me . . ."

As the bus drew into the stop, everyone swarmed forward, and Yin Jie was pushed up inside. It was difficult to get the doors shut. For a second as the bus moved off, Yin Jie saw the old couple still standing behind there. The old man was helping his wife tie her scarf on, his gray hair waving gently in the cold wind.

That afternoon the factory put on the film *A Sweet Cause.** Before it was half over Yin Jie slipped out. A few boys about fifteen or sixteen years old had collected on the stairs up to the cinema talking idly among themselves. As she went down past them, one of them turned his head and asked, "Hey, was it sweet?"

"Sweeter than wormwood," another said.

A burst of guffaws.

Yin Jie walked out into the main street, not knowing where to go. She did not want to go home immediately. Her girlfriends had become distant, most of them, after her marriage, and anyway she did not want others to acknowledge her unhappiness with their sympathetic glances. She felt a sense of loneliness. Ah, loneliness, it was no longer just a fashionable word for a young girl to write in her letters and diaries. It began to emerge in its full meaning. She was still young, how would she while away the days to come? She remembered how when she was young she used to eat Mickey Mouse lollies, each time first peeling off the thin rice paper and putting it on the tip of her tongue to let it melt there like a snowflake. At that time she felt it was sweet, sweeter than the lollies, because a foretaste of sweetness drew her on. What had she to look forward to now? She was tired and had a slight headache; it would be good if she could find somewhere to sit down and catch her breath.

She turned into a restaurant, but there were no empty seats. At a table in a corner a man was sitting with a young girl, their coats piled onto a stool beside them. She walked over.

"Could you move your coats somewhere else, please?"

*A farce about love and marriage.

"Where do you suggest?" he answered in a muffled voice, not even lifting his head.

Yin Jie went blank and stood there transfixed. It was him, Wei Hailin. She had always thought that she would run into him again at some point in her life, but she never dreamed that this moment would come so soon. She wanted to leave, since he hadn't noticed her yet, to hurry away, but her legs had gone weak and would not move. Gazing at the wrinkles in the corners of his eyes and the wriggling muscles in his cheeks, gazing at his thinning hair, half hiding the young girl's tender little face, she felt as if something was dying, dying in her heart. It had been another dream, but it had ended so quickly. In fact she really had no right to feel hopeless because she had not known what it was she was hoping for.

"You?" He lifted his head, rising to his feet in stunned surprise.

"You haven't forgotten?"

He laughed awkwardly, rubbing the back of his hand against his nose. Another constant. In the past Yin Jie had tried to make him drop this habit.

"Is that your daughter?" she asked.

"Say hello to auntie, Jiajia."

The girl popped her head out from under Hailin's elbow, a drop of oil still hanging from a corner of her mouth. "Hello, auntie, my name is Wei Jia, I'll be four in one month."

"What a good girl," said Yin Jie.

They sat down. Starting with his mother and the old friends they had both known, Yin Jie chattered about the government, international terrorist activity, flying saucers, internal movies, and literary magazines. "Keep on talking, don't stop on any account," she thought.

The waitress came over to take her order, interrupting their conversation. They fell silent, uncertain what to say. Yin Jie had been looking straight into his eyes, but suddenly flustered, she lowered her eyelids, looking at the bowl of leftover soup on the table, a few drops of amber-colored oil still floating around the soup spoon.

"Yin Jie," he said softly.

"Uh?"

"What can I say? Back in those days I . . . I was too ignorant about feelings . . ."

"What's the point of talking about it? Wasn't it all for the best, such a lovely child."

Hailin gave a forced laugh.

"Why isn't her Mama here?" Yin Jie asked.

"My Mama hasn't been home for ever such a long time," Jiajia butted in.

"Traveling on business?"

"Mama and Papa had a quarrel."

"That's enough, hurry up and finish off your soup." Hailin cuffed her lightly around the head.

"What, divorced?"

"Oh, no, no . . ."

"Mama comes home to see me on Sundays, she buys lots and lots of sweets," Jiajia interjected again, licking the spoon.

A long silence.

"Doing all right?" Hailin finally asked.

"Yes."

"I wish you happiness."

"Don't say things like that, they don't mean anything."

"Time goes so fast . . ."

"No, so slow."

Hailin gave her a swift glance. "Why?"

Yin Jie did not answer.

"A different way of looking at it?"

"Perhaps."

"Where do you live now?" Hailin groped in his pocket. "Here, take my telephone number. You can call me if there's anything."

"All right."

Hailin wrote down the number in a small notebook, tore out the page, and handed it to her. "We have to go . . ."

Yin Jie nodded.

"Can we meet again?" he asked.

"I don't know."

"Goodbye auntie!" Jiajia waved her little hand in its padded glove.

The door swung in and out a few times, then closed. Yin Jie kneaded her hands slowly, crumpling the paper into a ball. The door to the past had finally closed; then let it close. Behind that door was the dense night, and countless confused footsteps, but no signs of memories, none. With a slight flick of her hand, the paper ball landed against the corner of the wall and rolled down alongside a stained, spotted spittoon. It seemed she was not that unfortunate, everyone was the same, each in his or her own way was staggering ever more weakly under the heavy burden of marriage. Perhaps the only difference was in the ties that held the marriages together: between Dazhi and her it was housing; between the drinker and his missus their turn on a roster; between Hailin and his wife, presumably, the child; between the old couple who looked so fortunate there was only a form, nothing more than a monotonous, rigid form. The crux of the matter was habit, once you're used to it, it stopped being anything extraordinary. You stopped feeling the pain. But wasn't this the same as being numb? Numb! As her meal was being served, Yin Jie glanced at the waitress's apathetic expression and felt her heart grow cold. Was her own expression just the same? Perhaps each person is an icy mirror; others see themselves in it, from outward expression to inner feelings, and people live in these countless reflections.

In the crowded trolley bus on her way home, she suddenly thought of something from the past. Not long after she and Hailin had first met, they had gone to the evening showing of a movie. Coming back on the bus, the two of them were crowded together, pressed together so tightly that they couldn't move. About their heads was a dome light with one half painted red. In the red glow the people around them seemed static, immobile. Each face seemed very strange, flat, without dimension, utterly dissimilar and yet identical. Hailin's scorching breath blew on her face, and she lowered her head timidly. She did not want to speak or laugh, she only wished that the bus would never stop, just keep on going for ever and ever . . .

They reached her stop. Getting off the bus, Yin Jie caught sight of the old man, waiting patiently under the stop sign.

"Hello," she greeted him.

The old man gave a slight bow. "Just off work?"

"Still waiting for her?"

"This is the fourth, they're crowded today."

"Do you meet her every day?"

He straightened his glasses, and allowed himself the hint of a smile. "Except when I'm ill, plus when I was under investigation for eight months; ah, natural disasters, manmade calamities . . ."

"How long altogether?"

"Thirty-two years, it will be exactly thirty-two years in two months and seven days."

"That you've been married?"

"Yes."

Yin Jie felt astonished. But what astonished her was not the words themselves but his expression, which was very hard to describe.

"Are . . . are you very happy?" she couldn't help asking.

The old man chuckled. "That's an odd thing to ask, what should I say?"

Yin Jie also laughed. "Say the truth."

"The important thing is this," he patted his heart, "don't let it dry up, like an old well . . ."

The next bus had come, and the old man went forward to meet it. In a short while, he squeezed his way out through the crowd, drawing his wife with him. Nodding to Yin Jie, they walked on, disappearing into the gathering dusk. Yin Jie's eyes grew moist; the lines of mercury lights proliferated, becoming a single blur.

As she walked past beneath a block of apartments she heard a violin melody. She did not remember what piece it was, she only knew that it was very gentle and beautiful, and would reverberate in her heart for a long time.

Moon on the Manuscript

Sunlight slid onto the glass desk top as I lowered my eyelids. A warm band of orange trembled lightly. It was a still morning. At intervals the oppressive sound of popped rice spread through the lane. A war was going on in Afghanistan. A jumbo jet had crashed in southern France . . . I had been sitting here for three days now, without being able to write a word. The world was so concrete, it seemed as if it only had meaning at a given concrete time and place. The tired and drawn face in the mirror when I was washing this morning resembled a cornered beast. At the public lecture a few days ago, the university students had started to hiss, and someone handed up a slip saying "You represent us? How disgusting!" The grating sound of the microphone's alternating current gave me the opportunity of silence. What more had I to say to these fellows who considered themselves so superior?

I opened my eyes and blew lightly, and the snow-white cigarette ash on the glass top was like a flock of sea gulls skimming over the water. At low tide I would almost invariably go hunting for shellfish with my playmates. We would knock off oysters from the rocks one by one and pour them into our mouths. There were also small crabs that hid in the seaweed or under the rocks . . . I'm a fisherman's son, but it seems as if this was no longer a fact but only a line in a dossier. Had my mother not died and her brother taken me to Beijing, at this minute I would probably be sitting on the deck of a chugging, throbbing, motorized junk, smoking a long-stemmed pipe and surrounded on all sides by fishing nets full of salt rime and the odor of fish. I spread out a hand: pale, slender, not a single callus. Fate is incomprehensible, perhaps fate is the only thing that is incomprehensible . . .

Someone knocked on the door, so lightly that at first I thought I'd heard wrong. It was a girl with short cropped hair that had a brownish tint.

"Is Mr. Ding here?" she asked timidly.

"That's me."

"I . . ." her round face flushed.

"Come in and tell me what's on your mind."

She almost kicked over the thermos flask on the floor. "I'm sorry . . ."

"It doesn't matter. Please sit down."

After some hesitation she sat down on an old stool beside the couch, placing her old satchel on her knees. "My name is Chen Fang, I'm a student at the Normal College. I came because I like your stories." She laughed apologetically.

"Which ones do you like?"

She thought it over. "I like 'The Relic.'"

"As far as I'm concerned that's become a relic itself. What about the more recent ones?"

"Er," her tone was a little uncertain. "I haven't read them yet."

I got on my guard, thinking she might be one of the students who had been booing. "What's the reaction of the students around you?"

"I'm not sure. Some people seem to think they aren't as deep as before."

"A hole in the ice is deep," I said.

The girl seemed to be a bit nervous, continually fiddling with the frayed strap of her satchel, twisting it back and forth around her fingers.

"Would you like some water?"

"No, please don't bother, I'm going in a minute." She took out a thick manuscript from her satchel. "I tried to write something. It's fairly poor. I thought I'd ask you to read it, is that all right?"

I took the manuscript and weighed it in my hand. "Are you in the Chinese department?"

"No, physics."

"Your first try at writing?"

She nodded earnestly.

"Take my advice, stick to your own field and don't waste your efforts on this."

She shrugged: "Why?"

"It's sour grapes."

"Really?"

"I say that because I've tried."

She laughed, very sweetly, and for a moment her ordinary-looking face appeared beautiful. "But I've always liked sour things since I was little."

I bit my lip and remained silent.

"And you can make sweet wine with sour grapes."

"Sweet wine?"

She stood up. "Anyway, I'd still like to try."

"Very well then, I won't say any more."

At the door she turned her head. "I thought, I thought you would be full of confidence."

"Confidence? The word is too abstract."

"What is a concrete one then?"

"Life, writing," I grimaced, "and confidence, too."

After seeing my visitor off, I sat down again at my desk. Perhaps this was the beginning of a story, starting with the conversation about sour grapes, and then what? I picked up my pen, screwed off the cap, and stared at the metal nib. What was the matter? It was fine weather outside, and I was shut up in a room, like a fly in winter. I used to be able to write eight thousand characters a day, "like a fountain," to use the old lady's expression. She saw herself as my protector. One look at that stupid face would make anyone contemplate suicide. Perhaps a difficult labor is a good thing, a new beginning. How droll, a man approaching forty still talking about new beginnings. Emperors build their mausoleums when they're still in their teens. Ordinary people are lucky, you can go for a walk after work, or slip off and have a drink, you don't have a load of worries . . . The pen slipped between my fingers and poked a hole in the upper righthand corner of the manuscript, splashing a big blob of ink on it. Idly I drew a crescent moon.

The sight of Juan coming in aroused a feeling of time fleeting. It was as if in that second, memories of the past welled up and swirled around me, forming a background in disharmony with our everyday life.

"Why're you looking at me like that?" she asked.

"Nothing," I said dully.

She pulled out Dongdong from behind her. "Say hello to daddy."

Dongdong stood between me and Juan, looking glum and gazing blankly at the floor.

"Say hello," Juan's voice was a little impatient.

Dongdong still stood there, not budging.

"He had a fight with the other children this afternoon, he grabbed someone's car . . . I'm exhausted." Juan settled her bottom on the couch and sighed.

I went over and hugged Dongdong, prickling him with my mustache as I kissed him. Not saying anything, he dodged aside, detached himself from me, and toddled over to the desk.

"Moon," he muttered, stretching out his small hands to the manuscript.

Juan bustled over. "Ah, the great author, he can't produce a single word, but he knows how to doodle. There'll soon be a mountain of letters piled up demanding stories, I wonder how you're going to meet those debts."

"I don't owe anything to anyone," I said stiffly.

She smoothed a crease on her sleeve with her fingers, giving me a quick glance.

"I only owe myself," I said then.

"What's got into you?"

I stayed silent.

She walked over, patted me on the shoulder and stroked my face. "You're tired."

I looked into her eyes and gave a forced laugh.

"What's bothering you?"

"Nothing."

"Then why this?"

I grasped her hand. "I'm tired."

"You've got such a terribly gloomy expression. Shave off that mustache tomorrow. I'm going to chop up some meat, I bought some chives."

I sat down at the table and stroked Dongdong's downy head. This time he did not dodge away.

"Daddy will buy you a car tomorrow."

"I don't want one," he said staring at the paper.

"Why not?"

"Fatty said the car was his granddad's." He suddenly lifted his head and asked, "What's my granddad?"

"A fisherman."

Dongdong turned his head to look at the goldfish bowl on the side table.

"What sort of fish?"

"All sorts."

"Where does he live?"

"He's dead."

Dongdong raised his eyes in surprise.

"He drowned at sea."

"Wasn't he careful?"

I shook my head.

"Were you sad?"

"I was only three then."

"I'm four and a half."

"Yes, you're a big boy now."

Dongdong drew his forefinger back and forth on the manuscript. "Teacher says the moon is round."

"She's right."

"Why didn't you draw it round?"

"Each person has a different moon."

"Granddad's moon?"

"Quite round."

I remembered the small dark cottage piled with fishing gear. I often burrowed myself in there, to lie alone on the dried fishing nets. Moonlight filtered down from the cracks between the rafters, murmuring in the sea wind, an accompaniment to the monotonous sound of the waves.

"Posterity equals zero," Kang Ming smacked his lips and threw the matchstick into the ashtray. "Zero, old man."

I shook my head, reluctant to continue the argument. All arguments were meaningless. I knew he was needling me, trying to draw me into a game that I was already tired of. Every Saturday evening as a rule he would occupy our twelve-square-meter room in his own unique way.

"There's no need to feel any responsibility in regard to posterity. The question's very simple, no one has to feel responsible in regard to anyone."

"Do you have a responsibility to yourself?" I asked.

"That's a complicated question."

"No, it's also very simple. People now tend to put the responsibility on society all the time. In fact, society is composed of individual people. If each individual refuses to accept responsibility for his own acts, how can we expect any social progress?"

"OK, I give up. Your wife?"

"Taking the child back to her mother's."

"Writing coming along well this time?"

"No."

He turned his head and looked at me. One eye was very bright, reflecting the light from the standard lamp, the other was in a dark green shadow.

"You've changed," he said.

"Really?"

"Probably it's the conscience of the artist pressing on you so hard you can't breathe."

"I'm not an artist, never have been."

"Your name is big enough."

"It would be bigger if I started a fire on the street."

"Don't set your demands too high, old man."

I stayed silent.

"The question is not how you or I think, of course it's a good thing to develop your own brain." He got up and walked to and fro, his shadow slipping across the wall. "One thing should be understood, we are merely society's luxuries."

"I don't understand."

"It seems that only we 'commercial' editors know how the market works . . ." He walked over to the desk and picked up the sheet of paper. "Interesting. Do you know what a lunar eclipse is?"

I gazed at him.

He turned around and leaned against the table, smiling enigmatically. "It's the result of the earth beneath our feet blocking off the sunlight, common knowledge."

The paper at the end of the cigarette began to curl up, covering the red fire that was gradually darkening, the blue and brown wisps of smoke mixing together. Although technically deficient, the girl's story still touched me deeply. The tragedy was certainly her personal history, the beginning and the end of love. To search for love in this loveless world is very difficult, but loss is something instant and eternal. "The business about the apartment, haven't you been keeping up the pressure for it? The application's been in for months." A rustling sound, it was Juan taking off her clothes. The cigarette ash tumbled off, falling in separate flakes on the manuscript. "Go and see Xu tomorrow, one word from him is more effective than you making ten visits to the Association." "I'd prefer not to." Was that my voice? People can never hear their own voices accurately. How long can this voice linger in the world? At most seventy years, then it will disappear along with me. But the noise of the sea never ceases, never ends. I write something, it is printed in a book, but who dares guarantee that twenty or thirty years later people will still be reading it? Not even just twenty or thirty years, the younger generation have begun shaking their heads right now. "Ge's wife, he works in our factory, she's in a washing machine factory, they're having a trial sale, only a hundred and fifty . . ." What lasts forever? Eternity in art is too terrible, the sight of it strikes fear into people's hearts like a cold gravestone. It demands a writer stake everything on a single venture. The bed boards creaked, Juan was turning over. Sea gulls staked everything on a single venture. No one who has heard their full-throated doleful wail could doubt this. Why am I always thinking of the sea lately? I drew a deep breath, smoking relaxes me. A piece of cigarette ash fell near the moon. Ah, the result of blocking sunlight. Yes, artists are still men. I really shouldn't look down on Kang Ming, we're all the same. Besides, he's right in a way. Perhaps lying is man's basic nature, and being sincere is acquired, sincerity must be studied. Is the problem only in speaking truthfully? "It's getting late," Juan said in a muffled voice. This was a hint. She was waiting for me, just as primitive tribal woman waited for the hunter, no, fisherman. The fishing spear in his hand, an animal skin around his waist, he utters a full-throated cry answering the summons. "Yes, this month it's our turn to collect the water and electricity bill, last month the electricity was so dear, there must be someone stealing the electricity . . ." I wonder if the small dark cottage still exists? The pungent fishy smell, the slippery floor, the small iron bucket hanging from the ceiling to catch the rainwater. Haven't been home for many years, I really should go back and look around. "Tomorrow evening you should go to our place and pick up Dongdong. I may be working overtime." My father, to me, will forever be a mystery. How he drowned not even I know. He didn't leave a single thing behind. No, he left me. And what will I leave behind? I stubbed out the cigarette and switched off the lamp. Everything disappeared, the moonlight poured in, I remembered the girl's smile. "Why don't you say something?" Juan snorted and turned over facing the wall. She was angry, but it was a pretense. I turned down the quilt and pulled her over by the shoulder, watching her quivering eyelids in the dark. "All right," I said. She slowly lifted her arm, moving her face nearer. "The business about the apartment . . ."

"Here's to your creative work, may it be an eternal fountain!" said the old lady.

I put down my cup.

"What's up?" the old lady looked at me.

"We should drink to Xu's health."

"May as well, I suppose. To my reluctance to go to the grave," the old man said.

The old lady placed a piece of fish on my plate. "Try some, it's yellow croaker, my own work."

"Excellent."

"Compared with your stories?"

"Much superior."

The old lady moved closer, with a mysterious air. "There is something you must thank me for properly . . ."

"What?"

"Guess."

I shook my head.

"Go on, guess." She trod on me with the tip of her foot.

"That's enough," the old man impatiently knocked the plate with his chopsticks. "Stop making such a fuss, if you've something to say, come out with it."

"It's none of your business!" The old lady gave him a baleful look. "A few days ago, Mr. Zhang, the director of the press, was here, I mentioned you to him. He's agreed to publish a collection of your work."

"Oh."

She waited for me to make a better response.

"Thank you, but . . ." I knocked the table with my finger knuckles. "Why don't we wait a little, we can talk about it later."

"What?"

"I haven't put together anything decent yet."

"Ho, here am I burning joss sticks and the old buddha turns his backside to me."

"He's looking ahead," the old man mumbled, sucking on the fish head. "Mm, mm, wait and see."

"You've been waiting all your life, and in the end, all you've got is a name with nothing to show for it except your memoirs, huh?" the old lady said indignantly.

"What're you yelling?" The old man thumped the table. "At least I've got something worth putting into memoirs."

"Humph," came from the old lady.

The old man's good humor recovered after a minute. He dug out a dark brown fish eye and looked it over carefully.

"Think it over, don't let this opportunity slip by." The old lady clasped her arms around her shriveled chest and sighed. "I'm going to take a look in the kitchen."

"The old nag," muttered the old man, waiting until she had gone out the door. He turned toward me, "Don't listen to her gibberish."

"She means well."

"There must be something bothering you."

I gave a noncommittal smile.

"It doesn't matter, literary men are given to oversentimentality." He concentrated again on the fish eye.

"I'm just a little unwilling."

He lifted his head and gazed at me expressionlessly. "How old are you?" he asked.

"Thirty-seven."

"Do you know how old China's history is?"

I didn't answer.

"Five thousand years." He stretched out five crooked, trembling fingers. "There's no harm in waiting a bit longer, you young men." As he finished speaking, he downed the fish eye in a single gulp.

I sat down at the desk. I knew this would be the inevitable result. I could not go back to the deck, to the rocks, to the small dark cottage where the moonlight rang out from the rafters. I had a slight headache, it was the alcohol—the sun-dried grain was to blame, the sun was to blame. I felt a sadness I had not known before, and felt like crying although I hadn't cried for years. Perhaps my tears were saltier than others'. I was a fisherman's son. My father died at sea. His boat overturned, and there wasn't even a corpse, but they set up a wooden tablet for him in the village graveyard. There were many wooden tablets there, facing the sea, facing the sunrise every morning. I was fortunate. I wonder whether authors who have been published often go past bookshops and look at their own books behind the glass. Hardback and paperback. The hardback editions have characters stamped in gold on the outside, and the cover is made of soft, pliable leather. They are more fortunate than I. Fortunes can change, however. I shouldn't stop. I didn't choose this opportunity, it chose me. Actually, nothing is of much importance in the end. My nerves are weak, I'm always being troubled by nightmares, nightmares that trouble my peace of mind. That fish eye has seen everything there is in the sea: seaweed, electric eels, mother-of-pearl . . . yes, oysters, too. Don't stop, I'm only thirty-seven, that's still an up-and-coming age for writers. That girl's smiling face didn't hold purity and beauty alone. A smile can cover up everything. But where the smile has been, a scar or wrinkle will remain. I pulled open the drawer and gingerly touched the dog-eared corner of the manuscript. Sour grapes will only ripen and turn into wine if there is a sun. She had hope. Although the students' booing was not very pleasant, it nevertheless contained a sunlike sincerity and honesty. Oh, what's the point of these things, life is always concrete. I once knew love too, I have the right to describe this love too. It was a secret, a secret that couldn't be transcended in a tragedy, but I've had my brush with it. This isn't plagiarizing, nonsense, of course it isn't.

I spread out the sheet of paper with the drawing of the moon and began to write.

Holding a toy car in his hand, Dongdong was kicking a stone, humming snatches of a song which seemed to be a story about a cat and a butterfly.

"Hurry up, Dongdong," I pulled his small hand. "Stop kicking that stone." He looked around at the dark shadows of the pedestrians and traffic around us, still humming.

"Daddy, look at the moon," he said.

The moon was big and round.

"That isn't your moon."

"No, it isn't."

"Where's your moon?"

I said nothing. We were walking under the dense shade of a pink siris. I knew he was looking at me intently, but he couldn't see my face clearly.

Intersection

Fan Guandong took a sip from his glass. Stirring the plate of boiled peanuts with his chopsticks, he picked out a dark sliver of grass and placed it to the side. Lifting his small, slightly protruding eyes, he stared at the muddy road outside the window. A hen was looking for food along the ruts in the road, its dirty feathers blown upright by the wind. Pasted over the glass was a strip of faded green paper. He was illiterate, but he guessed it said "Beer sold out" or "Beer now on."

This place as a rule was rarely patronized by outsiders. Today, however, its peace was disturbed by a rowdy gang of kids. With not a single drinking pal in sight, he felt the drinks had lost their flavor. When the regular customers gathered here, the wisecracks would come thick and fast, and everyone would discuss freely the events of the past and present as the acrid smoke softly drifted to the ceiling.

A tall fat man was standing in front of the counter, wiping his face with a handkerchief. His back was a little hunched, his head tilted to one side, and his ears stuck out. A wrinkled white shirt was tucked into wide but neatly pressed woolen trousers.

What rotten luck! Fan Guandong spat on the ground and smeared the phlegm with the sole of his shoe. It was the engineer, Fat Wu, the technical manager on the construction site. Because of the slight defect in his neck, the fellows called him "five minutes to six" behind his back. He was an odd sort of person, this fellow. He had transferred from another company several years ago, but no one knew the details of his background. He looked like a bulldozer when he walked, his manner suggesting that nothing was worth his attention. Someone said of him half in fun, "Fat Wu must have drunk a lot of ink, his eyes have turned blue."

Fan Guandong had already had a run-in with him. That day they were tamping the concrete for the workshop's main engine base when Fat Wu appeared, wearing a white safety helmet. He walked around twice, and then suddenly started shouting and yelling, saying that everyone was disobeying the operating rules. Without uttering a sound, Fan Guandong shut off the vibrating machine, took off his boot, tipped out a small stone, and began to suck at his pipe. Fat Wu kept on yelling, but this act really got his temper up. He stamped his foot and swore violently . . . it was a pretty common event at the construction site. Naturally, all the workmen were on Fan Guandong's side. In their eyes, the engineer was a fellow who had "a screw loose."

Fat Wu turned around, and as their eyes met, Fan Guandong realized that the other man seemed to look rather down at the heels, his gray face and rumpled hair suggesting that he had suffered a serious illness.

After a moment's hesitation, Fat Wu slowly walked over. "Master Fan—"

Fan Guandong muttered a surly acknowledgment.

"Mind if I sit down here?"

"I don't own the place."

Fat Wu stood there dumbly, then sat down with a sheepish grin and pushed a plate of cold food toward the middle of the table.

"Try some . . ." he said.

Fan Guandong cast a look at his companion and silently undid the buttons on his work clothes, revealing a dark red chest. Suddenly he drew out of his pocket his sole ten-yuan note and slapped it down on the table. "Young Li, over here."

The pockmarked lad behind the counter was picking his teeth with a match. He grabbed easily at a cloth and walked over.

"What'll it be, Mr. Fan?" he asked, grinning.

"Get us some decent food and drink, this much worth."

The pockmarked lad was taken aback. Clutching the note in his hand, he flicked one end of it with his finger.

"What day is it today?"

"You don't need a day to spend money. Cut the cackle."

"Whatever you say."

". . . . . ." Fat Wu eyed him gloomily and stretched out a hand to pick up the plate. "I'll get another table then."

Fan Guandong grasped him by the wrist. "Don't move off, do me the honor."

"This won't do."

"You don't think I'm worthy enough?"

"Master Fan, you've had a lot to drink."

"What kind of language is that?" Fan Guandong shook his head in displeasure. "Round these parts we don't use that kind of talk."

Unable to stir from his seat, Fat Wu was obliged to sit back and relax. "You're trying to put me on the spot, aren't you, Mr. Fan?"

"Don't know what you mean."

The pockmarked lad brought a tray with a bottle of Feng River Distillate and six cold dishes, and laid them on the table.

"Pretty extravagant, Mr. Fan." he said, giving him a wink.

"So what, it's just to keep the liquor-worm in its place."

"The liquor-worm?" asked Fat Wu doubtfully, rubbing his smarting wrist.

"You wouldn't understand that, huh?" Fan Guandong was pointing his finger at his belly. "All good drinkers have this little joker, you'll take even a bowl of soup if there's nothing else to go with the drinks, or else you'll end up in trouble."

"Makes sense."

"This place's not bad, eh? Beats the big restaurants. Let's have a drink. Cheers."

They emptied their glasses. Within a few seconds Fat Wu's jutting ears had turned bright red, like two frostbitten leaves.

"What do you think, old Wu, the way we're drinking, is it in accordance with the operating rules?" asked Fan Guandong.

Fat Wu's cheeks quivered and he burst into laughter, the deep chesty sound reverberating around the cafe. The young men, who were playing the finger game, turned their heads to look.

"I suppose I've offended you, Master Fan?"

"It's nothing. We're like a mongrel and a jackass snapping at each other. But whichever way you look at it, if you'd show a smile on your face more often we'd fulfill our plan sooner . . ."

"Why?"

"You're the boss. When you go out you should see which way the wind's blowing." Fan Guandong turned to shout at the pockmarked lad. "Hey, Young Li, have you been fixed up with an old lady yet?"

"Mr. Fan, have you had too much to drink?" The pockmarked lad retorted sarcastically.

"If you haven't, let our Mr. Engineer act as a matchmaker for you."

"All right, all right," said Fat Wu unhappily, his face darkening.

"What's up?"

"You really don't know?" Fat Wu sighed and tugged at his sleeve, as if trying to cover the watch on his wrist. "My wife divorced me some time ago."

"What for?"

"Oh, it takes too long to explain. When I was in for correction, she really couldn't hold out anymore . . ."

Fan Guandong felt uncomfortable all over. He waved the other not to go on.

"Faithless bitch," he said angrily.

"It would have been a wait of more than ten years, it wouldn't have been easy for her either."

It was getting dark, and raindrops were drumming against the window, making a monotonous sound. Fat Wu pulled out his handkerchief and blew his nose noisily. Fan Guandong filled his pipe with slow deliberation, glancing frequently out of the window.

They drank the second glass in silence.

"It's raining." Fat Wu broke the silence.

"Let it," Fan Guandong grimaced. "You might say women's hearts are made of bean curd, I've had several rows with my old lady too . . . She never came back to you?"

"She came back just now, and had another cry."

"Well then, you shouldn't drag it out. Who hasn't made a mistake . . .?"

The corners of Fat Wu's mouth twitched, and he smiled bitterly. "She's already married."

"Pah, the faithless bitch!" Fan Guandong made a gesture as if trying to wipe this woman off the face of the earth.

"But you can't blame her entirely."

"Then blame who? You lot, you can't make a straightforward job out of anything."

Fan Guandong turned around again. "Waiter, your fish is a bit off, is it rat-killer or something?"

"Liquor-worm killer." The pockmarked lad, deep in his accounts, returned the compliment.

"Try the fish I catch in a couple of days, that'll be fresh," Fat Wu said proudly.

"How big?"

"Three or four ounces, the big ones."

Fan Guandong laughed so hard he choked, and then he had a fit of coughing. "Hey, waiter, do you have a cat here?"

"We've got cat piss."

"Get back to your bills."

"You're laughing at me," Fat Wu muttered.

"Tell me, where do you catch these fish of yours?" asked Fan Guandong, hooking his forefinger.

"In the park."

"Fish in that stinking ditch? Don't go there and be cheated."

"As a matter of fact I've caught quite a few there," Fat Wu said earnestly.

"Next Sunday come with me on a real trip outside, how about it? The hills are hills, the water is water, and we'll cook them as we catch 'em. Melonseed carp, black carp, silver carp, the big ones are over ten catties. And don't forget to bring a bottle."

Fat Wu moistened his thick lips with his tongue, his eyes shining with excitement. "Done."

"Let's have another drink, celebrate in advance."

"No more for me."

"Tell me where's the grave of a man who died from drinking? Come on."

They drank a third round. Fat Wu's head was tilting more and more alarmingly, and he had to prop it up with his hands.

"I really can't take any more," he said.

"Wait . . . waiter," Fan Guandong's tongue had stiffened, and it took him an effort to yell. "Give the crema . . . crematorium a ri . . . ring, ask them if they . . . they've got an empty bunk left?"

"I . . . I'm not going to the crematorium." There was a hint of tears in Fat Wu's voice.

"I'm going with you, we'll have a look around first."

"I'm not going!" Fat Wu screamed.

"Right, we're not going, good times are ahead, we'll have another round . . . Come to my place tomorrow, my old lady is at the vegetable market, I'll get her to introduce you to a young widow . . ."

"I'm not worth anybody."

"Don't you give me that rubbish, just leave it all to me and there'll be no problem. What year are you, old Wu?"

"Serpent."

"We're a pair. I'm a snake too. What day were you born on?"

Fat Wu swayed his head, but the only contribution he could make was to wave his hand.

"Don't remember? It . . . it doesn't matter, although we're not from the same mother, we're still brothers, aren't we?"

"Yes, yes." Making a great effort, Fat Wu nodded his head.

They drank the last round.

The rain had stopped. Under the dim streetlights, they

walked along the middle of the road supporting each other, swaying from side to side, and completely ignoring the hooting and cursing from the passing traffic. As they walked, they struck up a song, humming the words. Their voices got louder and louder, but no one would have been able to tell what they were singing. Fat Wu was bellowing in a low deep bass, and Fan Guandong accompanied him in the shrill falsetto of the local opera style. The two voices mingled, creating a sound both peculiar and harmonious. They were singing of life's joys and misfortunes, they were singing of friendship, friendship, and friendship.

The next morning, Fan Guandong was pushing the small cart filled with mortar when he ran headlong into Fat Wu, who was wearing his white safety helmet. Their eyes met, then broke away, and neither made the first move to greet the other. When he had walked some distance away, Fan Guandong turned his head around and gazed at the receding figure of the other man.

13 Happiness Street

1

A late autumn morning. The street was bleak and desolate. A gust of wind rustled the withered yellow leaves on the pavement. The dreary, monotonous cry of an old woman selling ices could be heard in the distance. Fang Cheng pulled his old black woolen coat tightly around him and kicked a stone on the ground. It wedged itself in the iron grate in the gutter with a clunk. The call from his sister just now had been really too fantastic: young Jun had been flying his kite in this street yesterday afternoon, yes, this same damn street, when all of a sudden, he had disappeared without a trace; in broad daylight! His sister's sobs, followed by the beep signaling the line was disconnected, had upset him so much that his head was still ringing. Sun, the section head, was sitting opposite him at the time, and had given him an inquisitive glance, so he had put down the receiver and done his utmost to look normal.

Across the road, a row of locust trees had been sawed down to the roots, the trunks lying across the pavement. A yellow Japanese forklift was parked by the side of the road. Four or five men were busy attaching hooks to the sawed-off trees and loading them onto a large truck to the tooting of a whistle.

Fang Cheng approached the old woman selling ices. "Such fine locust trees, how come . . ."

"Ices, three fen and five fen." The shriveled mouth snapped open and snapped shut again.

"Comrade . . ."

The old woman's strident voice robbed him of the courage to repeat his question. He crossed the road to the truck. A young fellow who looked like the driver was leaning against the front fender smoking.

"Excuse me, what's going on here?"

"Don't you have eyes in your head?"

"I mean, what are you sawing the trees down for?"

"Who do you think you are, going round poking your nose into everything? Are you building a house, and you want us to leave you a log for the roof beam? I'll tell you straight, I can't even get one for myself." Flicking away his cigarette butt, the driver turned round and climbed into the driver's cab, slamming the door behind him.

Fang Cheng bit his lip. A middle-aged woman carrying a string bag was walking past. He caught up with her. "Excuse me, where did you get those turnips?"

"At the greengrocer's over the way."

"Oh." He smiled politely and walked with her for a few steps. "How come these trees have been cut down? Such a shame."

"Who knows? I heard that yesterday a kite got caught in the trees, and some young rascal climbed up to get it . . ." She suddenly fell silent and hurried off nervously.

A long shadow slipped across the ground.

Fang Cheng swung around. A man wearing a leather jacket pulled a green army cap over his eyes, gave him a swift glance and walked past.

It was only then that Fang Cheng noticed the high outside wall exposed behind the stumps of the felled locust trees. The plaster was so old that it had peeled off in places, showing the large solid bricks underneath. He took a deep breath, inhaling gasoline fumes mixed with the sweet scent of locust wood, and walked back along the wall. Before long he came upon a recess in the wall enclosing a gateway guarded by two stone lions. The red paint on the door had faded and was covered with a layer of dust, as if it hadn't been opened for a long time. On it was a very ordinary plaque with the words "13 Happiness Street," and beneath it a cream-colored buzzer. Fang Cheng went to press it, but it wouldn't budge. On closer inspection he realized it was molded from a single piece of plastic and was purely decorative. He stood there bewildered.

As he drew back a few paces, trying to get a clearer view of the whole gate, he bumped into an old man who happened to be passing by.

"Sorry. Excuse me, who lives here?"

He stopped short. The terror that welled up from the depths of the old man's eyes made Fang Cheng's legs go weak. The old man stumbled away, his walking stick beating an urgent and irregular rhythm as he disappeared into the distance.

A young boy walked by, absorbed in whittling a branch from one of the locust trees with a penknife.

"Hey, where's the neighborhood committee office, young man?"

"Turn at the lane over there," the boy sniffled, pointing with the branch.

The narrow lane twisted its way through the shoddy makeshift houses. From time to time Fang Cheng had to walk sideways in order to prevent the boards and exposed nails from catching and tearing his overcoat. At the entrance to what looked like a rather spacious courtyard at the far end of the lane two signboards were hanging side by side: Neighborhood Committee and Red Medical Station. Both were covered with childish muddy fingerprints.

He pushed open the door of the room on the north side of the courtyard and stuck his head inside.

"Did you bring the certificate?" asked a girl busy knitting a sweater.

"What certificate?"

"The death certificate!" she said impatiently.

Everything in the room was white: the sheet, the folding

screen, the table, the chairs, and also the girl's lab coat and pallid face. Fang Cheng shivered. "No, no, I've . . ."

"Listen, if we don't sign it nobody's going to let you hold the funeral service!"

"I'm looking for someone."

"Looking for someone?" She looked up in surprise, lifting her hair back with one of her knitting needles. "Don't you know what's proper?"

"But this is . . ."

"The Red Medical Station."

Retreating into the yard, Fang Cheng noticed a dense crowd of people in the room to the south. He walked over and knocked on the door.

"Come in," a voice said.

Inside, about a dozen people were seated around a long wooden table, all staring at him in silence. The light inside the room was so dim that he couldn't make out their faces, but judging from their heavy bronchial wheezing, most of them were old women.

"Has it been signed?" The question came from a woman at the far end of the table. From her voice she seemed pretty young; she'd be the chairwoman or something.

"No, I . . ."

"Then they're still alive and breathing," she broke in sharply.

A howl of laughter. One fat old woman laughed so much she started gagging, and someone thumped her on the back.

"I'm a reporter," Fang Cheng explained hastily.

Instantly the room fell deathly silent. They gazed stupidly at each other, as if they were not too sure what he meant.

The chairwoman was the first to break the silence. "Your papers."

Fang Cheng had barely taken out his press card when it was snatched away by the person nearest the door. The card in its red plastic cover was handed round the table for everyone to look at and comment on. As it passed from hand to hand, some of them shook their heads while others spat on their fingers and rubbed it. Finally it reached the chairwoman. Gripping the card, she studied it carefully, then got the old man in glasses beside her to read it aloud. At last she gave a nod.

"Hm. Have you come to take photos?"

A buzz of excited confusion filled the room. Dull eyes flashed, people nudged and tugged at each other, and one old woman who had fallen asleep propped against the table actually woke up. It was as if something that they had been waiting a lifetime for was finally about to happen.

"You can take our picture now, we're in the middle of our political study," the chairwoman said haughtily. "Sit up everyone, and don't look into the camera!"

They all sat up straight, and there was a loud rustle as they picked up the newspapers on the table.

"Hold on, I haven't brought my camera . . . I'm here on another matter. I'm trying to find out who lives at Number 13 Happiness Street."

"How come you never breathed a word of this earlier?" said the chairwoman, obviously quite put out.

"You didn't give me a chance . . ."

"All right then, what do you want to know?"

"It's about Number 13 Happiness Street . . ."

"Someone alive and kicking? That's none of our business. On your way then, and next time don't give us such a shock again, these old bones can't take all the excitement."

"Whose business is it?"

"Quiet! Let's get on with our meeting. Now, where were we? Oh yes, this case involving Dumb Chen from over in the Fourth Xiangyang Courtyard. He'll live on in our hearts forever and all that, but people have started asking why he's still being issued with a face mask every winter . . ."

"Maybe his corpse is still breathing." A strange rasping sound came from the corner.

"We'll issue you with a cauldron to lie in when it's your turn to go to heaven, so you won't have to straighten that snake's waist of yours . . ."

They started to quarrel, their voices getting louder and louder. Fang Cheng took advantage of the confusion to slip out. When he reached the gate he breathed a long sigh of relief, feeling that he had actually almost died himself.

He took a wrong turn. The buildings inside another compound were being pulled down, and clouds of dust filled the air. A crowd of children pressed around the entrance, peering inside. In the yard the workmen were chanting as they swung a thick wooden pole against the gable of the house to the east. A structure like a well was under construction in the middle of a stretch of rubble.

"What is this place?" Fang Cheng asked the children.

"The local housing authority," a young girl replied shyly.

Stepping over a pile of lime, Fang Cheng ran into a young fellow carrying a bucket of cement. "I'm a reporter, where is your foreman?"

"Hey, Wang . . ."

A head popped out from a scaffold. "What is it?"

"The newspapers again."

Wang leaped down nimbly and put down his trowel, wiping his forehead and muscular neck with his sleeve. "Well, you lot are on the ball all right, it's our first go at this particular innovation . . ."

"Innovation?"

"Sounds as if you're here about cadres doing manual labor again. Your paper's carried that news a good half-dozen times already, and the only thing they ever change is my name. If you fellas keep it up it won't be long before I'll have trouble figuring out what I'm called. Take a look at this job. What d'you reckon?"

"What exactly is it?"

"A house, of course. The latest style."

"Actually, it looks like a . . ." he bit back the word "tomb."

"A blockhouse, right? But it doesn't have peepholes in the sides."

"What about the windows?"

"They'll all be on the roof." Wang rubbed his hands in glee, flicking off small pellets of mud. "Ideal in case of war, keeps out robbers, protects you against both wind and the cold, it's got lots of advantages. It's something we learned from our ancestors."

Our cave-dwelling ancestors, Fang Cheng smiled wryly.

"The thing is that houses like these are cheap, you can build 'em by the dozen with premixed concrete. They're easier to make than chicken coops, and they're more solid than a blockhouse. If this catches on, you and me'll both be famous. For starters I'll get a new house, and sit in an armchair at the bureau office. But don't put any of that in your story. Here, take a look at the blueprints. We're in the middle of a demolition job, so the air's not too clean. Hey, Li, are you taking that shovel's pulse or what? Look lively now and bring a stool over here . . ."

Fang Cheng felt a bit dizzy. "It's all right, I'll look these over back at the office. By the way, do you happen to know who lives at Number 13 Happiness Street?"

"Dunno, that's not our business."

"Whose is it then? Whose business *is* it to know?"

"Don't blow your top, let me think about it for a second . . . you could try asking around at the bureau, they've got a big map there, it shows everything down to the last detail."

"Good, I'll try them."

"Do us a favor while you're at it, take this blueprint with you and give it to the director. We'll get a pedicab to take you."

"No need, but thanks all the same."

"This time be sure you don't get my name wrong," Wang shouted after him.

Fang Cheng staggered out and stood in the middle of the road, staring at the sky.

2

The secretary darted out from behind the door, her heels clicking. "Director Ding will be very happy to see you, Comrade Reporter. The other seventeen directors would also like to talk to you, at your convenience of course. Director Ma would like to give you his view on the question of the revolutionary succession; Director Tian wants to give you a rundown on his war record; Director Wang would like to discuss the simplification of Chinese characters . . ."

"Which one of them is the real director of the bureau?"

"Here we make no distinction between the director and assistant directors, we simply list them all in alphabetical order."

"I'm sorry, but I'm a bit pressed for time. I'm here on another matter. Anyway, how do all the directors know I'm here?"

"They were at the board meeting together just now."

"Am I breaking it up?"

"Don't give it another thought. They've been at it for nine days already. They were only too glad to take a break."

The director's office was thick with smoke. A pudgy old man with a healthy-looking complexion standing beside the conference table extended his hand to Fang Cheng with a broad smile. "Welcome, have a seat. Look at all this smoke, it's a form of collective murder . . ."

"What?"

He waved his arms around in the air in an attempt to disperse the clouds of smoke. "The fact that I'm an optimist has been my salvation, let me tell you. Have you heard of a medicine called 'Anliben?'"

"No."

"It's a miracle drug used overseas for people with heart trouble. Does your paper ever send you abroad?"

"The chances are pretty slim."

"Then could you ask someone to help me get some?"

"I'll see what I can do. Do you have heart trouble?"

The director immediately looked glum. "I'm an old man, getting past it. Who knows, maybe the next time you come it'll be Director Ma sitting in this seat . . ." He cleared his throat. "But let's get back to the matter in hand. Major political campaigns bring about major changes, and major changes promote further political campaigns. In the current quarter we've completed 158 percent of our work plan; compared with the same period last year . . ."

"Excuse me, Director Ding, I haven't come here on a story."

"Oh?"

"I want to make some inquiries about a house. Who lives at Number 13 Happiness Street?"

Beads of sweat appeared on Ding's shiny red face. He pulled out a handkerchief and wiped his face."You're not trying to trick me with some difficult question, are you? A big city like this, how could I know every house on every street by heart, like a production chart?"

"I heard that you've got a big map here . . ."

"Yes, yes, I almost forgot." Groping for a small bottle in his pocket, he poured out a few pills and popped them into his mouth. "What do you think of the chicken-blood cure?"

"I haven't tried it."

He pressed a button on his desk, and the red curtains on the wall parted slowly. He picked up a pointer, whipped the air with it energetically, and went up to the map. "How about the arm-swinging cure?"

"I'm sure it helps."

"Yes, it's very effective. Happiness Street . . . Number 30 . . . ah, a coal depot."

"I'm after Number 13."

"13 . . . 13 . . . come and see for yourself, my friend."

It was a blank space.

"How come it's not marked?" Fang Cheng asked in surprise.

Director Ding patted him on the shoulder. "Look carefully, there are quite a lot of blank spots on this map. No one knows what these places are."

"No one knows?"

"Nothing to be surprised about. It's just like all the blank spots in our knowledge of medicine."

"Not even the Public Security Bureau people?"

"Why don't you go and see for yourself, we open out onto their back door; it's very handy. What do you think of gadgets like pacemakers, are they reliable?"

"Pacemakers? I don't know much about them." Fang Cheng

felt around in his pockets and fished out the blueprint. "This morning I went to the local housing authority, and Wang, the foreman, asked me to give this to you. It's the innovation they've been working on."

"That fellow's too active for his own good. He's like a goddamn magician, always coming up with some new gimmick. There's still a lot of major business here we haven't had time to get round to yet." Ding frowned, rolled up the blueprint, and threw it into a wastepaper basket in the corner. "It's thanks to people like him that there's never a moment's peace and quiet anywhere."

The secretary appeared at the door.

"A message for all directors. The meeting is about to resume."

Fang Cheng showed his press card to the guard standing at the opening in the iron fence which surrounded the Public Security Bureau. "I want to see the director of the bureau."

"Go to Interrogation Room I."

"Uh?"

"Up the stairs, first door on the right."

"I'm a reporter."

The guard looked at him blankly, not bothering to reply.

Fang Cheng went up the stairs, and with the help of the faint light in the corridor found a door with a brass plaque nailed to it: Interrogation Room I. He knocked. No one answered, so he pushed the door open and went in. It was sumptuously furnished, with a red carpet on the floor and some leather chairs set around a tea table. It was not in the least like an interrogation room. He heaved a sigh of relief and sat down.

Suddenly three or four policemen came in through a small side door escorting a man in a gray Mao suit. The man was of medium height, and his swarthy face was like an iron mask, cold and stern. A policeman wearing spectacles moved to his side and whispered something in his ear. He nodded.

"This is Director Liu," Spectacles said by way of introduction.

"Please be seated." The director's voice was deep and harsh. He and Spectacles moved to the chair opposite and sat down. The other policemen stood at either side of them.

"Director Liu, there's something I would like to ask you," said Fang Cheng.

"Just a moment, first I've got a question for you." After a moment's pause, Liu proceeded, "If I gave you five matches to make a square how would you do it?"

Fang Cheng stared at him in astonishment.

"Now, don't be nervous."

"I'm not nervous." He thought hard, but his mind was a complete blank.

Suddenly, Liu gave a harsh laugh, and turned smugly toward Spectacles. "This is typical of ideological criminals, they always try and find a way to use the extra match. Ordinary criminals are another case altogether . . ."

"You have a thorough grasp of the psychology of the criminal mind," offered Spectacles obsequiously.

"This is an outrage!" Fang Cheng protested.

"Don't get excited, young man, and don't interrupt me when I'm talking." Liu turned to Spectacles again. "The important thing to note here is that by using psychological tactics you can force the criminal's thinking into a very small space, or shall we say a surface, where he can't possibly conceal himself, and then he's easily overwhelmed. Do you see what I am saying?"

Spectacles nodded. "But . . . but how can you tell he's a criminal? From the look in his eyes?"

"No, no, that's all out of date. Ideological criminals can easily disguise their expressions. Listen, everyone you confront is a criminal, and don't you ever forget it."

"Everyone?"

"Yes. That's what class struggle is all about."

"But . . . then . . . that's . . ." Spectacles spluttered.

"All right, you ask too many questions, I have no alternative but to put you down as ideologically suspect." Rudely cutting Spectacles short, Liu turned and looked sternly at Fang Cheng. "State your business, young man."

"I . . . I want to make an inquiry about a house."

"Good, go on."

"Who lives at Number 13 Happiness Street?"

Director Liu froze, but in an instant a barely perceptible smile appeared on his lips. Spectacles, still looking crestfallen, opened his briefcase and took out some paper, ready to take notes. The two policemen stood next to Fang Cheng. The atmosphere in the room became tense.

"Your name?" Liu asked sharply.

"Fang Cheng."

"Age?"

"What do you take me for? I'm a reporter."

"Hand over your papers."

Fang Cheng drew out his press card and passed it to one of the policemen at his side.

"Examine it and take his fingerprints. Also, find his file and check his ideological status," ordered the director.

"What am I being accused of?"

"Prying into state secrets."

"Is Number 13 Happiness Street a state secret?"

"Whatever no one knows is a secret."

"Including you? You mean, you don't know either?"

"Me? There's a certain continuity to your case, you won't even co-operate during interrogation."

Fang Cheng sighed.

"Next question . . ."

Toward evening, Fang Cheng was released.

3

The municipal library was empty; a faint odor of mold drifted through. Fang Cheng leafed through the catalog, finally locating the book: *A Study of Grave-robbing Techniques Through the Ages.* He noted down the call number and rushed upstairs to the reading room.

A middle-aged woman with prominent cheekbones standing behind the desk looked at the slip and then studied him. "Are you an archeologist?"

"No, I'm a reporter."

"Are you planning to visit some tombs for a story?" she said half-jokingly.

"I want to uncover some secrets."

"What secrets can you possibly find in this book?"

"A place where life has ended can still contain all kinds of secrets."

"Doesn't anyone know what they are?"

"No, because even the living have become part of the secret."

"What?"

"No one knows anyone; no one understands anyone."

The woman with high cheekbones stared at him. "Good heavens, you must be mad."

"It's not me who's mad, it's heaven."

She turned away and ignored him after that. Nearly an hour later he heard the clickety-clack of the book trolley, and the book landed on the desk, raising a cloud of dust. Putting it under his arm, Fang Cheng went into the reading room and sat down at an empty desk in a corner. He leafed through the book, taking notes from time to time.

A pale square of sunlight moved slowly across the table. Fang Cheng stretched and looked at his watch. It was getting late. Without being aware of it he had become surrounded by other readers. Strange, they were all concealing their faces behind thick books. Looking more carefully, Fang Cheng shuddered. They were all reading the same book: *A Study of Grave-robbing Techniques Through the Ages.* He broke into a sweat and stirred uneasily in his seat.

As he slipped out of the library he was aware of a shadowy figure following closely behind. He went into a small lane and then suddenly turned back. The man didn't have time to conceal himself, and they met head-on: it was the fellow in the leather jacket he had bumped into the previous morning on Happiness Street. As soon as he emerged from the lane, Fang Cheng made a dash for a trolley bus at a nearby stop. He jumped on board, and the doors closed behind him with a squeal.

When he got off the bus he looked around anxiously and only relaxed when he felt sure he had not been followed. He thrust his hands into his overcoat pockets and did his best to regain his self-confidence and courage.

At a crossing a boy ran past flying a kite. The string in his hand was taut, and the kite danced in the air. A high place, of course! Jun had disappeared while he was flying a kite. It must have been because he had seen something from a high place. What an idiot I've been, he thought, why didn't I think of that earlier? How awful, he'd almost let himself be suffocated like a rat trapped in a hole.

He bought a pair of high-power binoculars at a secondhand store and set off in the direction of Happiness Street, working his way toward his target through a maze of lanes and alleyways. Finally he saw a tall chimney towering alone in a stretch of vacant ground, surrounded on all sides by broken bricks and rubbish.

He made for the boiler-room at the foot of the chimney. A wizened old man was stoking the boiler as an airblower droned in the background. His tattered sweat-stained work clothes were held together at the waist and swung back and forth in time with his monotonous movements.

"Can I interrupt you for a minute!" Fang Cheng called out.

The old man slowly straightened himself, turned his long, skinny body, and walked over to the doorway. His face was covered with coal dust and ashes.

"Who're you looking for?" he asked.

"I wonder if you could tell me where this leads to?"

"Heaven."

"No, what I mean is, who's the fire for?"

"How should I know. They pay me, I do the work, that's the way it is."

"If they pay you, there must be some evidence for it."

"Ah, yes. Now where's my pay slip got to?" he said, patting himself up and down. "Must've used it to roll a cigarette."

"What was written on it?"

"Let me think . . . seems it might have run something like this: 'Burn enough to make a thousand black clouds.' Hah!" The old man grinned, baring his teeth. Against his grimy face his broken and uneven teeth seemed extremely white.

Fang Cheng took off his black woolen overcoat. "Can I trouble you to keep an eye on this for me. I'm going up to take a look."

"You want to leave a note for your family?"

"What?"

"You're the twelfth so far. Just yesterday a girl jumped . . ."

The old man went back to stoking the boiler. Tongues of flame shot forth.

Fang Cheng gazed up at the chimney, which seemed to lean slightly. He went to the foot of the iron ladder and started climbing. The houses grew smaller and smaller, and it got so windy that his clothes flapped around him. When he reached the last rung, he steadied himself. Hooking one arm through the ladder, he turned around and began to survey the scene with his binoculars. Rooftops, date trees, courtyard walls . . . all came clearly into view. Suddenly he stiffened, and the hand holding the binoculars began shaking. He couldn't believe his eyes. Finally he managed to collect his thoughts and refocus the binoculars. He searched carefully in every corner, but didn't see even a single blade of grass.

"Oh damn it to hell . . ." he muttered to himself.

As his feet touched ground he heard someone calling out sharply behind him, "Don't move. Where do you think you're going now?" Not at all surprised, he brushed the dust off his clothes and turned round. The man in the leather jacket gave him a shove, and they walked toward a jeep parked some distance away.

Twisting his head, Fang Cheng saw the old man stoking the boiler while thick smoke continued to billow out of the tall chimney.

"Black clouds," he said.

4

Fang Cheng was sent to the lunatic asylum.

When he looked at the people running in circles around the desolate grounds and the outside wall covered with weeds, he finally understood: so now he too was inside the wall.

Waves

Main Characters in "Waves"

***Yang Xun**, a young man from a high-ranking official family in Beijing.*
***Xiao Ling**, a young woman from a family of Beijing intellectuals.*
***Lin Dongping**, a middle-aged official in a provincial town; an old friend of Yang Xun's mother.*
***Lin Yuanyuan**, Lin Dongping's daughter.*
***Bai Hua**, a petty criminal; about the same age as Yang Xun.*

The action takes place during the early '70s, toward the end of the Cultural Revolution, in a town in north China. Yang Xun and Xiao Ling have both spent several years in the countryside as "educated youths" before being assigned to work in factories in town. At that time it was still extremely difficult for "educated youths" to return to their homes in the big cities.

—B.S.M.

1

(Yang Xun)

We pulled into the station, the buffers screeching. Streetlights, the shadows of trees, and a line of pulsating railings flashed past. The train attendant opened the door, pulled up the handrail and yelled something indistinct. A stream of fresh air rushed into my face; I breathed in a deep draft and stepped down from the carriage.

The platform was deserted. In the distance the locomotive spouted jets of steam, and a sickly pale spotlight wavered in the rising fog. From the long shadow of the train came the clang of small hammers striking metal.

Night flowed softly along the breeze.

The old ticket-collector leaned against the railing, napping. A loose brass button hung on his chest, quivering a little. He stretched, pulled a fob-watch from his pocket, and said, "Huh, late again, the loafers." He turned the ticket over and over, then gave a long yawn and handed it back. "I've been to Beijing . . . , Tianqiao, Dazhala'r, the flower market . . . it's nothing much."

I handed him a cigarette. "When were you there?"

"In '34." He struck a match, sheltering it from the wind with his hand. The flame leaped from between his fingers to his forehead as he took a greedy puff. "I'd just got myself a wife that year, so I went shopping for a bit of printed cotton and stuff."

A sweet-greasy smell of mildew and decay hung over the little station square. A big cart was standing under the streetlight at the doorway of the waiting room. The shaft-horse snorted from time to time, sniffing about on the ground. The driver lay sideways across the top of the cart, one foot dangling down. I put down my bag, lit a cigarette, and threw the match into a pitch-black puddle nearby.

There were no streetlights and no moon along the road, only a faint gleam from somewhere reflected on the narrow blades of grass by the roadside. Suddenly, a mud-brick house with a light on inside flashed into view from behind some rustling sunflowers. It stood all alone in a vegetable patch. A bunch of red peppers hanging on the door was very distinct in the light.

I changed my bag from one hand to the other and walked up.

"Hey, pal." I knocked on the door. "Could you give me a drink of water?"

Not a sound.

I knocked hard. "Hey, pal—"

A scratching noise. I sensed someone standing behind the door, trying not to breathe. At last the door opened. The outline of a young woman's face was caught by a faint ray of light, and around it were translucent strands of hair . . . what on earth?!

"I'm sorry, I've just got off the train. The factory's a long way off, and I'm terribly thirsty . . ." I explained awkwardly. The shadows gradually faded, and I saw a pair of large, watchful eyes.

She gestured with her hand. "Come in."

The room was furnished very simply, and the wallpaper was peeling in places. A photograph of a little girl mounted in a glass frame stood on the table, a pen and a blue notebook lying carelessly beside it.

"Sit down." She pointed to a stool beside the door, and with one hand behind her back retreated a few steps and sat down on the bed opposite. As the light fell across her face, I was startled: what a beautiful girl.

"Pour it yourself, the thermos flask and the cup are on the box beside you." She opened the blue notebook, still holding her other hand behind her back.

The water was scalding. I blew on the steam and asked: "Do you live here by yourself?"

She raised her eyes and stared at me. After a while she nodded abstractedly.

"Have you just been sent back from the countryside?"

"What?"

I repeated my question.

"A year ago."

"Which team were you in?"

She raised her eyebrows in surprise. "Is there anything else you'd like to know?"

I was taken aback for a moment, then smiled. "Yes. What have you got in your hand, for instance?"

"You must have been brought up on *Ten Thousand Whys.*" She produced a glinting knife from behind her back and laid it on the table.

"On the contrary, I wasn't at all studious when I was young."

She betrayed a sarcastic little smile. "So you're starting now."

"Yes."

"Hurry up and drink your water." She frowned and waved her hand impatiently, the knife tracing flashing curves in the air.

Silence.

She tapped softly on the table with the knife handle in a rhythm that was now fast, now slow. She bent her head to one side as if the sound contained a unique significance. Clearly she was following some familiar train of thought . . . Bang! She threw the knife down on the table, crossed to the window, and opened it. A little poplar stretched its clusters of glistening triangular leaves toward the window, leaping joyfully at her shoulder as if it were welcoming its long-awaited mistress.

I watched her figure from behind, the cup in my hand shaking. Perhaps I should say something to break this awkward silence and break down the barriers of sex, experience, and darkness. Perhaps some fateful relationship was in store for us, but these relationships were always so fragile, so easily missed.

The little girl on the desk smiled mischievously, calling to me silently.

"Is this a photo of you when you were small?" I couldn't help asking.

She seemed not to hear, her arms folded as before, staring out the window. What could she see? Night, fields, trees . . . or was there only the dark, the boundless dark. I asked again, this time realizing how inappropriate my questions were.

Her slender shoulders rose and fell slightly. Suddenly she turned, staring at me coldly, even with a touch of hostility. "How can you be so tactless . . . don't you know how to respect other people's ways? You've finished your water, now go, I want some peace and quiet!"

I stood up. "Sorry to have bothered you. Thank you."

She nodded, and in that instant I saw the glistening of tears.

(Xiao Ling)

Mama is playing the "Moonlight Sonata."

The lights in the room are out. I sit quietly by the piano like a kitten, my plaits loose, the scent of soap drifting out.

Moonlight falls across the floor and begins to dance to the music like a girl in a white silk dress, everything around humming a soft accompaniment to her.

"Mama, Mama—" I suddenly cry out involuntarily.

The moonlight congeals.

"What is it, Lingling?" Mama puts her hand on my forehead. "Don't you feel well?"

"Mama, I'm afraid."

"What are you afraid of?"

"I don't know."

It's true, I don't know whether it's because of the dark, the moonlight, or those mysterious sounds.

I put down my pen. Did the past start from here? Sometimes memory is quite strange; the things it picks out are often insignificant little things. But perhaps it is really these little things which contain concealed within them the portents of an irreversible fate. It's so long since I've written anything it feels strange to start writing now. And besides, what is this? Autobiography? An outline for a novel? No, neither of these, nothing but a recollection of the past.

A siren shrills in the distance. Sometimes I'm like a weary traveler cast out at a small station along the way, thinking neither of my starting point nor of my destination, just thinking of peace and the chance of some lasting rest.

"Fantasy, now, is an intolerably stupid idea. It only makes people stupid, drives them crazy, so they attempt things beyond their ability." The physics teacher in his creased black uniform paces up and down the lecture platform, rubbing his blue-shadowed chin. "Class, what is science? Science is reason, as is every other subject . . ."

I raise my hand.

"Yes, what is it?"

"Teacher, what about poetry?"

"Hm, sit down, what I'm saying includes all fields. Of course, I'm fond of poetry too. In fact, I sometimes try my hand. I've sent stuff to several magazines, and the comrade editors have hailed the rigor of my logic. These lines, for instance:

'The earth has gravitation,
And we have musculation,
No fear then are we feeling
Of bumping into the ceiling.'"

The whole room bursts out laughing.

"How's that, class, not bad, eh?" The teacher pulls modestly at the corners of his jacket. "Any more questions?"

"Hey, you really climb fast."

I turn my head. A boy from another class comes climbing up, leaning on a staff. With his bare arm and sleeve tied round his waist he looks like a Tibetan. Now I remember; last summer holidays I helped him make up lessons.

"I'm afraid this is the long way round," I say.

"No, this is a shortcut. Come on, I'll lead the way." He pushes ahead, using his staff to beat back the clumps of thorns. "Hurry up, the top's not far off."

Dark clouds are gathering, pressing down low, and the wind blows into my skirt. Suddenly there is a clap of thunder which seems to burst right beside my ear. My legs are caught up in my skirt, and it's quite hard to keep going.

"What's up?" the boy calls, turning his head.

"You go first."

He springs down to me like a mountain goat and hands me

his staff. "Here, take this, it'll be easier. Don't be frightened. Look, it's a real storm. When I was small I often came to this hill to pick wild jujube, all by myself. If I got caught in the rain, hey, that was a real thrill! I'd strip off my clothes," he strikes his chest, "just like this, I'd stand on the top of the hill, with the clouds swirling and rolling under my feet, the thunder roaring, and I'd shout and yell until my voice could be everywhere. Guess what I'd shout?"

"What?"

He clambers onto a rocky outcrop and lets out a great shout across the valley: "Oohwaa . . . ooh . . . waa . . ."

The echo rings in the valley, lingering a long time.

Then came this uninvited guest, bringing with him exhaustion, cold, and an unfamiliar breath.

What's the matter with me? My whole body feels ill at ease, my thoughts are confused, all because of this wretched fellow. What's he got to do with you? He only came here for water and light. And then? Well, on your way, however far and long all roads may be . . .

The black night and I are face to face.

Emptiness, obscurity, purposelessness, are these what I give to the night, or what the night gives to me? It's hard to distinguish which is night and which is me, as if these two have blended into one. It's always like this. It's only when living things are in contact with nonliving things that there can be harmony, calm, no conflict, no desire, nothing.

Oh little poplar, what is it you keep saying?

"What are you looking at, Lingling, are you watching a sea gull?"

"I'm watching the sun, Mama."

"Don't be naughty, you'll hurt your eyes."

"It doesn't matter."

"Do as I say, Lingling." The drops of water are like diamonds against Mama's tanned skin. "Aren't you coming for a swim?"

"You go, Mama, I'm sunbathing."

I lie on the burning sand, watching the sun without blinking. The sun's roar is deafening, covering the falling of the waves and the cries of the crowd. I shut my eyes then open them again, and the colors shift and change rapidly.

The sky becomes so dull and small, like a dirty piece of rag carried high up by a sea gull. The sun is wealthy, after all.

High tide . . .

2

(Lin Dongping)

"Cigarette—" I said.

He reached into the tin box and took out a cigarette, striking a match unhurriedly. Both of us were used to such awkward silences. A dead leaf fluttered down outside the window, striking against the pane with a light, brittle sound.

"Everyone well at home?"

"Papa's very busy . . ."

"Oh yes, I saw in the papers. Foreigners elbowing their way in, what can you do . . . and your mother?"

"She plans to retire this year."

"Retire?" I murmured to myself, my fingers drumming on the glass teatable top.

The door opened with a bang and Yuanyuan rushed in, her face all red; whether she'd tied her scarf too tightly or whether it was because of the wind I didn't know. "Oh, it's you, Xun, when did you get back? You know, it's really strange, whenever you come, our house goes as quiet as a grave . . ."

I glared at her reprovingly.

She promptly covered her mouth with her hand, laughing. "It's unlucky to say that, right? I ought to put it like this: 'As quiet as an unruffled pond. Suddenly the cock crows, breaking the . . .'" Yuanyuan flung her scarf into the air, and it dropped like a parachute onto the top of the clothes stand. "That's what we were reading in class."

"Go and make us some tea."

"All right. 'The old farmer Zhang shoos the animals out of the yard . . . '" Yuanyuan pushed open the door and left.

The phone rang. I picked up the receiver, winding the cord round my hand. "Yes, it's me, yes, what time? I'm just leaving."

Yuanyuan came in carrying the cups. "Pa, another meeting? Oh, these Party meetings never end . . ."

"Yuanyuan!" I called out sharply.

"Everyone says so . . ."

"Who is everyone? And who are you?"

She stuck out her tongue, winking at Xun.

"Let Xun stay here for a meal, I'll be back soon."

I wound down the window, and at once a cool rustling wind filled the car, the curtains flapping against my face. That was better, that cold, aching feeling. In the side mirror everything turned from large to small, rapidly dissolving. "Retire"; the word was so unfamiliar, especially for her, even a little frightening. Her image was still as I remembered from our first meeting, still as young and sharp-tongued. Time was unreal. It would soon be thirty years. What were we arguing about in that District Committee Enlarged Session? Was it the prospects for co-operation between the Nationalists and Communists, or the electrical plant workers' strike? She was gripping her cup, twisting it around and around in her hands but never actually touching the water. Then when the debate intensified, the water spilled and she hurriedly drank a mouthful. Perhaps it was the excitement, or because the light was too dim, but I didn't see her clearly at the time. After the session was over, we met on a bend of the stairs. She put out her hand so naturally and gracefully, smiling ironically at me for a moment . . . ah, why do I want to torment myself all over again? Who was it that said pain is a sign of life? Now I remember; it was in our first lecture at medical college. An old American-educated professor told us, then wrote it on the blackboard in English, chalk dust floating gently down.

It was an autumn morning, the sunlight seeping through the dim old-fashioned windows . . . that tousle-haired student and I, what had we still in common? My hair was white now.

Outside the window, two young workers, their clothes covered in grease, clutching lunchboxes, arguing about something as they walked, looked up; a young girl in a red-checked scarf, nibbling a sweet potato, looked up; the woman washing clothes at the tap wiped her hands on her apron and looked up. What did that look of theirs mean? Perhaps they never wondered who was sitting in the car; what did it have to do with them? But the police turn on all the green lights and even raise their white gloves.

A black Zym sedan was parked at the gate of the Municipal Revolutionary Committee. I recognized the owner from the number-plate: the current second secretary to the Provincial Party Committee. When I held the post of Provincial Propaganda Department Chief, he was just the section chief under me; his rise came after my transfer, owing, it was said, to an article he had in the Party newspaper.

Inside the dingy gatehouse, two people were engaged in conversation.

". . . Secretary Wu, there's been a fair bit of obstruction, and a poor bloody soldier like me can hardly handle it. There are always a few blockheads you can't budge . . ." It was Wang Defa's Shandong accent.

Wu Jiezhong laughed. "Perhaps I'm one of those blockheads too?"

I coughed, and they turned round.

Wu Jiezhong stuck out a thin, bony finger. "Old Lin, you've sprung an ambush on us."

"Then I'll come to a sticky end," I said.

We all laughed, but each of us laughed in a different way, making an unpleasant noise.

"Secretary Wu's come to investigate our work," Wang Defa said.

"Let's not say 'investigate,' just passing by to have a look; how's the production situation this quarter?" Wu

Jiezhong adjusted the black woolen overcoat draped over his shoulders.

"Bad," I said.

An awkward silence. Wang Defa fished a large handkerchief from his pocket and blew his nose noisily.

"Has the Zhang Village coal mine resumed production?" he asked. "The central authorities take a very serious view of this matter."

"Since the cave-in we've been organizing rush repairs, but the crux of the matter is that the causes of the accident still haven't been cleared up. This point is very important, otherwise similar accidents . . ."

"My view is we shouldn't stop eating because of a hiccup." Wu Jiezhong shook his head in dissatisfaction. "Very well, look into this matter again; get onto it as quickly as possible, because the whole country's watching this mine as a model. What's important is the influence . . . you go back, I'll see myself off."

"Is the other matter settled?" Wang Defa interrupted.

"Oh. I think we'd better not go ahead with it."

"The comrades from the drama troupe have already got the costumes and props ready."

"But don't do anything extravagant, just a get-together . . ." Wu Jiezhong glanced at me. "Are you coming too, Old Lin?"

"No, I'm not feeling too well today."

There were still twenty minutes before the meeting started, so I walked into the office and sat down at the desk. The stamp pad, pen rack, and paperweight on the desk gleamed in the sunlight. Let me be quiet for a while, I'm tired. When I was a child, Blind Zhang from East Street in town shook his head over me, saying I'd have no reward for a lifetime of toil. For that Nurse nearly boxed his ears. I still remembered that scene: I stood on tiptoe with my chin on the ice-cold datewood counter, watching his eye sockets sealed with a black plaster and his trembling hands with their large joints. He threw the bamboo slips into the barrel, shaking them with a rustling sound, muttering incantations. The red-beaked canary hopped impatiently back and forth . . .

I looked up; the sun shone on the huge detailed map of the city. The maze of lines, circles, and symbols gradually blurred until there was only the eye-catching Town Hall looming up in silence, looking down over the entire city. The third-story windows of the East Wing burned in the twilight sun, as if concentrated at the focus of a lens . . . strange, I needed only sit down behind this desk to have my confidence restored. It was as if only now, amidst this pile of shining stationery, that I found my legitimate place . . .

The door opened and Miss Zhang walked in very quietly. "Chief Lin, some letters from the masses . . ."

"Hand them over to the Postal Inquiries Section."

"It's the Postal Inquiries Section that sent them over." She smiled mysteriously.

"Very well, leave them here."

The envelopes had been stuck down again, so I slit them open with scissors one by one. Most of them had been written by local disaster victims (thinking of the floods this summer really made me shudder), asking for an investigation of where the national disaster relief funds had gone. The position of chief of the flood relief subgroup was held by Wang Defa: at every meeting of the standing committee he held forth about the concrete figures for each item, and the sweat stains on his faded army uniform, which he never washed, exuded an evil smell, as if he could thereby give people the impression he was working his guts out. In the pile, unexpectedly, was this inexplicable letter: ". . . on any Wednesday and Saturday evening please go to 75 People's Road East and catch the adulterers in the act." These people were mad, to send such a letter over to me out of the blue, it was simply a joke! I locked the letters in a drawer. A hundred letters were already lying there; what did a few more matter.

It was time for the meeting. I went downstairs and opened the supply shop door. Su Yumei had her head buried in a book, a strand of hair hanging down.

"A packet of cigarettes," I said.

In the instant she looked up, her eyes were very focused; evidently her concentration just now was a kind of pretense. "Chief Lin?" She smoothed her hair, smiling prettily.

"What are you reading?"

"*Bitter Herb.*[1] It's very moving."

"Do you have any Front Gate cigarettes[2]?"

"We have everything. Some high-quality milk sweets have just come in. The brand name sounds really nice. Would you like some?"

"What brand?"

She blinked flirtatiously. "Purity, Purity milk sweets."

(Lin Yuanyuan)

"Any news about your job allocation?" Xun asked, sipping his tea.

"Huh, don't mention it, my teacher claims they're taking care of it, they've made such a fuss the whole school knows about it, so there's still no sign of it. Besides, what's the point of working?" I leaned against the bookcase, loosening and then plaiting again my wretchedly meager pigtails. Mama said that in all my life I'd never be able to grow long plaits. Ah, it's nearly seven years since she passed away, and this plait was still short and blunt like a rabbit's tail.

"Hey, look who's here." I don't know when she arrived, but Fafa, wearing a red sports jersey, was leaning languidly in the doorway, her arms folded across her chest. "Look at Yuanyuan, her voice has gone all sweet."

"Do you mind!" I glared at her.

Swinging her backside, Fafa walked up to the teatable and nonchalantly took out a cigarette, turning it round and round in her hand. "How are things in the capital, Comrade Yang Xun?"

"In what respect?"

[1]A novel by Feng Deying, first published in 1958.
[2]One of the highest-quality brands of cigarette in China.

Fafa blew out a big thick smoke ring. "The basic aspects of life, of course, like . . ." she brushed her knee.

"Dresses," Xun smiled mockingly for a moment. "I'm sorry, I didn't take much notice."

"Typical bookworm. You can only understand girls from books . . ."

"That's enough, Fafa!" I cut her short.

"What other ways have you tried?" Xun asked unhurriedly.

"Me? I prefer observation and experience." Fafa pulled over a chair and sat down. "In accordance with the principle of sexual attraction, I have a special interest in men . . ."

What a nerve! I gave her a discreet kick.

"Why are you kicking me? It's always bad luck for those who tell the truth, but I'd rather die than surrender." Fafa laughed sharply, like a knife scraping on glass. "After investigation and research, I've found that men are selfish creatures, and it's only we women who are great."

"Why?"

"Women are richer in sacrificial spirit."

Oh, I got fed up listening to that sort of nonsense ages ago. I honestly felt like jumping up and shouting, "Fafa, that's not your idea, it's just something you've picked up. You're not worthy of it, you'll never know what sacrifice is."

Xun laughed lightly. "And you? Fafa, are you preparing to sacrifice something? Faced with a beggar, for instance, are you prepared to sacrifice your family status?"

"Of course, I love the poor . . ."

"Hearing that sounds the same as if you'd said you love money."

Fafa flushed red. "Don't lecture me. My father gives me political classes at every meal."

"Only at mealtimes? That's wonderful, it helps the digestion . . ." Xun got to his feet. "Yuanyuan, I'm going for a walk."

The door closed. The room went from light to dark as a cloud drifted past outside. I went to the window, watching his solid figure recede.

"That creature's covered with prickles," Fafa said.

"Fafa, it's you who's wrong . . ."

"Oh, I'm always wrong, and he's right. Isn't it obvious? You're in love with him."

"What rubbish!" My face flushed hot immediately, right down to my neck. Was it true, perhaps? My heart was thumping wildly. What did love mean? Was it liking? But I liked lots of people.

Fafa walked over and squeezed my shoulder. "You can't fool me with that."

"Go away!"

"Are you angry? O.K., so I was wrong. Calm down, my dear Yuanyuan. Look, here are two tickets to the reception, the Public Security Bureau only got three. I've heard all the big shots from upstairs are coming. Let's go together. O.K.?"

(Yang Xun)

I was wandering aimlessly down the street.

The goods in the shop windows were covered with dust, with little signs hanging in front of them: "For display only—not for sale," "Service for valid coupons only." A disorderly crowd was pressing around the grocery shop door. Children banging enamel bowls pushed in and out through the throng. A young fellow in a greasy white cap stuck his head out the door, shouting something in a loud voice. A row of pedicabs was parked at the corner of the street under the slogan "We have friends all over the world." The drivers lounged in the back seats smoking, chatting, and napping, battered straw hats half-hiding their bronzed faces . . .

Suddenly a girl blocked my way. Her hands stuck in her coat pockets, she was smiling, her head to one side. "Don't you recognize me?"

I stopped, startled. "It's you . . ."

"That's right, trust your own memory. Are you sure you weren't sleepwalking that evening?"

I smiled. "I was thrown out for a drink of water."

"I was in a bad mood that day; it was evening, too."

"What does evening have to do with it?"

"People are influenced by their environment, as the materialist saying goes."

"Aren't there any other kinds of sayings?"

"You have a bad habit of asking questions." She stopped, looking at the people all around. "Look, we can't just keep standing here. Are you free now? Walk a little way with me, I feel like going for a walk now."

She spoke so frankly and naturally, I couldn't help smiling.

"What are you smiling at?"

"Do you often invite people like this?"

"It depends." She frowned and looked away. "If you have something else to do, forget it."

I almost shouted, "No, nothing, I was just going for a walk too."

We walked on ahead. A kite caught on the overhead lines fluttered like a piece of fallen white cloud.

"Let me introduce myself. My name's Yang Xun. And yours?"

Silence.

"Are you afraid I'll pollute your name?"

"Pollute? I haven't heard that word for a long time."

"In this glorious new world, pollution doesn't exist." A truck thundered past, drowning my voice.

"What?"

I repeated myself.

"Nor does man exist," she said.

"Are you always in a bad mood?"

"My mood's fine at the moment."

"And that evening, why was it bad then?"

She stopped, raising her eyebrows in surprise. "So, this is your splendid tradition, you cadres' kids?"

"My father drives a pedicab."

She laughed sarcastically and drew a circle in the air with her finger. "You left out one wheel."

"What's your evidence for saying that?"

"Intuition." She paused for several seconds, and in that time I sensed she was saying something to herself. "The bad habits you people have make me sick."

The paving stones underfoot slid past: blurred, distinct, blurred . . . I stopped. "Since that's how it is . . ."

"Since what? You promised, you have to finish our walk!" she said almost savagely.

"That's not what I mean."

"Forget it, there's no need to explain."

We passed the dilapidated city gate, walking silently along the moat. The oily greenness of the water adrift with black weeds exuded a rich autumnal smell. A bird nesting in a tree twittered and flew off with a rustling sound.

She pushed aside the dangling willow branches, the dancing sunlight filtering down onto her shoulders and arms. "Hey, why don't you say something?" she asked suddenly.

"I'm doing hard labor."

She laughed. "Is it really so hard? Oh, you're hopeless. Look, this is a wonderful place for exile."

"This is a stinking ditch."

"Huh, come and look." Suddenly she grasped a willow branch and gazed across the moat. Several children were skimming stones. The stones stirred up rings of ripples, and the sunlight was shattered into fragments, a glittering silver coin floating on the crest of each wave. She was completely captivated, counting them excitedly and tearing off the willow leaves beside her. "Four, five, six . . . look, that little dark kid's really terrific . . . nine, the highest score . . ." She tore off a willow leaf and held it in her mouth, her voice becoming indistinct. A willow branch beside her swayed back and forth, like a green pendulum. She turned round abruptly, with a wink that just hinted at ridicule. "Hey, prisoner exiled to a stinking ditch, aren't you interested."

"I was just thinking how unlucky adults are. Even if they have everything, they can't change their bad luck . . ."

"Do you think children are fortunate? Don't forget, these are all poor children," she said. "People are born unlucky."

"So why do you want to go on living?"

"Living is just a fact."

"Facts can be changed too."

"The pity of it is that people have enough inertia to keep lingering on, eking out an existence to their last breath, and that's what normally passes for life force."

"Why are you so pessimistic?"

"Another of your whys." She looked at me intently, her eyes, almost severe, flashing green stars, a strand of hair dangling over her forehead. "Are you trying to expound some truth?"

I did not answer.

"Tell me something, please." She brushed back the stray hairs, speaking slowly and emphatically. "In your life, what is there worth believing in?"

I thought for a moment. "Our country, for example."

"Ha, that's an outdated tune."

"No, I don't mean some hackneyed political cliché, I mean our common suffering, our common way of life, our common cultural heritage, our common yearning . . . all of these make up our indivisible fate; we have a duty to our country . . ."

"Duty?" she cut me off coldly. "What duty are you talking about? The duty to be an offering after having been slaughtered, or what?"

"Yes, if necessary, that kind of duty."

"Forget it. I can just see you sitting in a spacious drawing room discussing the subject like this. What right have you to say 'we,' what right?" She was becoming more and more agitated, her face growing flushed, tears filling her eyes. "No thanks, this country's not mine! I don't have a country, I don't have one . . ." She turned away.

A few clouds along the pale green horizon were dyed red by the evening light like unextinguished coals, leaving their last warmth to the earth. The river had turned an inky green, breathing out faint, rhythmic sounds.

She turned her head, brushing the willow leaves off her plaits, and glancing away evasively she forced a smile. "I shouldn't be like this, let's go back."

We passed a small liquor shop.

"Let's go in," I suggested. "Do you drink?"

She nodded. "Yes, but only spirits."

A drunk was flirting with the waitress at the counter. "My old woman's a bad egg, you, you think she hasn't played round enough?"

I shouldered him aside. "Half a catty of Fenyang Spirits and two cold plates."

The drunk shouted at my shoulder, "I say it's enough, it's enough!"

I paid, collected the bottle and plates, and stopped halfway back. A fellow of about my age was sitting next to her, hugging half a bottle of spirits and babbling: ". . . come on, I'll tell your fortune, for free, I'll make an exception for you, cross my heart, I never lie . . ."

I dropped my hand on his shoulder. "Hey, what's going on?"

He cast a sidelong glance at me, his eyes dull, his cheeks flushed red. He was obviously a little drunk. "Boss, you want your fortune told too? Line up, line up, priority to women comrades. Oh, it's very busy today, very busy."

She compressed her lips in a smile, indicating that I should sit down. I sat down.

"You're intelligent, no doubt about it, extremely intelligent. A pity you have such a hard life, no one to cheer you up . . ."

I banged my fist down on the table and stood up. He turned, looking sideways at me, an evil glint flashing in his eyes. "Impatient? It's good, good to be alive. Know who I am? Bai Hua, go ask around . . ."

"I don't care who the hell you are, I'll smash your face in . . ." I had grabbed an empty bottle beside me when a small strong hand pressed down on mine. I looked down at her.

"Sit down! Don't you see he's drunk?" Her raised eyelashes cast long shadows across her cheeks.

I sat down.

"Are you really a fortune teller?" she asked.

"That's right."

"You don't look like one to me."

Bai Hua grinned, took a half-smoked cigarette from behind his ear, molded it straight, and struck several matches before lighting it. Shreds of smoke curled out from between his teeth. "Where are you two from?"

"Heaven," she said, fanning away the smoke with her hand.

Bai Hua gazed intently at the ceiling and shook his head. After a while he asked again, "What's between you two?"

"You try and work it out," I said.

"Going steady?"

She laughed loudly and clearly. "No, falling out."

"Have a drink! Have a drink!" Bai Hua impatiently tossed the half-smoked cigarette onto the floor, stuck the neck of the bottle into his cup, and began to sing in an affected voice: "Just swallow a mouthful of wine honey-sweet, in your plain, simple life no sorrow you'll meet . . ."

"Don't have any more." She caught hold of his cup. "Look how drunk you are."

"Who's drunk? Drunk? Me? What a laugh . . ." He tore her hand away from around the cup. "Don't dirty your little hand." He raised the cup to drink when he was arrested by her hand. With a bang he placed the cup heavily on the table, spilling the liquor. "Do you dare control me?"

"I'd like to try," she said calmly.

"You? Try?" Bai Hua looked her up and down in surprise, then sighed deeply, his shoulders drooping. "All right, I, I won't drink."

The street was enveloped in a damp night mist, and the haloed streetlights looked at each other across a distance. An alley cat flew like lightning across the street. Suddenly she stopped. "Do you like poetry?"

"Yes."

"If I recite a poem, will you listen?"

"Of course."

She gazed straight ahead, her voice at once gentle and fervent:

> "Green, how much I love your greenness,
> Green wind, green branches.
> The ship upon the sea,
> The horse in the mountains.
> . . . .
> Green, how much I love your greenness.
> Myriad stars of white frost,
> Come with the fish of darkness
> Which opens the road to dawn.
> The fig tree scours the wind
> With the sandpaper of its branches,
> The mountain, like a wildcat,
> Bristles its angry bitter-aloes.
> . . . ."[3]

A leaf fell under her foot, spun round, and flew away again. She shook her head. "I recited that badly."

"It was good. By Lorca?"

"'A Sleepwalker's Ballad.'"

"It's a beautiful dream. What a pity it only lasts an instant before it dies."

"On the contrary, our generation's dream is too painful, and too long; you can never wake up, and even if you do, you'll only find another nightmare waiting for you."

"Why can't there be a happier ending?"

"Oh, you, always forcing yourself to believe in something; your country, duty, hope, these pretty lollipops always luring you on until you bump into a high wall . . ."

"You certainly haven't seen the end either."

"That's right, I'm waiting for the end, I must see it, whatever it is, that's the main reason I go on living. There are two

[3]Federico García Lorca, "Romance Sonámbulo," from *Romancero Gitano* (1928).

kinds of people in the world; one kind adds to the world's glory, and the other kind makes scars on it. You probably belong to the former kind; I to the latter . . ."

I gazed at her narrowed, unfathomable eyes in silence. "Is your own life very unhappy."

"My own life?" She closed her eyes slowly. "When they get to this point, people will separate you from the world . . ."

"No, I don't mean that, I was only trying to ask . . ."

Her expression darkened, and she glared at me fiercely. "Lots of questions are not to be asked, do you understand? That's the simplest common sense these days, understand? Why? Why? It's as if you've just come from another planet!"

The one lighted window in the street had gone out, and all was pitch-black. The road was all bumps and hollows. Some women nightshift workers came toward us, chattering about something in low voices, and gradually faded away in the distance.

"I have a bad temper," she murmured to herself, sighing.

"That's understandable, it's evening now."

"Oh," she laughed softly, "but one evening's not the same as another. There's a moon tonight."

"And poetry."

"Yes, and poetry. I'm on nightshift, we must say goodbye."

We stood at the crossroads, facing each other. The mist floated behind her like a huge iceberg. It rushed up in the darkness, enfolding a wave of silence which drowned us in its midst. Silence, a sudden silence. At last, unwillingly, it quietly withdrew.

She held out her hand. "My name is Xiao Ling."

(Xiao Ling)

The light was flickering in a battered green enamel bowl on the toolbox. What did he really mean by what he said? Perhaps it was just another kind of deception. The country, huh, none of these ultimate playthings exists, it's just those yesmen pretending to be emotional; they need a cheap conscience to reach a cheap equilibrium . . . but why be so fierce? Surely you don't really detest him? But don't forget, you were with him for a whole evening, a misty evening, and besides, you're so excited, like a girl on her first date. My head aches, I'm drunk. The little coach in the music box (when I was little I often broke off the wheels) speeds out into the distance, toward the end of the earth, loaded with my anguished dreams. And what is there out there? I'm afraid there's nothing, only a continuation of here . . .

"Hand me the pliers."

Meaning, why does there have to be meaning? Don't meaningless things last longer? Like stones—where is the meaning in them? Children laughing: let them laugh and break this endless stillness . . . I was reciting poetry. Fool, when did you become so emotional, even carefree and romantic? Was it the night mist? Was it the moonlight? I love poetry; in the past I loved it for its beauty, now I love it for castigating life, for piercing the heart, but how did I never realize the value of these two aspects together? Perhaps because everyone sees life from only one angle . . .

"Spanner, did you hear? Pass me the spanner!"

Autumn has come, and the leaves flutter down one by one like the listless flowers of spring. It's an imitation, a clumsy imitation, full of human vulgarity, just like flames in a mirror, an empty fervor that lacks warmth, which will always lack warmth but never fail to set those blood-red haunches swaying . . . everywhere there are stage props covered in dust, even people become part of the props, the laughing ones laughing forever, the crying ones crying forever . . .

"Change two six-ring screws . . . Cat got your tongue?" Firecracker stopped work and stuck his head out from under the shadow of the revolving machine. The acne on his face and the scars around his mouth showed up clearly. I turned my head away. Several flies alighted on the light bulb.

"Hey, what are you thinking about all the time?"

A fly climbed up the light bulb with extreme caution. Its

flimsy wings glimmered with a pale purple light, their pattern clearly distinguishable. I opened the door of the duty office and went out.

In the sky above the narrow path around the factory wall starlight rippled and moonlight rolled along the top of the wall overgrown with weeds. I stopped and drew a deep breath. How I yearn for somewhere to belong: as long as it were more permanent, more peaceful, I'd rather not think of anything at all. No yesterday and no tomorrow, no pain and no happiness. Let my heart unfold toward the outside world like a dark-red sponge, quietly soaking up each transparent drop of water . . .

Someone's shadow flashed at the end of the passageway, and a moment later Firecracker walked up to me.

"What's up?"

"I'm a bit tired."

"You've been drinking, you can't fool me." He rolled a cigarette, taking his time, the cigarette paper rasping in his rough fingers. "The divorce procedures are all finished, and that bitch of a woman squeezed a lot of money out of me, huh!" He struck a match and stopped in midair, the flame illuminating the drooping corners of his eyes. He lit the cigarette. "What's on your mind, young Xiao?"

"What business is it of yours?"

The tip of his cigarette dimmed, and he blew on the ash. "A matter of mutual concern, why not? Can't you give me any suggestions, Xiao, about what I should do?"

"Look, is the overhead beam in the duty office strong?"

"It's iron, of course it is."

"Then go hang yourself." I laughed heartily.

The steam hammer beat up and down.

"O.K., I'll make you see if this Horse King[4] has three eyes or not." He stubbed his cigarette out fiercely, the sparks scatter-

[4]A popular name for Buddha, whose divinity is manifested in his third eye.

ing on the ground. "After all, you're just a provisional worker, you saunter into work, you drink . . ."

"Go and report me then. Beat it," I said.

(Bai Hua)

I walked up to the counter, eyeing the sleek red and green bottles on the shelf. They were almost in convulsions, bouncing and jumping, as if all I needed to do was to close one damned eye and they'd fly away.

"Look, see this? Credentials, the upper ranks' confidence in me . . ." The blabber-mouth standing in front of me was pestering the waitresses behind the counter.

I tapped the fellow on the arm. "Ssh—quiet down."

He turned round, staring at me, baffled. "But what can I do if they won't acknowledge my invention? Poor we may be, but that's all part of building our great Socialism. Now these girls, they only know how to stand and giggle like idiots, but it's a big problem, it should be treated as a matter of basic political principle . . ."

The devil only knows what stuff the old crab had been knocking back. I gave his backside a kick. "Beat it. Back to your hole."

He nodded, grinning and smiling at me, then waddled off to the door. Suddenly he turned round and shouted: "It's a political frame-up, I'll go to the provincial authorities and the Central Committee and complain about you people! Old Marx, if he knew . . . hmph!"

Where did those two kids come from? I lost a trick there, damn, if the bastards in West River saw they'd laugh their heads off all night. That chick, she's really got something. Forget it, let it go.

I went out and limped across the road. A sleekly shining sedan was parked in a patch of light at the gate of the Municipal Party Committee hostel up ahead, and a dozen policemen were marching cockily up and down. The swine, out for a good time as usual.

All at once, two chicks walked out from the side gate, scarcely more than fledglings not yet out of the nest, but very smartly dressed.

"Yuanyuan, what *is* up with you?" the tall, thin one said. "I was just starting to enjoy myself . . ."

"I didn't drag you away."

"That is an admirable attitude, comrades." I pinched my cap, squashed it down on my forehead, and caught up with them.

They stopped, staring at me in surprise.

"Who are you?" the one called Yuanyuan asked timidly.

"Me? Responsible for security work."

"Plainclothes," the tall thin one said hurriedly. "You're under my father."

"Oh, you're Director Liu's little treasure? I know your father very well."

"What a way to talk, huh! Don't try to chum up with me. What's your cap doing squashed down like that, and you smell of drink. I'll tell my father when I get back and make him demote you."

"Ah, I'm nothing," I struck a wounded pose, "but what about the five children?"

They looked at each other and burst out laughing.

I ducked down a lane and stopped by a pitch-black doorway with a wooden sign hanging beside it: "Warehouse Site; Workers Only." I reached for a rope behind the sign and pulled it hard: one long, two short. In a moment or two someone asked, "Who is it?"

"Step on it!"

The door opened a crack, and a big forehead appeared. "Come in, Boss, there's a show on."

I walked into the room with its boarded-up windows. Number Four's smooth round shoulders were swaying slightly amidst the choking cigarette smoke. She was strumming a guitar and singing in a husky voice. The fellows crowded around her, all drunk as lords.

"Here comes the Boss."

"Sit over here, Boss."

I sat down on a wooden box in the corner and lit a cigarette.

When the song came to an end the party fell into an uproar at once, with a great din of shouts and whistles. One bastard with big cheekbones staggered and shoved his way across, sitting down next to Number Four and putting his arm around her waist. He whispered something to her. There was a great cackle all round. Number Four shook her head, fondling the guitar strings with a sultry smile.

I felt for a kitchen chopper in the corner, stood up, and walked over. The fellows automatically made way for me. I went up to them and put my hand on Number Four's shoulder. "She's mine."

The room fell quiet instantly, and you could hear the sound of a cup breaking. Big Cheekbones was dazed for a second, then bent down and pulled out a knife. I ducked sideways, and the back of the chopper struck his wrist. The knife fell to the floor with a clatter. As the chopper turned in the air it cut into his shoulder. He clapped his hand over the wound, blood seeping out through his fingers.

"Any more of you with bright ideas?" I asked, my gaze sweeping round, and all the young melonheads turned away. I fished out ten yuan, crumpled it into a ball, and threw it in Big Cheekbones' twisted face. "Go and buy some medicine, worm, and then grow bigger eyes . . . come on, Number Four, let's go."

3

(Yang Xun)

She was sitting on the edge of the bed, leafing through a book, the white reflection of the pages shining on her face. Her name was Xiao Ling, she was twenty-three this year. Besides that, what else did I know? She was an enigma. Rose, Little Swallow . . . the girls I'd known before paled before her. They belonged in the drawing room, like a painting or a vase of flowers; you didn't think of them once you'd left. What was she thinking? She certainly had a great many secrets, secrets which didn't belong to me, or to anyone. The book with the blue cover, for instance, lying on the table, might be packed with secrets, as if her entire life was stored in these secrets, sealed up forever . . .

"Hey, haven't you looked enough?" she asked suddenly.

I smiled, "No."

She snapped the book shut and raised her head. "All right, look." Our eyes met. Her chin trembled, unable to hold back a smile. She smiled so naturally and openly, it was like a horizontal blue streak flashing out in every direction. "Say something, the silence is getting on my nerves."

"Don't you know how to respect other people's ways? You've finished your water, now go, I want some peace!" I said.

"Sorry to have bothered you. Thank you," she said.

We burst out laughing.

"Hey, beggar," she waved her hand, "don't laugh, talk about yourself."

"What is there to say? My curriculum vitae is simple: father, mother, sister, school, work in the countryside, factory work . . . about ten words altogether."

"Which is also to say, politically reliable."

"Except that I was in the county jail for a few days when I was in the countryside."

"For robbery?" Her eyes widened in surprise. "Or for hooliganism?"

"You have a rich imagination."

"But there always has to be a charge."

"Another student and I opposed collection of the grain tax, there was a drought that year, and many of the peasants had absolutely nothing to eat."

"What a fine champion of idealism. And afterward, did you bow your head and confess?

"An old comrade-in-arms of my mother got me out."

"That's how it always ends, that's why people like you always believe in happy endings; standing at every crossroads there's some protector or other." She drummed on the book with her fingers. "That day when you were talking about our country, I was wondering, is our country the lifelong protector of you and your kind . . .?"

"You mean our country protects us, or we protect our country?"

"It's the same thing."

"No, it's not. If the former is true, then in order to achieve the latter we must always pay a higher price in our efforts and endeavors."

"What price?"

"The price of the heart."

"But people like you, in the end, never do pay the full price, you never have to suffer hunger and cold, be subjected to discrimination and insults, lay down your life for a few words . . ."

"That depends. During those years of . . ."

"That was only temporary, like our smiles."

I leaped to my feet. "You, we. You have a very interesting way of dividing things up. Since the two of us aren't on the same road, what's the point of seeing each other? I'm sorry, it's time for me to be leaving."

"Sit down." She blocked my way, defiantly biting her lip. "I tell you, you mustn't go because I talk like this!"

We stood at a deadlock. She was so close, her breath blew lightly against my face. The cross of the windowframe was reflected in her eyes. Crickets chirped softly in the corner.

"You're really hospitable," I said.

"Let me ask you something. What is courtesy?"

"Respect for other people."

"No. Courtesy is just a kind of indifference."

"A certain degree of indifference is necessary."

"Well, is truth necessary? A person can't have everything, first this, then that . . ." She stopped, and gave a little smile. "Aren't you tired?"

I smiled too, and sat down.

She shook her head. "All right, let's have some courtesy. Would you like some water? Oh yes, and there's some black tea here too . . ." She put on an apron, took a jar out of the box, went to the corner, and lit the kerosene burner on top of the earthen stove. The blue flames flared up, licking the black base of the pot. Sometimes fire doesn't remind you of its untamed violence, or the way it makes things collapse, it reveals instead that other face: beauty, warmth, kindness . . .

She stirred the pot with a spoon, making a clear, crisp clinking sound. Her back to me, she suddenly asked, "Yang Xun, am I strange?"

"How can I say; I get a different impression every time."

"To tell the truth, I thought that now I was old I should be relatively stable. Don't laugh. But I'm still changing; sometimes I don't recognize myself at all. What are you laughing at?"

"You don't look more than eighteen or nineteen."

"Don't flatter me. Women always like to be told they look younger than they are, isn't that so? They live for others. Really, I feel old, like an old grandmother sitting in the doorway in the sun, sizing up each passer-by with cold detachment . . ."

"Well, I'm a passer-by."

"You're an exception."

"Why?"

"You didn't just pass by, you broke in . . . clear the table, the tea's ready." She poured black tea into two cups and took a packet of biscuits out of the drawer. "Please, have one."

"Now *that's* courtesy."

"Is it? Then I've progressed a little." She blew gently on the steam in the cup. "Strange, how did we warm up all of a sudden?"

"Yes, we've got very warm."

"You haven't answered my question at all."

"No one can answer it. It's a question with a history of thousands of years."

She blushed. After a little while she said, "Yang Xun, have you ever been to the seaside?"

"Yes."

"Between each high tide and low tide, there's a period of

relative calm. The fishermen call it full tide. It's such a pity the time is so short . . ."

"I don't really understand things like that."

"You should understand!" She raised her voice, and there was deep pain in it. I stared at her, and suddenly I had the feeling that her hair had gone gradually white in the sunlight.

Silence.

"Is it sweet enough?" she asked suddenly.

"It's a little bitter."

She pushed over the tin of sugar. "Add more sugar, if you like."

"There's no need, I like it a little bitter," I said.

(Xiao Ling)

I love walking alone, walking unrestrained along the street, seeing how the earth is flooded in twilight. He left as suddenly as he came. I didn't detain him, but how I hope he'll come again, and sit and talk of the brief full tide, and why the sea is salty . . . You speak to him sarcastically, answer him coldly, yet you long for him to stay longer; how do you explain it? I don't like dropping hints, but one can only answer a hint with a hint, because the reality is sometimes too depressing, frighteningly depressing . . .

"Don't press your nose against the window, Lingling, did you hear me?"

"Mama, look at the frostwork, how do they get like this?"

"Because of the cold."

"But look, they're so pretty."

"Lingling, will you have to get your nose frozen before you learn? Why won't you do as I tell you."

A crossroads. Which way to turn? Choices, choices, but I'll keep straight on. A crowd of schoolchildren with schoolbags on their backs runs by, making a great racket. A motorized pedicab is parked by the side of the road, the driver in a red jersey leaning against the door, smoking and staring at me. A mother with a basket on her arm, pulling her noisily crying little boy along, says over and over. "Wanwan, stop fussing, Mama will buy you a sweet . . ."

I've left this world far behind. I've walked out in silence. I do not know where home is. Sometimes, when I turn and look back at this world, I feel a kind of happiness in my heart. It is not pleasure in other people's misfortunes, no, not that, still less nostalgia, or yearning, but a pleasure of discovery that it seems can only come through distance, through the separation and connection of distance.

The dusk is changing something. The sunlight is climbing onto one roof after another. Each of the people hurrying by in this instant forms an aspect of your life. This aspect is forever changing, and yet you are still yourself. Things that last, that last . . . those intense eyes again, how many times is it now? Yes, I crave another's love and help, even a few considerate words would do. I once had a father, a mother, and friends . . .

It was dark. The streetlights were very dim, like a row of fireflies slowly flying past. The moon rose, a new moon, growing an artist's chin. It was lost in thought. In the distance, under a faint canopy of light, a swaying figure appeared and quickly vanished. It wasn't long before the closer canopies revealed . . .

"It's you, Bai Hua."

"Oh, Xiao Ling . . ."

"How do you know my name?"

"I always get to know what I want to know. Believe me?"

"You've been drinking again."

"What of it?" He swayed violently and grabbed hold of a telegraph pole. "What of it?"

"Tell me, where do you live?"

He stopped, blinking his bloodshot eyes with difficulty. "Where do I live? Let's just say, somewhere underground. Huh, a rat who can dig a hole, a rat . . ."

I cut him short. "Come on, I'll see you home."

"My place? I mean, you're not, not scared?" Rather bewildered, he stuck his hands in his trouser pockets and pulled them out again, then rubbed his damp hair. "Oh, that's a good idea, cross my heart, I mean, miss . . . walk, walk, take a big step, take a small step, cross the mountain, cross the stream . . ." he chanted haltingly.

Darkness. Brightness. Darkness. We walked along under the streetlights. Following his wavering and the wavering of the streetlights, the road was not very steady, as if it too was starting to waver a little. What prompted me to go and look? Curiosity? What nonsense, hasn't Time played enough tricks on people? So what was it? Could it be in retaliation for yearning for warmth just now? That peculiar shadow of his slipped under his feet one moment, slanted on the roadside the next, then bumped against the wall. Why did I want to see him like this? In one's own eyes, it's always easy to avoid oneself.

Someone in the distance was singing, but the song was hard to make out. Bai Hua seemed to sober up a little. "What's that bleating? We're not all dead yet, so why the bleating? Like mud stuck on your body. I'll sing something for you fellas . . ."

Sure enough he started to sing, a bit faintly at first, then rising to his full strength. It was as if he and the song were one, passing the streetlights and the curtain of night, flying away toward another world.

> "Wandering fellow,
> Hey, so merry!
> Treading the world's mountains and rivers,
> Marching on in thunder, wind and rain,
> Singing beneath the sunlight,
> The earth gives me freedom,
> Freedom makes me merry.
> . . . . . ."[5]

We turned into a square behind a block of apartments and entered a pitch-black clump of trees. He bent over and pushed open a concrete slab on a pulley, revealing an air-raid shelter

[5]A popular song among the educated youth sent to the countryside.

staircase. I glanced at him and plunged down. It was damp and cold inside, so dark you couldn't see anything. Click! He flicked his lighter on. We followed the stairs down and pushed open an unlatched steel door, the damp vault spreading out in front of the jumping flare. Utter silence but for water dripping somewhere.

We turned into a little room. He groped around and lit a kerosene lamp on an old wooden table. Only now did I discover that there was a woman of indeterminate age sitting on a bedspread with a straw mat in the corner of the room. She was propping herself up with her hands behind her back, her eyes flashing like a wildcat's.

"Where've you been?" she asked.

"Number Four?" Bai Hua scratched his head. "Who let you in?"

"You drank a lot again, Boss. Come here." She held out her arms.

"Get lost," Bai Hua snarled.

"I'm not going, this is my place!"

Bai Hua drew a knife from his waist and pressed forward a few steps. I leaped across to block him. "Aren't you ashamed?"

At this moment Number Four caught sight of me, and slowly got to her feet, "Oh, so that explains it, you've found another one now. Ha ha." She laughed sarcastically. Bai Hua pushed me away and rushed toward her. Number Four slipped to the door in a flash. "Look at that, such a delicate little face, eh? Ha ha . . ." The wild nervous laughter turned into a crashing echo and gradually faded away.

Bai Hua walked toward the table, his shadow growing bigger and bigger, wavering on the walls and ceiling. Bang! He stuck the knife into the table and sat down slowly, cradling his head in his hands.

"Is this the freedom and merriment of your song?"

Bai Hua banged his fist on the table. "Shut up."

"Answer my question."

"All right, I sang about what I haven't got, everyone does that!" He brought out a bottle of spirits from under the table, knocked the top off on a corner of the table, and poured himself a cup.

"Bai Hua, you can't drink any more," I said, going up to him.

"Have one with me." He poured another cup and pushed it toward me. His eyes gradually filled with tears, then he sighed deeply. "You're a good person, Xiao Ling, I couldn't hurt you, I only wish I could look at you every day, listen to you talk, and if anyone touched you, look, this is what I'd do—"

He pulled out the knife fiercely and thrust at his own palm. Blood flowed out, dripping into the cup. He stabbed himself again, and the spirits in his cup turned red. I grabbed his wrist and snatched the knife away. "You're mad!"

"It doesn't matter." He laughed shrilly. "The blood of people here isn't worth money, cross my heart."

"That's enough nonsense, grip this, raise your hand, hold still! Did you hear? Do you have a bandage and ointment?"

"On the box, genuine knife wound ointment."

When I'd finished dressing the wound I sighed deeply and sat down. "Are you always like this?"

He shook his head. "Huh, it's nothing, it's just the same old story."

"Yes, that's actually the truth."

The snuff spattered, releasing beautiful arc lines which immediately turned into wisps of blue smoke.

"Bai Hua, have you seen the stars?" I asked.

"Of course."

"Have you thought about them? They're old and yet new. Here we only see yesterday's light, while they're still sending out new light . . ."

"So what?"

"We're only accepting something as a kind of accomplished fact, without ever wondering whether these things, which have been dissolved into one with our lives, have any value."

"Value? That's money again, and that's nothing."

"I suddenly feel that people are so pitiful . . ."

"Pitiful." He nodded in agreement.

Did he understand what I meant? Well, it didn't matter one way or the other, it had nothing to do with him. This was purely my own state of mind. A kind of mood, a kind of endless crumbling touched off by small stirrings. Yet this crumbling was not the same as it used to be, but peculiarly quiet; so quiet it almost makes one grieve, like a mountain slowly subsiding from the flow of an underground river . . .

The silence whirred. Remote and gentle at first, then gradually turning into a piercing din, as if this little room could no longer hold it.

He raised the cup. "Come on, let's have a drink, my head's bursting."

The cup glistened in the air. Stars. Who would have thought there would be such a feeling, they must be everywhere then. Even in these places where starlight could never reach, there could be another radiance. But it all depended on these bright rays joining. Yesterday and tomorrow, life and death, good and evil . . .

"All right then, I won't drink," he said, hanging his head.

I raised my cup. "Come on. Cheers."

(Bai Hua)

I was dreaming, dreaming of stars.

"Wake up, Boss." Someone was pushing me—it was Manzi.

"What's up?"

"The one-twenty express'll be here soon, Boss."

I pulled out my pocketwatch and tapped on the glass. "What are you panicking about, there's still another hour to go." A burning stab of pain. Glancing at my bandaged left hand I couldn't help grimacing. I went over to the bucket, splashed my face with cold water and wiped it, using my right hand. Then I glanced at the chair where she'd just been sitting. "Come on, don't forget the gear."

The street was deserted; only a cat was wailing on a rubbish heap. I looked up; stars, sparkling and glittering. Huh, good-for-nothing lumps, wasn't that all they were?

"What are you staring at, Boss?" Manzi looked up too.

"Have you ever seen stars?"

"Sure, those are stars, aren't they?"

"They're old and they're new, understand?"

Manzi stared at me, baffled. "No, I don't get it."

"You can pity people . . ." I said.

"Sure, that's right, and you can hate them too." Manzi nodded, to show he understood this time. "Hey, Boss, you've grown learned."

Reaching the West Station, we followed the shadows round the outside wall. Not far ahead, someone was talking in a low voice.

"We only want five yuan, that's not much at all," said a girl with a thin, shrill voice.

"That's the old price." That hoarse voice sounded like Lanzi.

"Three yuan, that'll keep you in food for a few days," said some bastard with a Manchurian accent.

I gave Manzi a wink and walked up. Lanzi and another girl, no more than thirteen or fourteen, were leaning against the wall, bargaining with a couple of fellows in their forties.

"If I say no, I mean no, our money doesn't grow on trees either," said the bastard with the big chin. Suddenly catching sight of us, he nudged the other with his elbow and turned to sneak away.

"Hold it!" I called in a low voice, as Manzi blocked their way from behind.

"What's up?" Big Chin ran his tongue over his lips, pretending to be calm.

"Fix the price before you go."

"What price? I don't get it.

"Enough goddamn play-acting!" I said. "Ten yuan each."

"What's the idea?" snorted Big Chin, unconvinced. "Are you threatening me?"

"You bet we are!" Manzi pulled out his knife and held it at Big Chin's back. Big Chin started to shake.

"Brothers, take your hands off and let us go," whined the other one. "We're new, we didn't understand the rules here."

"The rules here are simple," I said. "Your cash or your life."

"We'll pay, we'll pay." The shivering mongrel took out two ten-yuan notes and handed them to me.

"Now get lost." I waited till they'd gone far enough away, then turned to the small white faces of the two girls and handed over the money. "Go on, take it."

"Boss," Lanzi smiled wryly. "The last couple of days haven't been too good."

"Manzi, how much have you got on you?" I asked.

"Sixty."

"Give them thirty."

Manzi unwillingly pulled out the money and gave it to Lanzi.

"Thanks, Boss."

We jumped the wall, skirted around the piles of goods, slid over to the dispatch office, checked no one was around, and opened the door. Old Meng was rocking his scrawny head, humming a little tune. He walked nervously to the door and looked around. "Anyone see you?"

"Don't worry." Manzi clapped him on the shoulder. "What've you got for us this time?"

"Satisfaction guaranteed." He looked at his watch. "She's coming in in twenty minutes, on Track Three, stopping ten minutes. First-class goods are in the third section. But be careful, there are guards . . ." His Adam's apple rolled up and down, like a date he couldn't swallow.

"Some money for smokes." I gave him a few banknotes. "I'll bring the drinking money next time."

"It's my honor, Boss."

We crossed the tracks silently and crouched down in the

shadow of a heap of cement. Crickets chirped ceaselessly in the thick clumps of grass.

In the distance a whistle blew and the tracks vibrated, clanking. There she was, damn it, pulling into the station.

4

(Bai Hua)

There was a big plate-glass window with all kinds of things shining inside: lights, tablecloths, bottles of liquor, guitars, scarves, military uniforms, and even a basket of beautiful fresh flowers. Now that was odd, where did fresh flowers come from on a cold day like this? That Yuanyuan rushed busily in and out. Would she still recognize me? I heard Yang Xun say that today was her birthday. Good God, when the hell was I born? Xiao Ling was sitting all alone in a corner, well away from that scum. No, Yang Xun was keeping his lecherous eye on her. I'd have to lay things on the line with him.

I pressed closer to the window, and the scene changed completely: a full moon, a cypress bent in the moonlight, like an old man dying. Not a star in sight.

"Quiet, quiet! Who's going to sing first?" someone shouted at the top of his voice. "Bring the guitar . . ."

The guitar crashed out, some people yelling along with it, stamping madly on the goddamn floor. I'd really had a bellyful of this. Damn it, why should I suffer like this for nothing?

I stepped back, and the moon and the old man flew away. She was still sitting there, not moving at all. Black eyes, red mouth, white face, as white as paper. Something sour and aching pierced through me. Ah, that was ten years ago . . .

A morning in early winter. The wind had dropped. The rough, pitted surface of the road had been swept clean by the wind. As usual I stepped across the creaking ice fragments into the waiting room, shouted hello at Old Jia the cleaner, then went behind the seats and pulled out a stick with needles on the end—my cigarette butt collector. A thin little girl was sitting there, wrapped in an old coat with the padding falling out, no more than eleven or twelve years old by the look of her. She smiled at me, I grinned back too, took my stick and left.

In the evening I slipped into the waiting room as usual. The fire in the stove was crackling, reflecting on half a dozen crooked figures. Suddenly I gave a start; she was still there, crouching as before behind the seat, listlessly smiling at me.

"You haven't left yet?" I asked.

She shook her head.

"You're on your own?" I asked again.

She nodded and smiled again.

"I asked you a question. What are you smiling at like an idiot? Are you dumb?" I was getting a bit angry.

"I'm not dumb," she said softly, enunciating each syllable.

"So what's the idea, not saying anything?"

She stared at me for some time, and ran her tongue over her dry, cracked lips. "Water, I want a drink of water."

I fetched a bowl of steaming hot water. She clasped it in both hands, her teeth chattering against the rim. I felt her forehead. "Hey, you're really hot! You've got a fever."

Big teardrops rolled down into the bowl.

"What is it? Tell me."

She spoke falteringly, half in tears. "My stepmother, she brought me to see the doctor . . . We came here on the train. The doctor said I couldn't get better, it would be wasting a lot of money . . . My stepmother, she brought me here, she said she was going to get me something nice to eat, and then she didn't come back, she never came . . ."

"The old bitch!" I ground my teeth. "See if I don't beat her flat!"

She stopped crying and blinked at me. "She's not old."

"Old or not, she'll cop it anyway."

"But she's really fat, you couldn't beat her flat."

"Then I'll smash her flat with a brick. Do you believe me?"

"Yes," She smiled. Round dimples appeared in her cheeks.

Early next day, me and my pals pooled some money and I took her a bit of medicine and food. I soaked some steamed bread in hot water and fed her piece by piece. She was very obedient. Every evening I told her stories, and she'd always ask, "And then? And then?"

Once, combing out her plaits, she said to me: "I've got a big brother, he's great."

"So what?"

"He's like you, really."

I caught hold of her little hand. "I'm your big brother, do you hear?"

She looked startled for a moment, then lowered her eyes shyly. "Yes, big brother."

Several days went by, and she actually seemed to be getting better. I found a "doctor" to look at her. He walked out of the waiting room with me, rolled the money we'd given him into a ball, stuffed it into his cap, thought for some time, then sighed. "The medicine's too expensive, brother, there won't be change back from . . ."

"Write out the prescription. I can afford it, I can!"

I wandered about in the cold wind for a long time, walking, walking, biting my lips till they bled. I'd do anything for her, even if it meant dying!

Night deepened, and I went back to the waiting room. She was still awake, waiting for me. "Big brother, why are you back so late?"

"Oh, I had something to do."

"You're shivering . . ."

"It's cold outside."

"Come on, sit over here, let me warm you up." The firelight from the stove lit up her little face. She hugged me tightly, but I shivered even more violently. "Are you still cold?"

"No, I'm not cold."

"As soon as I'm better, I'll sing for you. The people at home in the hills all like listening to me sing, even the calf at home blinks his eyes, he can't get enough . . ."

I could not stop myself from breaking into tears.

"What is it, big brother?" Bewildered, she smoothed my disheveled hair with her little hand, the tears streaming down . . .

When morning came I sat up quietly, unclasped her hot little hands from my arm, and stared intently at her for a while. Only when her eyelids flickered did I slip away.

It went pretty smoothly in the beginning, but something kept shouting in my mind; more, just a bit more, and she'll get well, she'll sing her pretty songs . . . Suddenly, on the bus, a fat-headed bastard twisted my ear and dragged me off to the local police station. An emaciated cur with his cap stuck crooked on his head jangled a bunch of keys and jabbed me in the head with his finger. "Five days inside, that's cheap for you!"

I grabbed hold of his collar like a madman, imploring bitterly, "Uncle, I don't care what you do, beat me, break my arm, only let me go. Don't lock me up, Uncle, please, my little sister's sick, she's going to die . . ."

"She's going to die?" he snorted. "With little beggars like you, one dead is one less!"

With a crash the jail door was locked. I flung myself at it, beating my head against the door. My fingernails grasped at the wall until covered in blood, and I fainted.

Five days passed. I ran madly down the road, the startled crowd parting to make way for me. I burst through the door of the waiting room and rushed to the corner. It was empty. "Where's my sister? Where is she?" I shouted at the people gathered round. No one uttered a sound. Old Jia slipped out, trailing his broom along the wall.

On the wall where she'd been leaning, a fingernail had carved thirty or forty uneven lines: "Big brother, I miss you! Come back, big brother . . ."

(Lin Yuanyuan)

At long last the song came to an end. The singing had upset me terribly. I wiped my hands on my apron, walked round the table, and went up to Yang Xun. He was standing at the bookcase, turning over the pages of a book.

"What is it, Yuanyuan?" Yang Xun asked, raising his head.

"Who is she?" My throat was so hot and dry, it was an effort to swallow.

He kept on turning the pages, as if his answer were written there. At length he said, "Her name's Xiao Ling."

"Your girlfriend?"

In the reflection of the window, I saw just the hint of a smile. "You could say so. Isn't she welcome?"

"Welcome!" I stared at him fiercely, turned and walked off.

In the kitchen the girls were talking and laughing like twittering sparrows. A stream of choking soot floated on the ceiling. I went to the cupboard, took out an empty bowl at random, and wiped it with a rag. The inside of the bowl was glazed with a brilliant red camellia. So this was it: the answer to days and nights of agitation and nightmare at last: I loved him, but he? Didn't he have feelings too? I mustn't cry, today was my birthday. I was eighteen. I cast a glance at the murky mirror above my head. Oh, I was ugly, what of it? Her beauty was her business, why bring her here? Answer, oh, don't smile hypocritically. The camellia blurred, like a pool of blood. Torn flower, it's all false, I hate you, I hate everyone. If I had an atom bomb I'd drop it and turn everything into ashes. Oh, torn flower . . .

Fafa thrust her head toward me. "Do you add sugar to Chicken Foo-yung?"

"I don't know!" I turned away petulantly.

"What's wrong now?" She grabbed me by the shoulder.

"I've got pepper in my eye."

"Come on, you don't even know how to lie, tell me—" She snatched away the bowl, staring into my eyes. "Oh, so it's the same old thing, but you never admit it. Tell me, what are you going to do? Take revenge?"

Revenge! Revenge, revenge? I considered it in different tones. But how to take revenge? And what would it prove? "Fafa, just drop it."

"O.K., we'll talk about it later. It's a day of celebration, cheer up, think of happy things and you'll feel better. We're going to eat right away, come and have a look . . ."

I looked around at all the faces; they seemed remote and

unfamiliar. What, had they come to celebrate my birthday? But what else did we have in common, they and I? I was eighteen, it was truly hard to believe, like a lantern slide in the wrong order; a whir, and it was pushed in front of you. What came before it? And afterward, what else would come? Ah, life was so boring . . .

Fafa drummed on a bowl with a spoon. "Quiet, comrades, stub out your cigarettes, the other half of the room's population wants to stay alive."

Laughter. Was it funny?

"Lin Yuanyuan was overcome by gas, she's not feeling too well." Fafa raised the spoon. "Now let me announce . . ."

Clinking of glasses and uproarious laughter. Everyone was extremely happy, except me. Very well, be happy, laugh, forget about me, but don't hang up false signs.

My gaze fell again on the violent-looking fellow, and I shivered. Who was he? I seemed to have seen him somewhere before. It was frightening to watch him drink, as if he were drinking water.

Those two were prattling about something. They noticed my attention and drank to cover their confusion. Why bother? This isn't a church, you can even kiss!

Calm down, Yuanyuan, perhaps life is just like this. It certainly hasn't been arranged for your benefit.

(Yang Xun)

"Xiao Ling, aren't you feeling well?"

"The truth is, I shouldn't have come."

"Drink up, Yuanyuan's watching us."

"How old is she?"

"Eighteen, five years younger than you."

"I'm a hundred years older than she."

"Why not even more?"

"That's the limit, a century only has a hundred years. Oh,

the great twentieth century, the mad, chaotic, utterly irrational century, the century without faith . . .

"We used to have faith."

"Those broken fragments still clinking behind us. Perhaps we are moving forward, but where's the road?"

"Why must there be a road? If vast fields can hold humanity, why crowd along one narrow road?"

"Fields. But I was thinking of a place beyond the horizon . . ."

"Such a place doesn't exist."

"No, when you think of it, it exists."

"You're evading something."

"Perhaps. I'm evading happiness, evading beauty, evading light . . ."

"Slow down, Xiao Ling, you'll get drunk like that."

"I'm also evading being sober, because this world's too clear, so clear it makes me sick. I want to blind myself, even if only for a little while!"

"This is not the way."

"I hope those people who have a way also have a little conscience; what those who live in this world have is ways, ways, ways . . ."

"Don't drink so much."

"Yang Xun, have you ever noticed the old women in the street who collect waste paper? Actually, they're dead, they died long ago. All that's left is a body, and this body has no connection whatsoever with the original person, it's only keeping up certain basic habits to survive, nothing more. This is my situation at present."

"No, you can still think."

"No, that's a sort of basic habit too, exactly the same as my drinking."

"Look at Bai Hua . . ."

"Why change the subject? Is it disagreeable? Doesn't it suit this elegant atmosphere? Mm?"

"Xiao Ling, we all have times like this, it will all pass."

"It won't pass, it never will, you needn't console me."

"Talk about it then, I won't stop you."

"I don't feel like talking."

The guitar struck an intense chord. The lights began to spin slowly; people's shadows flickered against each other on the walls, rocking and swaying, as if these shadows were a backdrop behind footlights, provided especially to emphasize the unreality of it all.

I stood at the window smoking. Bai Hua walked up.

"Got a cigarette?" he asked.

I handed one to him. He lit it, drawing back in silence, staring at the slowly lengthening white ash, saying nothing for a long time. At last, the ash fell and he raised his head and looked at me, one eye narrowing a little. "You, you like her?"

"Who?"

"Do I have to give her full name?" His eye narrowed even more, almost closing. "Something got your tongue?"

In that instant I saw in that narrowed eye of his what I'd seen that day in the liquor shop: foulness, cruelty, and the thirst for blood. It chilled me. "I like her."

"People like you shouldn't ever play around with her." He hissed the words from between his teeth.

"You should say that to yourself."

"All right." He was stricken for a moment and sighed. From the wisps of smoke curling slowly from his mouth, I sensed that he was very nervous. "Let's get it straight from the beginning; let's not get in each other's way."

". . . I know that guy." Fafa was sitting on the table smoking, several young fellows standing around her. "Although my father's after him, we keep on seeing each other as usual . . ."

"Where does he live?" one young brat said.

"Huh, a dog like that, with no father or mother, how could he have a home?"

"What's his name?"

"Bai Hua . . ."

I watched Bai Hua anxiously; his face was quite expressionless. He finished the last drag of his cigarette, slowly tore the butt into pieces and tossed it onto the floor, squashed it with the toe of his shoe, then threw off my restraining hand and approached the group. All eyes gradually collected upon him, and the room fell silent. Fafa stopped talking too and looked around in bewilderment. At that moment Bai Hua walked up to her.

"Looking for me?" Fafa asked, slipping off the table.

"That's right, I'm looking for you."

"What for?"

"I'm thinking of getting married, to you, how about it?"

Fafa stepped back, bumping into a chair. A moment of dead silence. "Who, who are you?"

"How come you don't know me? That dog you just mentioned." Bai Hua cupped Fafa's slightly quivering chin in his hand. "Let's go home and discuss it with your old man, have a chat, eh?" Bai Hua let his hand drop, swept his gaze indolently round the room, and walked out the door.

The room was plunged instantly into chaos. Fafa sobbed uncontrollably. Some people shouted about giving chase, and others suggested ringing the Public Security Bureau, but no one dared leave the room. Yuanyuan ran up to me breathlessly. "Huh, this is all your fault!"

People drifted off, until only Xiao Ling and I were left in the room. She sat in the same place as before, her cheek in her hand, staring at the clock on the wall.

"What are you thinking about?" I asked.

She shook her head. Then she walked over to an old piano in the corner, pulled off the checked cover thick with dust, and sat down on the piano stool, moving very slowly like an elderly invalid.

A clear strong chord broke the silence, and the windows in the room trembled in fervent response. The swift notes streamed and flowed like a boat on a river . . . she stopped, turned, and begged, "Turn off the light, do you mind?"

She played Beethoven's "Moonlight Sonata." The moonlight streamed in through the window, falling on her white cheeks and neck. The seaside under the moon. Surf beating gently against the cliff spat out gold and crimson bubbles. A horn blew in the distance . . . a roar, like a clap of thunder; she leaned over the keyboard, a slight spasm seizing her shoulders.

"Xiao Ling—" I went up to her.

Looking as if she'd just woken from a dream, she slowly straightened her back and tossed her hair. She gazed at me with rapt attention, tears in her eyes. In the moonlight, a deep warmth crept back into her ice-cold face.

(Xiao Ling)

"However you put it, anyone who's against the work group is against the Party!"

"What's the use of sticking labels on people like that? Work groups obviously stifle the masses, what right have they to represent the Party?"

"Well, anyway, that's, that's . . ." she stammers, her pretty face reddening. "You, what's your class origin?"

The sunlight dances on the red-and-green wall poster, dazzling me. I squint painfully. "High intellectual."

"Huh, rotten egg, little bitch, you've got ulterior motives!" She hits me a fierce blow on the ear, her pretty face twisting crookedly. She looks at her reddened palm in surprise.

A bang on the door.

"Who is it?" Mama puts down the watering can, wiping her hands on her apron. A crystal drop of water rolls down the violet's clustered leaves.

The door opens and about ten people swarm into the room. Leading them is a baby-faced youth. He wipes his sweating nose with the back of his hand. "Hey, stand still, no messing around . . . let's start."

"Why are you raiding our home?" asks Mama in terror.

Baby-face brandishes his leather belt, and the violet petals come fluttering down. "Because of this!"

The wall mirror is smashed, and leather boots trample back and forth over the glass, crunching it underfoot. Clothes and books are flung all over the floor. One fellow walks up to the piano and kicks it. "American made. Take it away, get some more people . . ."

"You're nothing but bandits!" Mama mutters, her hands clasped together, the knuckles showing white.

Baby-face turns round, smiling. "Are you talking about us, eh?"

I try to stop Mama, but it's too late. "Yes, you, bandits! What of it?" Mama's voice rises to a pitch.

"Nothing." His smile vanishes and he waves his hand. "Come here, teach her how to speak to Red Guards."

I throw myself toward Mama but am roughly pushed aside. Half a dozen belts fly at her.

"Mama!" I cry, struggling.

The belts whistle, the buckles flash back and forth in the air. Suddenly Mama breaks through the tight circle, runs to the balcony, and jumps nimbly onto the other side of the railing. "I'm going to die anyway. If anyone comes near I'll jump!"

Everything comes to a standstill. The sky is so blue, the wisps of white cloud don't move, the sunlight strokes the wounds on Mama's temple.

"Mama—" I cry out.

"Lingling—" Mama's eyes turn to me; her voice is very calm. Mama. Me. Mama. Eyes. Drops of blood. Sunlight. Clouds. The sky . . .

Baby-face seems to wake up, pokes the peak of his cap with his belt, and steps forward. "Go on, jump, jump!"

I rush forward and kneel on the ground, clasping his legs tightly and staring up at him with desperately entreating eyes. Looking down he hesitates, his slightly parted lips showing his shining teeth. He swallows and shoves me aside.

"Mama—"

The clouds and the sky suddenly turn upside down.

I close the door and glance sideways. "Papa, take that placard off your neck."

"No, they might come and check. It doesn't bother me, Lingling."

Dusk filters into the room as Papa and I sit in the dimness. I feel his gaze fixed on me. "Don't look at me like that. I can't bear it."

"Just this once, Papa doesn't usually look at you enough." Suddenly he asks, "Lingling, what will you do, if Papa's not here either?"

"What nonsense are you talking!" I cut him short indignantly.

During the night I wake with a start and tiptoe to Papa's door. In the moonlight, the bed is empty. A note held down on the desk rustles in the breeze. "Lingling, my child, I'm too ashamed, I can't go on living, please forgive my weakness. Don't look for me, I don't want you to see what I look like when I'm dead . . . When I was looking at you this evening, my heart broke. You're still so young, what will you do in the future? Goodbye, Lingling!"

Lonely streetlights. Fallen poplar leaves crunch underfoot. I stop and lay my hand on the cold stone railing. The river pounds under the bridge, swirling and spinning under the light from the mercury lamps, spurting out chains of bubbles. Its voice is serene and peaceful, yet full of a dignified and irrefutable strength. It's a language as old as the world.

Far away a train shrills out a long whistle. A wind rises, and the fallen leaves fly up and are blown into the somber river. I turn and walk back along the pitch-black road.

5

(Lin Yuanyuan)

Whistling a tune, Fafa glided around, dancing by herself, twirling about the room, her leather shoes tapping on the floor. Suddenly she stopped and asked, "That guy hasn't come back?"

"Yes, he came back one afternoon, the day before yesterday. He jumped in through the window, right there." I never thought I could lie so easily.

"What happened?"

"He asked about you." I compressed my lips to stop myself laughing, pulled an aired shirt from the wardrobe, and spread it on the bed to fold it.

"And what happened?"

"He asked your address."

"And?"

"And nothing." Fafa's face was green, it really was. "Of course, I said I didn't know," I said, straightening up.

She sucked in her breath slowly, just like a fish which, stuck at the bottom of the water for half its life, has difficulty floating to the surface. "Has he done anything to you?"

"What?"

"I mean, to sleep with that sort of guy wouldn't be bad." She pressed her hands on her hips and made an obscene gesture.

I shook with anger. "Fafa, you've got no self-respect."

"How come you're being so fierce? Have you just eaten human flesh?"

Just at that moment Papa walked through the door. Fafa slid to a halt without a word. I flung the folded clothes fiercely onto the bed. This was all so meaningless. Was this life, were these friends? Was this me? It was so infuriating. The window was shut tight and the central heating boiled with a hissing sound . . . I kept feeling there was something hiding outside the window; only open the window and it would come whistling in. But what was it?

Papa's big heavy hand fell on my shoulder. "Yuanyuan, you should be working, idle people get into trouble."

"You've been idle for years, and you haven't got into trouble," I retorted.

"How do you know I haven't?" said Papa. "All right, since it's such fine weather, we'll go to the Tomb of the Martyrs Park, how's that?"

Were we in class? Mr. Mu's big melon-face: "This is where

we salute the memory of the revolution's martyrs . . . eyes right!" Drum roll. Recite poems. Lay wreaths . . . All right then, we're born to obey.

The motor was humming softly. I sat in the front seat, staring out of the corner of my eye at Fat Wu's big hairy hands sliding up and down around the steering wheel. He drove really fast, scattering the pedestrians. If it were me, I wouldn't bother to dodge, who'd dare run into me! Once people were in a car, their attitude became quite different, they were only interested in greater security and speed.

"Stop." Papa tapped Fat Wu on the shoulder. The car screeched to a halt. He poked his head out. "Where are you going, Xun?"

"Just for a walk."

"Get in." Papa's hair was all twisted about by the wind. "Come for a walk in the Martyrs Park with us, we seldom get such fine weather."

Yang Xun raised his hand, and the watch on his wrist glinted in the sunlight. Did he have an engagement? Huh, don't let us delay you!

The back door slammed shut. "Has Yuanyuan gone dumb?"

I turned round and glared at him. "You're the dumb one!"

"Don't be silly," Papa said reprovingly.

The motor started humming again. The pencil-straight white lines bored under the wheels, as if they were being wrapped around the axle. The little mirror above my head was tapping, reflecting Papa's eyes, so feeble and weary, as if he hadn't slept for a lifetime . . . the side-view mirror reflected another pair of eyes. I could not restrain a shiver, a breath of coldness creeping up my spine. What was it? But I'd seen nothing, nothing, except a pair of eyes . . . White lines. White lines. White lines.

The early winter sunlight brimmed with warmth. Several peasant children gathering firewood crowded up to the car, gesturing and giggling; and old fellow in a worn-out sheepskin jacket reclined at his ease on a bench not far away, sticking his hand inside his greasy collar to scratch himself; a pair of lovers crossed the square, heading toward the pine grove.

"Yuanyuan—Yuanyuan, come over here—" some voices called out in chorus. Oh, it was the kids from the Municipal Committee's compound, dressed in loud colors, cameras slung over their shoulders. They were standing on the steps of the martyrs' memorial beckoning to me, the girls waving their bright scarves. "Go on," Papa said. "Wait, why don't we go and have a look together."

We mounted the stairs, and they came crowding over: "Hello, Uncle Lin!"

"Hm, are you putting on a fashion show?" said Papa.

"Are you against it?" said Monkey Xu, pushing forward. Today he was wearing a black leather jacket and a pair of brown stovepipe trousers.

"At least I wouldn't say I approve."

"Clothes should have individuality, people should wear whatever they like . . ." As Monkey Xu finished, he pulled a face.

Papa tapped him on the shoulder. "Let me take a look at this individuality of yours. This is an order: squat! Now then, if there's a war, what will you do?"

"What's it got to do with war?" voluble Fatty Wang interjected. "We hate war!"

"What will you do if the enemy comes?"

"Me?" Fatty Wang counted on her fingers. "In the first place, there's not the slightest sign . . ."

"In the second?"

"If they really do come, we're not cowards. But I don't understand, what's that got to do with wearing a few clothes that look smart?"

Papa smiled. "I'm not against looking smart, but you should try to acquire a little taste."

Monkey Xu stuck his head out again. "And if our idea of taste happens to differ? Then you'll simply give us an order: change into standard blue uniforms . . ."

"Actually we dressed up specially today because we feel

we're too old," Fatty Wang sighed. "Uncle Lin, what did your generation do when you were young?"

Papa's expression suddenly became grave, and he turned towards the martyrs' memorial. "Ask this. Under it lie one thousand one hundred and . . ."

"Fifty-seven martyrs, I know, I've known that since I was three. But I don't believe they charged around fighting every minute of their lives. After all, they were human beings as well. And besides, if there had been no love then there'd be no us!"

They all laughed.

"What a bold girl!" said Papa.

"As far as I can see, in those days you were more casual than we are. Everything was as plain as daylight, you didn't have to feel uncertain about anything. But for us, either there's just no way out, or all of them have been arranged by you. So where's the interest in living? Yuanyuan, what do you think?"

I winked secretly.

"Don't exaggerate our role; whether there'll be a change or not, still depends on you. What's your name? Fine, Comrade Fatty Wang, we'll have another chat sometime. Stay here and enjoy yourself, Yuanyuan, Xun and I are going for a walk."

Feeling utterly empty, I chatted with the others for a moment or two, then slipped into the shadows behind the martyrs' memorial. Looking at the sky from here, it seemed even bluer. A few crows flew past cawing. The ugly creatures were quite happy; I'd heard that in some countries people even regarded them as sacred birds. It seemed that even crows had different destinies, though their cry was about the same: caw . . . caw . . .

The two of them vanished into the dense forest.

(Lin Dongping)

We followed the path through the wood up to the ridge. Dry leaves covering the path crunched underfoot. A light breeze sprang up, and the bright, sparse gray branches swung a little.

I hadn't been here for a long time. This memorial park was

built in '55; I signed the approval myself. The then Municipal Committee secretary, Old Han, had no inkling that he would one day be the one thousand one hundred and fifty-eighth name. Several hundred teachers and cadres of the city also died a violent death around the same time. Their names ought to be carved on the memorial so that their children would remember them, and remember that period of history. Amongst the names of the dead on this long, long list would be that of Yuanyuan's mother. She was sent here as a member of the Provincial Committee work group and was dead after barely a month. She died in a criticism session, from another heart attack it was said. I felt guilty toward her, that years of disharmony had added to the burden on her heart, especially after she knew of my affair with Ruohong. But there was no court of feelings in the world, only conscience. And there were too many kinds of conscience nowadays. For me there was only one; there absolutely could not be two. And where was my conscience? . . . "They were human beings as well. If there had been no love then there'd be no us!" It was as if Fatty Wang's sharp eyes had seen right through what was in my heart, the wretched girl! Yes, we were all human beings, with our own history, our own secrets of happiness and pain. Others could never know, except those with whom you have entered into secrets. Why didn't Xun like to talk? He was not at all like his mother. When the organization sent Ruohong to help me with my work that evening we chatted nearly the whole night. Afraid of attracting other people's attention, we didn't turn on the light in the room. The moonlight poured through the skylight, illuminating the brass knobs of the old-fashioned iron bed on which she sat. At last she grew tired, and fell asleep against the bedstead. I covered her with a blanket, then went to the storeroom to send the last telegram . . .

The white poplars brushed against us as we passed, each a white memorial. We ought to set up a memorial for our unhappy love affairs, and tell the children: we've sacrificed everything for your happiness. Was that really true? Facts are often blown out of proportion. At least we left the fruit of love, and lasting memories.

Xun had walked on ahead. A few crows cawed noisily, flapping their wings in the treetops and flying off. Blasted creatures! You have no scruples about all that people cherish, it would even give you satisfaction to destroy them. Fortunately the world was big enough to contain everything. What was the meaning of this containment? Was it just co-existence? But could I co-exist with a creature like Wang Defa? He lived with such confidence, taking not the slightest account of me, speaking in front of me without any restraint. Like that scene in the office just now . . .

". . . this is the basic situation with the problem of co-operation in the engineering work on the Jinyin River." Wang Defa shut his notebook, leaned over, and pushed a packet of cheap cigarettes at me across the table.

"No thanks, I've just put one out."

"And I have another idea." He rubbed his unshaven chin and hesitated for a moment. "The new financial year will begin soon. Our supply situation's always a problem. Can we improve it? I've made a calculation: if everyone's monthly ration for oil, sugar, meat, and eggs is reduced to the lowest limit, then we can depend on the surrounding counties to supply us, and we won't have to go begging anywhere . . ."

"The lowest limit?"

"Be patient. This is calculated on a scientific basis. Last time I was at the provincial capital for a meeting, I asked a medical authority—you should have seen his big beard." Wang Defa grew excited and pulled a sheet of paper from his pocket. "I've made out a full report; if we achieve some success, who knows, the whole country might learn from us . . ."

I put on my glasses and looked at the report. "Three ounces of white sugar?"

"The human body can get sugar from grain and vegetables high in starch, it's scientific!"

"Hm, it's all very well as an idea." I took off my glasses and blinked. "What about the peasants? There's just been a flood; what revenues can we collect?"

"Ah, as the saying goes, 'there's no blessing you can't enjoy and no suffering you can't endure.' I grew up in the countryside, I understand them better than you. You ink-drinkers, you're too sentimental. How was it in '58? That was done by you lot. That winter I happened to be on home leave from the army. You couldn't count how many had died from hunger, but we got through somehow, didn't we!" He scratched at a greasy stain on his sleeve with his fingernail. "Tighten your belts a bit, that'll solve the problem."

"Tighten whose? Does that include you and me?" I asked.

He smiled knowingly. "Old Lin, you get more and more confused the older you get! Of course it doesn't include us. Don't worry."

I placed my hands on the table, then slowly clenched them again.

"Come on, Old Lin, sign," he said.

I put on my glasses and looked at the report again, then from over the rims I caught sight of his hand holding the cigarette. What was that hand capable of? Pounding the table, making telephone calls, even strangling . . . what, was I afraid? Just because he had real power, connections at the top? I was an intelligent person; it simply wasn't worth destroying myself over this small thing. I could still make many contributions to the people . . . What a lie! Behind this piece of paper, how many pairs of eyes are watching you, watching your every move, watching your conscience. Yet you still boast unblushingly of "the people" and "contributions" . . . for shame!

"I won't sign," I said, taking off my glasses and pushing away the report.

Wang Defa rapped on the table with his knuckles. "Old Lin, you and I are both experienced men . . . I can't do anything either, it's come down from a higher level."

"So why won't they give a proper order?"

He smiled just a little. "You still don't get the point, do you? From the bottom to the top, that's your glorious tradition from the days of guerrilla warfare."

"If that's the case, we should take up the discussion with the Party Committee and listen to their opinions."

The last trace of a smile vanished from his face. He looked at me expressionlessly. "Very well," he said.

Several tall poplars had been planted on the ridge. The sunshine lit up their pencil-straight trunks; in contrast to the surrounding gray tone, they appeared unusually clean, erect and stalwart. The wind blew the dry leaves into hollows. I sat down on a wind-weathered rock, drawing deeply at my cigarette, chewing the bitter shreds of tobacco that had fallen into my mouth. A light thread of sorrow drifted about in the quiet net woven by the path, the fallen leaves, and the poplars and was carried away by the wind to the mountain wilderness.

Xun walked over to a poplar and gazed into the distance.

(Yang Xun)

The city and she were over there. Where was she? Streets and roofs were faintly visible under a thin smear of mist, and a hundred thousand windows glinted in the setting sun, shining with a strange light.

I turned round to find Uncle Lin staring intently at me, the loneliness of an old man in his eyes.

"It's beautiful here," I said.

He nodded.

"You couldn't tell it was winter except for the fallen leaves."

"The change of seasons is always like that, subtle." The wind blew the wisps of smoke away from his mouth. "Look at that cloud, it might snow at any moment."

I glanced at my watch. "I should be going, I have something to do."

"What is it?"

"Going to see a film."

"A date?"

I smiled and did not answer.

"A fellow student or a local girl?"

"Neither."

"Oh." He fell silent for a while, then motioned with his hand. "Off you go then, and give her my regards. I'll sit here for a while longer."

The snowflakes were spinning, the whole sky dancing with them. The night faded. The two of us stood on the cinema steps, watching the black tide of people, a floating mass of gaily colored scarves, flowing past like waves, parting and converging again, and gradually vanishing into the vast whiteness of the flying snow.

"It's strange, apart from us, how can so many people bear to sit through a film like that?" Xiao Ling said.

"Like enduring life, it's not so hard," I said.

"But it's supposed to be art, after all." She took a red gauze kerchief from her pocket and tied it over her head. "It always seems to me that the people who make these films must be sick in the head . . ."

"It's the state apparatus that's sick."

"Shh—" She put her finger to her lips and looked around. "Didn't you spend enough time in the county prison? I mean, don't push all the problems onto the top. Even if there were a change, how much effect would it really have? When the Nazis seized power, the majority of German intellectuals refused to co-operate. The crux of the matter is that the earlier generations of Chinese intellectuals have never formed a strong social stratum. They have always submitted to political pressure; even if they resisted, their resistance was extremely limited."

"And our generation?"

"I can't explain exactly. Still, each generation should be stronger than the last. Really, I can't quite explain." She shook her head. "Let's change the subject."

"The snowstorm was very sudden," I said.

Xiao Ling greedily drank in a mouthful of fresh air. "I signed a contract with the snowflakes to fall when people aren't expecting it."

"Where did you sign?"

"On the windowpane, with my breath and finger."

"When?"

"When I was four or five."

"Then you were this big." I pointed at a little girl in a green padded jacket walking past us.

"Then you were that big." She pointed at a plastic toy dog in the little girl's hand.

We both laughed.

"Haven't they torn up the contract?" I asked again.

"Only once."

"When?"

"This time. Today, I thought it would snow, I thought it would." She sighed, and the snowflakes disappeared from round her mouth. "Nature has this sort of power; it can reconcile us with ourselves, with others, with life . . ."

The crowd dispersed. The lights at the cinema door went out one by one. The earth, covered with white snow, grew bright, like a dark mirror.

". . . I'm so tired, I just wish I could have a rest, a home, a nest to go to." She closed her eyes sorrowfully. "So I can lick my wounds and have pleasant dreams."

"A home," I repeated.

She nodded. "Yes, a home."

"Xiao Ling," I said, catching hold of her hand.

"What?" She hung her head, blushing.

"Suppose there were someone willing to help you shoulder everything?"

"Everything," she said softly.

"Yes, everything. Suffering and loneliness, and happiness too."

"Happiness," she answered like an echo.

"That's right, happiness."

She drew her hand away. "Idiot."

We were separated by a row of tall white poplars. The snow crunched underfoot. For a long time neither of us spoke.

"Recite a poem, Xiao Ling," I said.

She wore a somewhat abstracted expression, but after a while, she bit her lip, and began to recite in a low voice:

"The sky is beautiful,
The sea is serene
But I see only
Darkness and blood . . ."[6]

"Why did you choose that poem?" I asked.

"The poem chose me." She bit her lip, and shook her head. "This is the only kind of fate I deserve. What can I do?"

"You were just talking about resistance."

"That's another matter." She forced a smile. "First I have to resist myself: unfortunately I haven't even that ability."

"So according to what you say, this generation has no hope?"

"Why wander so far from the point? All that can be said is that I have no hope."

"No, there's a hope," I said with determination. "We have hope. Where there's life there's hope."

"Who is 'we'?" She stopped by a tree and rested her cheek against the trunk with a captivating smile.

"You and I."

"Oh." She pulled off her scarf, all wet with snowflakes, gave it a shake, and tied it to the trunk of the tree, gliding her finger up and down on it. "Who gave you the right to talk like this?" she asked in a hurried, low voice.

"You and I."

Suddenly she raised her eyes, almost grim. "Do you understand me?"

"Yes, I do."

"Based on what? These few meetings?"

"This isn't something that can be measured in terms of time . . ."

"No, no, don't say that, you'll pay a price." She hastily cut short my speech, and released the scarf from the tree trunk. "It's late, let's go."

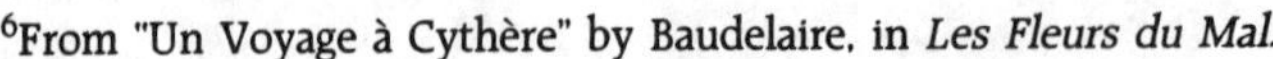

[6]From "Un Voyage à Cythère" by Baudelaire, in *Les Fleurs du Mal.*

The snow had stopped. The rays from the mercury lamps reflected on the snow shone with a deep blue light. She bit her lip, staring straight ahead, her steps hurried then slow, stumbling along, kicking up puffs of powdered snow. At the last poplar she stopped, looking at me silently, hesitation and distress in her eyes.

"Let's say goodbye," she said.

"When shall we meet?"

"We won't." She looked away. "Never . . ."

"Don't make jokes."

"I'm not in a joking mood."

"What's the matter, Xiao Ling?"

"Don't bear a grudge against me, don't . . ." Her lip trembled as she turned her head abruptly and walked away with rapid steps, gradually disappearing at the crossroads ahead.

I stood in the snow for a long time. How did this nightmare begin? How had it ended so carelessly? I scooped up some snow and rubbed it on my face, letting the melted snow soak down my neck drop by drop. The wind whistled in the distance. No, the wind was over my head, in the treetops, flowing in a firm direction, like an invisible arm enfolding this miserable world. It was true, it could not be seen, there was only darkness and blood . . . I walked back past the poplars, brushing each trunk with my hand; perhaps a little of her warmth remained on them—no, her warmth was zero, it was snow and ice . . .

I walked haltingly. Narrow streets, crooked houses; they crowded in on me until I couldn't breathe. I stopped beside a telegraph pole. Not far ahead, a man and a woman were talking in low voices. What, was it Bai Hua and her?! She glanced hastily in my direction and said something to Bai Hua in a low voice. Bai Hua put his arm round her waist and walked into the shadows.

Bang! Everything spun round with a humming sound, in a string of dazzling lights and foul black snow . . . I grabbed the telegraph pole, swearing savagely.

(Xiao Ling)

The wind blew the tears out of my eyes, and a corner of the scarf flapped against my face as I walked on, never turning my head, never! Ahead lay an abyss, but there was no way I could stretch out an entreating hand. No one could save anyone else, so what was the sense in perishing together? One should always leave behind something; a shred of warmth, a scarp of fantasy, a corner of clear sky, even though the boundless darkness and pools of blood cover them over unceasingly like pounding waves. Ah, you drifting stars, pure and beautiful, let me find a place to shelter in your endless radiance.

I turned into a small park by the side of the street and sat down on a bench half-hidden by a fir tree. It was utterly secluded and quiet here; you could hear the sound of the wind shaking the snow from the branches, and once in a while the blasts of distant car horns. With a plop, a black fir cone fell to the ground and rolled to my feet. I buried it gently in the snow with the toe of my shoe.

"Well, it's young Xiao." The sudden voice in the stillness gave me a fright. It was Firecracker lounging on a bench not far away, his feet propped up on the armrest. "And how's it going now?"

I took no notice of him, turning away to stare at the rows of apartment blocks like steep cliffs behind the stand of firs.

He staggered over to me, reeking of liquor. "Not at work, eh?"

I glared at him.

"Don't look at me, I've got a certificate for sick leave, temperature of 38.6, I need to take a stroll." He narrowed his eyes, the big creases at the corners of his mouth slackening and tightening.

"In the village I heard donkeys get the same treatment."

"That's enough smart talk." His smile suddenly disappeared. "Why aren't you at work?"

"That's none of your business."

"Ha, don't be so unsociable, you're my apprentice, we should have a bit of a chat now. Come on, have another drink with your teacher." He pulled a half-bottle of spirits out of his pocket, shook it in the air, and moved closer.

I sprang to my feet. "What do you think you're doing?"

"Hey, everyone at the factory says you're so tough, you don't give a damn about anything, what's so shocking about a drink with your teacher?" Blinking his bloodshot eyes, he put out his hand to touch my shoulder. I turned in a flash and slapped him fiercely across the face. He froze, spat some bloody saliva on the ground, and forced himself toward me. Trembling with anger I retreated from tree to tree, at last bumping into the iron street railing. "I want you to know the next time, look, has this Horse King got three eyes or not," he rasped harshly.

"Hey, I've been burning incense and kowtowing and at long last the Buddha's appeared. Who's this Horse King?" someone suddenly interjected from the path outside.

I turned round to look and let out a sigh of relief. "Oh, Bai Hua, give me a hand, he's a bit sick."

"I'm just back from making housecalls. I've cut off an arm and beaten a pig, and I'm pretty tired, but I'll carry out revolutionary humanitarianism."

He leaped over the railing and patted Firecracker on the shoulder. "What's wrong, brother?"

"Don't touch me!" Firecracker recoiled as if he'd received an electric shock.

"Epilepsy. Come on, we'll have an examination here." Bai Hua seized his arm and shoved him behind the grove of trees.

"Let me go, or I'll knock your head off!" Firecracker howled.

"Quiet down. Got a pain in your gut? Your liver? Kidney? You don't understand what a kidney is? You trash . . ."

Utterly weary, I leaned my face against the ice-cold iron rail. Everything was finished. Was he still standing under the white poplar? Hate me, hate me, it's better that way. The wind whistled through the air, the sky was so black, the snow so white, ah, such a violent contrast. I have to brace myself and go on, risking the cruelty of the winter wind and the harshness of the burning sun, and at the end of the road I'll set up for myself a little headstone . . .

Bai Hua came back, brushing his hands. "All cleared up."

"Did you kill him?"

"Hardly. But I've busted his jaw and dislocated his joints. He can crawl back into his hole, anyhow."

We walked the street. The snow was melting, and the silver-white world was being broken into fragments. What you were originally, you will return to; illusions always come to an end, so end, I don't care!

"Come to my place for a while," Bai Hua said.

"It's too late."

"Do you think I'm beneath you?"

I shook my head.

"Say one word, just say it, and I'll follow you for the rest of my life. Do you believe me?"

"Bai Hua, do you respect me?"

"Of course."

"The direct meaning of respect is not to say things I don't wish to hear . . ." Suddenly I saw him. He was standing by a telegraph pole not far away, staring at us. My heart contracted violently. "Bai Hua, give me your arm, I feel faint . . ."

Bai Hua's lips parted slightly, as if something were forcing him to gasp for breath. At last he stretched out his arm, and leaning on his shoulder, I entered a dim laneway.

"Let me go," I said in a low voice.

Bai Hua trembled and didn't move.

"Let go!" I pushed him away roughly, turned, and ran.

The streetlights flashed. There was mud everywhere.

6

(Lin Dongping)

6:20: the Extended Session of the Party Committee had been going on for a whole three hours.

". . . for more than two months, we've spent the whole day

here bickering without being able to implement the spirit of the provincial government, and the supply of commodities remains in confusion." Wang Defa swept his gaze around the room and then continued. "We've just taken off our military uniforms and haven't had enough local work experience, so some people have wrongly appraised the situation . . ."

It had begun. I balanced a match between two fingers. This was a dangerous road; to what end would it lead? I'd been through many "ends." Some looked frightening at the time, but when the matter was all over, time broke everything into fragments and remolded them. Perhaps one shouldn't think so much, but concentrate. The room was heavy with cigarette smoke, each face seeming to sink and re-emerge in the cloud of smoke. What were they thinking? People's thoughts were hard to see clearly. Miss Zhang cast me an anxious glance. Thanks, my dear, but it doesn't matter. After all, the smoke can't hide everything. The wind blew in from an open window, carrying away the threads of smoke, flying away to some far-off place. Spring . . .

"Some people are thinking of giving the masses small concessions in order to gain their own unspeakable ends. Why has the Zhang Village coalmine been out of action for so long? Who is responsible for these things?"

The match snapped, and I raised my head. "It's my responsibility."

Wang Defa gave a start, then opened a packet of cigarettes and drew one out. "Good, let's ask Chief Lin to speak to us."

"First I'll discuss the Zhang Village coalmine," I said. "More than two hundred people were killed or injured in last year's cave-in. Even countrywide a mining accident on this scale is rare. Yes, the mineshaft has already been repaired, but to this day the cause of the cave-in hasn't been cleared up. How can we rush the workers into a dangerous job at the risk of their lives? Comrades, all of us here are members of the Communist Party, and we ought to have a conscience . . ."

"Conscience?" Wang Defa snorted. "The proletariat speaks of Party spirit."

I ignored him and continued speaking. "As for the supply of commodities, we cannot fail to consider the people's hardships. In the last few years production has not risen, for many reasons, but the crux of the matter is this: if the people have no strength, how will they work? Recently I went to several factories and chatted with workers and foremen about their daily lives. It distressed me. As for giving small concessions, I don't know what that refers to . . . giving charity to whom? For several years, many of our accounts have been incomprehensible. Last year, 50,000,000 yuan in flood relief . . ."

"What does that mean?" Wang Defa snatched an unlit cigarette from his mouth. "The chief of the Accounts Bureau's here, Old Lü, you tell us, which accounts aren't clear, eh?"

Old Lü adjusted his spectacles and hung his head. "How should I know? It's a mess, red-tape, hmph . . ."

"So what do you do for a living?" Wang Defa thumped the packet of cigarettes down on the table.

"Chief Wang, is this a good practice?" I said slowly, shredding the match into little pieces.

"I don't need you to train me! If we stand firm and act correctly in whatever we do, what's there to be afraid of? On the contrary, it's those self-styled veterans who should take stock of their own accounts . . ."

"Chief Wang, please don't bring personal prejudice into the Party session," Miss Zhang retorted heatedly.

"Personal prejudice?" Wang Defa let out a scornful laugh. "Let me ask you, Chief Lin, that house of yours cost 150,000 yuan—where did the money come from?"

"There are funds for building the Municipal Committee's living quarters," said Old Lü.

"How much a year?"

"200,000."

At once the meeting broke into confused discussion.

"So you see," Wang Defa leaned back, spreading out his hands. "You in fact appropriated most of it. How many workers and administrative staff does the Municipal Committee have? The people, conscience—they sound better said than sung . . ."

There was a whirring in my head. When Ruohong entrusted young Xun to me, there was the hint of some other emotion apart from a mother's love. Young Xun had grown up, and that time he spent in jail eroded much of his childish enthusiasm, making him a lot more sober. What made me anxious was that he was easily influenced by others. What sort of lass was this girlfriend of his? I hoped she was not a local; these local girls were too vulgar. Yuanyuan still hadn't lost her childishness, which worried me . . . no, it wasn't the time, I must concentrate.

". . . where have eight carpets gone? Two high-quality sofas? Even a Japanese television set allocated to the provincial government has found its way into Chief Lin's house," Wang Defa was saying.

"Chief Wang, why do you know so much about it?" I asked.

"I've made an investigation . . ."

"No, it's because these matters were handled by you. In October the year before last when I went to Beijing for a meeting, you approved the use of 150,000 yuan for building my house, have you forgotten?"

"Oh, that, that . . ." Wang Defa mumbled vaguely. "But it's you who lives there."

"It's I, but after all the money had a source. And the fifty million for flood relief . . ." I said.

"Slow down." Wang Defa pulled out a notebook and noisily flipped through the pages. "Here it is item by item, not a single discrepancy. Don't you try to pin anything on me."

"Why do the flood victims send letters, and why are so many people, even now, camped in the streets, begging for food?"

Wang Defa slammed his hand on the table, and the cups rattled and clattered. "You think this bit of money can provide these people with gulps of sesame oil?"

"I never mentioned sesame oil. Chief Wang, we can set up a special subcommittee to sort out the accounts for the last few years, to avoid anyone falling under suspicion. What do you think of that?"

"By all means," he said.

Wang Defa raised his eyelids and stared at me rigidly. I met his gaze. I'd rather like to see what you can do to me, relying on threats is no use, no use at all, it's the other way round, you should take care: are your own nerves reliable? His eyelids flickered, and he shifted his gaze.

I went down the stairs. In the wide-open gateway, stars, the night sky, and the damp wind were kneaded together. There was the sound of footsteps behind me, and Su Yumei caught up with me breathlessly.

"The meeting really went on for ages. I want to make a suggestion," she said.

"Haven't you left yet?"

"We're standing fast at our posts. At times like these, no one can do without us." She put on a pair of red nylon gloves, watching me provocatively. "Is there anything you need?"

I said nothing.

"Chief Lin, why don't you look for someone else?" she asked.

"I hadn't thought about it, and anyhow, who'd want an old man like me?"

"Come on, these days it's fashionable for a girl to look for an old fellow."

"For his money?"

"That's of secondary importance. Young kids don't understand feelings, but old ginger's hot." She broke into a loud giggle.

"And you, why don't you get married?"

"A single person has more peace and freedom. Besides, I don't like being managed." She paused, and blinked her eyelashes suggestively. "I've heard, I've heard you're not one to go by the rules; you played around a lot in the past . . ."

"Is that reliable?"

"Bureaucratic gossip, don't take any notice of it, I'll keep your secret." She ran down the stairs. "Bye-bye."

As I walked to the car, I drew a deep breath. Spring; it always made you aware of its existence. In fact, the ice hadn't even melted completely; perhaps it was merely some kind of call from the heart. People who are past the prime of life often become even more attached to the season of blossoms. Bureaucratic gossip . . .

I opened the car door.

"Finished?" Fat Wu yawned, stretching.

"Turn on the radio. See if there's anything to listen to."

The dial lit up. He flicked the knob back and forth. It was all dry news and ear-piercing model operas.

"Turn it off," I said.

Streetlights. Shops. Cinema. Streetlights. Restaurant. Rubbish heaps. Little mud-brick huts. Streetlights. . . . I shut my eyes. It was such a broken-down city, even the night couldn't hide its shabbiness. The creatures living in these mud-brick huts, searching through the rubbish, were these "the people"? Once the image stepped down from the propaganda posters it appeared far more pallid and frightening. 150,000 yuan, sofas, carpets, television sets . . . no, they didn't mean anything; in a class society people can't possibly be completely equal. While we went through fire and water, they lived in peace, content with their work, their days passing full of tranquillity. There's no need to have a guilty conscience. And besides, if you went to the provincial capital, or to Beijing, whose house was not better than mine, a hundred times better. When I listened to such talk, it was just as if I were persuading myself.

Arriving home, I told Auntie Chen to send dinner to the study, then rubbed myself down in the bathroom, changed into pajamas, and went into the study. Under the soft blue light of the desk lamp, young Xun was reclining on the sofa, reading a book.

(Yang Xun)

I raised my head. In the dimness, Uncle Lin was standing in the doorway, his hand on the brass doorknob as if he'd been standing there a long time.

I got to my feet. "Aren't you feeling well, Uncle Lin?"

"Oh, it's nothing, I'm just a bit tired." He passed his hand over his brow. "Where's Yuanyuan?"

"She's not back yet."

He walked to the window and drew the curtain. "Had a letter from your mother?"

"One came yesterday. She wants me to go back to Beijing. She's just entrusted someone with making arrangements for a discharge for me."

He was lost in thought at the window for a while. "Go back, your mother needs you. I'll take care of the formalities."

"I don't want to go back."

"Why not?"

I remained silent.

"Because of your girlfriend?"

I smiled wryly, put away my book and lit a cigarette.

"It doesn't matter, we can arrange for you together; is she from Beijing too?" Uncle Lin came over and sat down on the other sofa.

"She has no home."

"An orphan?"

"I'm not really sure, besides . . ."

"She's not willing to talk about it?"

"No, things like that . . ."

"Xun, you should consider your mother more, she's getting on and she wishes her son to be near her." He leaned forward, his tone rather unusual. I had the sudden feeling that in the past he too had been a child demanding sweets from his mother, and that he too had broken his heart over a girl and shed secret tears.

Just at this point, Auntie Chen brought in the dinner, put it on the tea-table, and left.

"Have something more to eat," he said.

"No, I've had plenty, I should get back to the factory. You have an early night," I said, standing up.

"Think this matter over carefully."

"All right." I walked toward the door.

"Xun—"

I turned round.

"Nothing. Close the door as you go out." He waved me away.

I walked along the dimly lit passage, reached the doorway, and was about to go down the stairs when I realized someone had slipped into the shadows of the pine trees. "Who's there?" I asked.

Yuanyuan emerged, her face turned away, and walked furiously toward the stairs. I blocked her way.

"Go away, let me go!"

"Hm, what a temper. Tell me, what's the matter?"

"I haven't got time."

"When do you have time?"

"Go and ask her."

"Her?"

"Come on, don't pretend to be completely stupid."

It suddenly dawned on me what she was talking about. "Yuanyuan, listen to me . . ."

"I haven't got time." She slipped past me, fleeing up the stairs. "And don't come to our house so often!"

The door slammed shut.

On the way back to the factory I went into a liquor shop. Inside, clouds of smoke, the mingled smell of smoke and spirits filling the air. A middle-aged beggar wandered up and down amongst the tables littered with cups and plates, tipping leftover soup and rice into a greasy plastic bag. Several young fellows were drinking and playing the finger-guessing game, shouting deafeningly:

"Two . . . six . . . nine . . . ten . . ."

I ordered half a catty of corn spirits and was just looking for a quiet corner when suddenly a hand fell on my shoulder. "Where are you going, brother? Park yourself here if you don't mind the company," Bai Hua said, wiping his mouth.

I sat down opposite him.

"Haven't seen you for days. Come on, have a drink first," he said.

I glared at him.

"What a long face. What's eating you?"

I glared at him. He put down his cup and drummed on it with his fingers, a deep furrow appearing on his brow. I raised my cup and drained it at one go.

"Not bad, have some more," he said, taking hold of the bottle.

I blocked the bottle with my hand, moved round the table, and went up close to him. He stood up slowly.

"What about her?" I asked under my breath.

He didn't say a word.

"What about her?" I asked again.

"What the devil, I was just going to ask you."

"Bai Hua," I grabbed him by the collar. "Don't try to play this trick on me . . ."

He shoved me away, his eyes narrowing ferociously. "If you're bored with living, just say one damned word!"

"I'm asking you, what was going on that night?"

"Which night?"

"The first snowfall of winter."

"Hey, wasn't that weird, I'm as puzzled as you are. I've got nothing to hide. You be the judge. I'd rescued her from a louse, and I'd hardly said two words when she complained she felt sick. She asked me to give her a hand, but the next minute she'd run off again . . ."

I grabbed the edge of the table to keep myself steady. Big cups, small cups. Bai Hua. Glinting nickel-plated pipes. Bai Hua. Fingers stretched out in the guessing game. Bai Hua. A propaganda poster on the wall ripped in half. Bai Hua. . . . I stumbled out.

I sat on the embankment, gazing at the lighted window in the ripples of the water, trying desperately to put my confused thoughts in order. Plop. A pebble rolled into the channel, and the lighted window was shaken into a patch of dim yellow. I scooped up a half-wet clod and crumbled it slowly, letting it sift through my fingers, then got up and walked toward the mud-brick cottage.

I knocked on the door, found that it was off the latch, and pushed it open. She got up from the table without a word, her face pale, almost expressionless, only her hands fiddling with the top of a fountain pen.

"You've come," she said finally, after a long pause.

"Yes, I've come."

"Sit down."

I remained standing.

"Apparently neither of us understands courtesy very well." She attempted a smile, which only made her lips tremble. She looked away fiercely, turning toward the window. A blue vein twitched on her snow-white temple.

"Xiao Ling." I stepped forward and turned her round by the shoulders to face me. "Why are you being like this?"

She lowered her eyelids. A glistening teardrop hung on her lashes, quivered, and rolled slowly down her cheek.

"Tell me why?"

She opened her eyes, shook her head, and smiled miserably. I stretched out my fingers and brushed away the tear from the corner of her mouth.

"Look, the moon's risen," she said softly, as if telling me a long-hidden secret.

I looked up. "The moon's red."

"Yes."

"Why?"

"Listen to you, still the same old fault."

"Xiao Ling, do you know how I've spent these last months?"

She sealed my mouth with her hand. "No grievances, all right?"

I nodded.

Suddenly she clasped my neck, trustingly pressed her lips against me, and without waiting for my response pushed me away, dodged over the other side of the table, and pulled a mischievous face. "Just stand there, I want to look at you like that."

I started to move round the table.

"Don't move!" she warned.

"This place has turned into a prison," I said.

"How is it compared to the county prison?"

"A bit better."

"I'll lock you up here," she pointed at her heart. "How about that?"

"That's much better."

We both laughed.

"What's this?" I picked up the notebook lying on the desk. "May I have a look?"

"No!" She snatched it away, clasping it to her breast. "Not now," she added.

"Later?"

"I'll definitely let you look."

"What have you written? Epigrams and mottoes?"

"No, just some of my thoughts, and recollections of the past."

(Xiao Ling)

High noon. Li Tiejun and I walk along beside the steaming river, followed by two Red Guards from the Red Headquarters Brigade, automatic rifles slung upside down over their shoulders. Under the burning sun, several young fellows are listlessly digging a trench by the bank.

"Maybe those bastards will plan an attack for tomorrow." He lashes the air with a willow sprig. "Then you people from Beijing will see something."

"We haven't come to watch a play. Give me a machine gun, I'll stay in the forward position," I say.

"You?" His lip curls in a sneer.

"Don't underestimate us. See how we perform on the field of battle." I stop for a moment, then suddenly ask, "Are you a strong person?"

"What does it mean to be strong? Not to be afraid of death, right?"

"That's not enough."

"What else is there? Killing someone without batting an eyelid?" he says half jokingly. "You don't believe me?"

I shake my head.

"Let's make a bet," he says.

We reach the head of the bridge on the highway. In the middle of the sandbag defenses the enameled mouths of heavy machine guns point straight ahead. At the wire-netting roadblock, some Red Guards are checking on the passers-by.

We lean on the stone balustrade of the bridge, chatting about this and that. Suddenly, Li Tiejun's eyes turn toward the crowd. He points to a young fellow, beckons with his finger, and calls him over.

"Where are you going?"

"Into the city to see my aunt, she's sick."

"Not taking anything, eh? Another detailed search."

The search produces a girl's photograph and a badge.

"Who's she?" asks Li Tiejun, taking the photograph.

"My girlfriend."

Li Tiejun picks up the badge, looks closely at the back and laughs grimly. "Taking a Red Cannon Brigade badge to see your aunt? Let's have the truth."

"I really am going to see my aunt," the youth persists.

"Kneel down!" Li Tiejun gives him a kick from behind, and he falls heavily to his knees. "I'll give you one last chance."

"I'm telling the truth."

"Then get ready to say goodbye." Li Tiejun throws the girl's photograph down in front of him and pulls out his pistol.

The youth picks up the photograph and presses it to his breast, then turns his head, his face deathly white. His beseeching eyes sweep from the muzzle of the gun to me.

"Tiejun, just a minute . . ." As I'm about to rush forward to hold him back, the gun goes off.

In the burning-hot noon, beside the quiet river, the gun is so loud the report hovers for a long time. With the sound of each gunshot, the youth's head strikes against the hard concrete road. Blood spurts out, dyeing the girl's photograph, running into the river . . .

Tiejun gives the body a kick, puts his gun away, and turns

proudly toward my stunned face. "This time you lose, that's one you owe me."

"You, you butcher, bastard!" I shout myself hoarse, turn and run, tears blurring my vision.

"Hey, get up."

I rub my eyes; a little old man wearing a patrol officer's armband is standing in front of me.

"Get up. Come with me," he says.

I fold up the raincoat I'd spread on the ground, step over the people curled up everywhere, and follow him into the station duty office.

"Sit down." He points to a stool beside the desk.

I remain standing.

"You're from Beijing?" he asks.

"You could say so."

"So why do you come here to sleep every evening?"

"This is the first time."

"Do you think I'm an old fool with no eyes, eh?" He starts to cough, holding a big handkerchief to cover his mouth. He coughs for a while, then asks suddenly, "Where's your home?"

"I don't have one."

He nods. "No relatives or friends?"

"Who could I go to? I'm wanted by the school," I say irritably. "What do you want? Go and report me . . ."

The old man's Adam's apple bobs up and down. He reaches into his pocket and brings out a little paper packet. "Here, take this."

I hesitate, then take the packet—it's ten yuan. Something salty and astringent blocks my throat. "Uncle . . ."

"Take it, child, don't try to be so superior. Get some more clothes or something, it's getting cold. Otherwise I'll just use the money for drink. Go on, take it. I haven't told the missus, but she'll be sure to agree. She's not much to look at but she's got a good heart . . ."

"Uncle," I say.

"Go on, go on."

"Uncle Shen, I just don't believe these lies anymore." I shut the book and leave it on my lap. "But this period of history . . ."

"Young people, ah, you always want to go forward. Remember, whatever the verdict, it's never the final verdict." He walks round the pile of books on the floor, closes the only window in the little room, comes back, and leans back in a creaking old cane chair. "Lingling, when I met your parents, I was studying Oriental History at Harvard. Now that may seem rather funny, but in fact it's not." He points to the book in my lap. "Old Hegel says this: 'All forms of existence bind themselves to their own self-created history; furthermore, history as a kind of concrete universal determines and transcends them. . . . ' That is to say, it's very difficult for man to transcend his own body and recognize history, and those on the crest of the historical wave recognize this even less: this, then, is the lamentable position of certain great men."

"It's also the lamentable position of our nation," I say.

"No." Uncle Shen makes a resolute gesture. "The life of one person is limited, but the life of a nation has no limit: the latent energy of our Chinese nation has never shone forth. Perhaps it's got a bit old, and as a result it has become rather slow in the process of self-recognition. But this process is now underway and is being carried through by a chain from one generation to the next. If a country blows an out-of-tune bugle, that symbolizes the decline of a certain kind of power. It is also the prelude to the rising up of the whole nation . . ."

The bell rings, and the clamor of leave-taking on the platform reaches a pitch, shouts and sobs mingling into one. An accordion plays frenziedly, while young fellows arm in arm sing themselves hoarse. I sit by the window, watching it all with cold indifference.

"Xiao Ling," Yun, who has come to see me off, takes my hand gently. "Come back this winter. Stay at our place, my mother's very fond of you."

"No, I'm not coming back."

"So when will you come back?"

"I'll never come back."

"Why? Xiao Ling . . ."

Suddenly, the whole station shudders and slowly withdraws. Yun's voice is drowned. She stretches out her hand, runs forward a few steps, and is engulfed in the crowd.

Goodbye, Beijing! Forget me, Beijing!

7

(Yang Xun)

Violet sunlight, trapped in the mist, sank into the hollows of the valley floor, revealing a forest of towering, blue-gray firs. From some unseen place a brook clamored, mingling with the sweet warbling of birds. Wildflowers were scattered like stars beside the stone-paved mountain path. On the cliffside the withered branch of an old tree disgorged a layer of delicate green moss.

Xiao Ling walked along, picking all kinds of wildflowers. "I remember when I was in primary school I wrote a composition about how I'd be a botanist when I grew up and associate only with flowers and grass . . ."

"Lucky your wish didn't come true," I said.

"Why?" she asked, raising her head.

"Then what should I do?"

She smiled. "I'd pretend you were a green bristlegrass, and press you in a book."

"If I were pressed in a book, I could only read one page."

"No, whenever I read a page, I'd change your place." She laughed, and even the solemn mountain valley could not but respond softly.

A clear mountain spring cut across the stone path, falling away into a deep valley. A dim white vapor rose from the pool at the bottom of the valley. She stood at the edge of the drop and looked down, as if listening to the tumbling roar. A few gray birds cried plaintively in the spray.

"Is it death down there?" She looked up, her mood now solemn and sad.

I did not answer.

"It's very close to us." The color drained from her eyes, and the sunlight in them shivered a little.

"What's wrong?" I asked.

She leaned against me silently, gazing down again. "I'm afraid . . ."

"Afraid of what?"

"Afraid of parting," she said in a muffled voice.

"Impossible, nothing can part us."

"Even death?"

"Impossible."

She gazed trustingly at me.

I stroked her shoulder. "Let's not stand here, all right?"

She nodded, turned, and squatted down by the spring. Gazing at her reflection she sighed. Then scooping up some water she washed her face and turned her head. "How shall we cross?"

I lifted her up and leaped across.

"I shouldn't go on like this, you must have felt disheartened just now," she said, lying in my arms.

"No."

"Truly? Now, look at me, don't turn away . . . good, now let me go."

A flight of stone stairs weathered by the wind led up to a carved white marble archway. The gold lacquer had peeled off the words "The Wheel of the Dharma flies round" on the dilapidated screen wall; all was sadness and desolation. The tortoise with the stele on its back was buried deep in mud, revealing only half a head. The rough stone path was covered over with last winter's dry leaves and sheep droppings. Most of the side hall on the right had collapsed, and from the broken arms of the Eighteen Disciples grew tall weeds, rustling in the passing breeze. We entered the main hall, into a faint odor of mold and decay. In the dimness, a shaft of sunlight fell on the long slender hand of the central Buddha.

"Hello, Guan Yin—"[7] Xiao Ling shouted like a child, and the dark, gloomy hall sent back a low, muffled echo.

"This is Sakyamuni," I said.

"An Indian?"

"That's right."

"Mr. Sakyamuni, welcome to our country. But do you have a passport?"

"He has the Scriptures," I said.

"There are more than enough of those here already. If you break our commandments you may get a term of labor reform." Xiao Ling suddenly turned and asked, "Are you interested in religion?"

"One can't help being interested: in these last years, we've been living in a kind of religious atmosphere," I said. "And you?"

"Me? I've just become interested," she said, closing her eyes. "But I wish that in the darkness there were a god to bless and protect us . . ."

"Why not Buddha, or Our Father in Heaven?"

"Anyone will do, as long as it's some sort of god."

"Do you really believe in such things?"

"It's hard to say." She winked and smiled mischievously. "My religious feeling is pragmatic . . . oh look, there's a cave."

Sure enough, there in the corner was the mouth of a cave as tall as a man. Xiao Ling popped her head in. "It's very dark. Did you bring a lighter?"

Holding up the lighter I walked forward. The cave was very deep; after a dozen or so steps a flight of narrow stairs appeared. Xiao Ling grabbed hold of my sleeve. I turned around, and in her wide eyes shone two little dancing flames. The stone stairs rose slowly in the firelight. Suddenly it became light and roomy. We had reached a small attic; inside, eight ferocious-looking monsters were placed around the walls.

"Oh! What a weird place. From the top you'd think it was

[7]The Goddess of Mercy.

Heaven, but in actual fact it feels more like Hell." Xiao Ling looked the monsters up and down one by one. "It's all right, not too scary after all, really rather sad; they must have suffered a lot to turn into things like this."

I went to the window. "Come and see, this is the lookout point."

We looked down from the height. The remnants of a wall stood solemnly in the overgrown grass, as if recalling past glory. The flashing stream flowed past outside the courtyard wall, eroding the exposed roots of an old cypress tree. Blue mountains were faintly visible in the distance.

She turned sideways and gazed at me, a kind of wonder in her eyes. Sunlight stroked her shoulders and arms, as if it wanted to seep right through her body. The red gauze scarf she wore was tugged by the wind, one moment blocking out the sun, the next fluttering back. Little rainbow-colored rings leaped before my eyes.

"It would be wonderful if we were like this forever," she said, resting her hands on my shoulders.

I drew her toward me and held her tight. Her head fell back, and her lips parted slightly, her breath coming rapidly. Suddenly big teardrops came rolling down . . .

"Xiao Ling," I called softly.

She simply lay on my shoulder and cried. After a long while, she pushed me away, wiped her eyes, and shook her head in embarrassment, smiling.

"Are you upset?" I asked.

"You're really an idiot. You don't know anything," she murmured, running her fingers through my hair, ruffling it then slowly smoothing it again.

With a flurry, two swallows flew out through a hole in the roof. "We must have disturbed them," Xiao Ling said.

"No, they disturbed us."

"But this is their home."

"It's our home too."

"Don't talk nonsense." She glared at me fiercely, covering my mouth with her hand. I caught hold of her hand and kissed it. She withdrew it and smoothed her hair. "I'm hungry."

I opened the bag, spread a sheet of plastic on the floor, then laid out the wine, cold food, and fruit. I also took out a little aluminum tin, shaking it in my hand. "I'll go and get some water and collect some firewood while I'm at it."

"I'll go too." On the way she jostled me with her elbow. "You see, I don't know why but as soon as you leave me I'm afraid. Aren't I a coward?"

"You're a brave girl."

"In these last few days I keep feeling that I'm changing, changing into something I don't quite recognize myself."

"You've become more like yourself."

"Could there be two mes?"

"Perhaps more than two."

"It gets worse and worse. So which me do you actually love?"

"All of them."

"You're being slippery." Her lips curled slyly. "In fact you only love the me in your mind's eye, and that me doesn't exist, right?"

"No, that's the combination of all the yous."

She laughed. "It's just as complicated as a mathematical calculation, if you end up with the three-headed, six-armed me, could you stand that?"

"Let's try it and see."

"I wonder, how can we go on like this? Walking along this little path, as if nothing had happened, as if all along we lived by the rules; birth, school, work, love . . . once in a while getting out of town and letting our cares drift away—do you understand what I mean?"

"I understand."

"If you could choose your life over again, what sort would you choose?"

"Still the one I've had."

"That's because you haven't paid a high enough price."

"No, it's because otherwise I wouldn't have known you."

"Oh, that reason's quite sufficient." She nodded with satisfaction.

We reached the spring.

"I feel like washing my hair." She stretched out and tested the water with her hand.

I looked up anxiously at the darkening sky. "Watch out you don't catch a chill. It looks as if it'll rain soon."

She hummed a light-hearted tune, undid her hairpin, and her hair spilled into the water without a sound. "Yang Xun, our treat won't be eaten by rats, will it?"

"If there are rats, they'll probably turn into demons."

"Don't try to scare me, I'm not that easily frightened. Come here, help me squeeze this dry." I rolled up my sleeves and gave a couple of squeezes. She threw off my hand. "You think this is a piece of rope; let me do it myself."

The branches crackled into flame, and the light from the fire flickered over her face. In the dancing shadows of the flames, her appearance was a little eerie.

"Are you sure the floor won't catch fire?" I asked anxiously.

"What are you talking about? Heat rises," she said.

Heat. Why had I never realized it before? Perhaps that was what I was feeling at this very moment, heat, slowly rising, rising. We always felt cold before, a coldness spreading outward from the heart, a coldness discharged through the need for heat, through the absorption of heat; finally they condensed into dewdrops on the blades of grass and rose as mists in the valleys.

Xiao Ling knelt on the sheet of plastic, opened the wine, poured two cups, and handed one to me. "Come on, let's drink."

"First let's think of some toasts," I said.

"To you, and that allegedly brave girl, happiness to you and her . . ."

"To the two survivors of these tragic times . . ."

"May this pair of survivors, like the swallows, still return to the nest together after being so rudely disturbed . . ."

"May the guns not aim at swallows . . ."

"To the indestructibility of swallows . . ."

"To beautiful fairytales . . ."

"To the health of Mr. Sakyamuni. Cheers!"

We drained our cups.

At that moment a clap of thunder roared. She got up and went to the window, her hair blowing in the wind. "It's going to rain," she murmured.

"We won't be able to get back," I said.

She turned her head and darted a peculiar look at me.

Night, night full of menace, full of thunder and lightning and rustling whispers, pressed down upon us. The lightning flashed, and in that instant her clear silhouette was thrown against the shattered sky.

"The wind's too strong at the window, come over here," I said.

She remained leaning against the window, staring into the distance.

"Xiao Ling," I called.

She turned, looking at me as if just woken from a dream, walked over silently, and sat beside me. The flames gradually died down, the last embers reflecting on her calm face, delineating a gentle curve. I drew her over, and she yielded silently. Her lips were freezing. She was rather thinly clad.

"Are you cold?"

She shook her head, watching me blankly. I bent down, kissing her forehead. Her snow-white throat stretched down, swelling a little inside her collar. A row of white buttons glistened in the dimness. My fingers touched the first one, gently unbuttoning it.

"Don't do that . . ." she said in alarm, grabbing my hand.

I touched the second one.

Slap! She fiercely threw off my hand, clutching her collar together tightly. "Get away! Didn't you hear me? Get away!" The lightning illuminated her trembling chin.

I got up and walked angrily to the window. Raindrops drummed on the window lattice. The wind gradually dropped, the invisible river thundered . . .

Suddenly I was blindfolded. I pulled her small hands away, turned round, and she rushed into my arms.

Lightning. The demons appeared over our heads, grinning ferociously. Darkness.

(Xiao Ling)

Love stands up trembling in the quagmire of pain. This liberation is as violent as death, so that I keep wanting to open the floodgates and let the tide of happiness escape with a roar.

Have you gone mad?

Yes, I've gone mad. If I haven't yet been stifled to death by mediocrity, I'd willingly be a madman, a cheerful madman, because faced with so-called normality, madness is a kind of opposite, and any opposite is beautiful.

Have you forgotten your own duty?

No, but in the midst of duty I still think of what lies beyond duty. I think of love, which bathes in a different sunlight.

Enough, I'm getting too abstract!

I like the abstract things of life. They have not been confined by callous and dirty reality, and because of that are more true, more lasting.

Tell me, are you happy?

What is happiness? Is it just a kind of contentment? Contentment leads to boredom. Perhaps genuine happiness leaves no aftertaste, or else is like storm that has passed by; you only see the traces left on the ground.

Could it be the resurrection of hope?

There is always hope, even in the darkest hours I still set aside a radiant corner for it. It has significance in itself, even total significance. Of course, it is by no means an illusory hope, but a hope that seeks a goal. Now, in the midst of destruction, it is caught tightly by the hand of a child and raised up high again; may it gain its heart's desire and smash the boundless and impenetrable darkness!

What kind of a goal are you seeking?

This is exactly the question our generation has raised and

must answer. Perhaps the search itself is what already epitomizes our generation. We will not easily accept death, nor silence, nor obedience to any preconceived judgment! Even though separated by high walls, mountain ranges and wide rivers, each person struggles, hesitates, becomes depressed and even weary; but taken overall, faith and strength are eternal.

You're getting too far from the point. Why haven't you mentioned him?

I loathe this tone of yours. Stop interrogating me like an old woman. Leave me in peace.

I opened my book, read a few lines, then shut it again. As soon as I picked up my sewing, the needle slipped and pricked my finger, and a smooth round drop of blood seeped out. I smiled and sucked it dry. It was as if I'd only just begun to grasp the true meaning of that experience; to feel astonished, to be intoxicated, to be shy. In fact, the reason for excitement like this wasn't in love alone, it was also in finding a new starting point. There were so many things I could do—the little piece of sunlight still left in my heart hadn't grown cold and could warm others . . .

I shivered, and my gaze rested on the little glass frame on the table. Jingjing, are you laughing at me? Yes, I should find a chance to tell him, tell him all this. Would he understand?

I walked into the workshop. The grinding-wheel motor was humming. Firecracker was absorbed in working on a knife, testing the blade with his hand over and over. Recently he'd become very slow; did Bai Hua really hurt him?

"Hey, what's the work for today?" I asked.

He didn't hear and went on grinding. I stretched out my hand and turned the machine off with a clatter. He jumped with fright, quickly hiding the knife behind his back. "Oh it's you, I, I was just going to trim my toenails, nothing else . . ."

"Who cares about your private business, I asked you what's the work for today?"

"There's work all right, but anyway, anyway the Political Work Section wants to see you," he said hesitantly.

"What's up?"

"I, I don't know."

I knocked twice on the door of the Political Work Section.

"Come in." A fat old woman was sitting behind a large specially made office desk. She took stock of me for a moment from behind her spectacles. A little wooden sign, "Please Don't Offer Cigarettes," was propped up on the desk. Beside her sat a girl copying out something. The girl put down her pen and eyed me curiously.

"Your name is Xiao Ling?" the old woman asked at last.

"Yes, what is it?"

"Sit down, Xiao Ling, this is . . ." She was about to introduce me to the girl beside her, then stopped. She took a large shawl from the back of her chair and wrapped it around her shoulders. "Aren't you two cold? This room really is like an icebox. Er, what's your name?"

"You've already used it twice," I say.

"Have I?" She adjusted her spectacles and looked at a card. "Oh, Xiao Ling. You're a provisional worker?"

"Yes."

"The contract period is three years, is that correct?"

"Correct."

"Well, it's like this; we want to look into your situation . . ."

"It's all in the file."

"No, there are a few additional questions."

"What are they?"

"What relatives have you in Beijing?"

"None."

"Abroad?"

"None."

"Well, after your parents died, who brought you up?"

"I looked after myself."

The old woman exchanged a glance with the girl and made a mark on a piece of paper. "Another thing. When you were kept apart for investigation in school in '68, was there a verdict?"

"I don't know."

"And something else. The years you were in the village, er, did you have a boyfriend?"

I got to my feet. "Excuse me, you have no right to concern yourself with that."

"Comrade Xiao Ling." The old woman tapped on the desk with her pencil and raised her voice. "You should correct your attitude . . ."

"You've taken a lot of trouble. There's nothing I can say."

I pushed open the door and walked out. Behind me the old woman's voice still carried on: "Hmph, hmph, see how fierce she is, she wanted to hit me . . . last time she beat her foreman half to death . . . we run big risks in our line of work . . . aren't you cold? . . ."

8

(Bai Hua)

Eyes half closed, I relaxed comfortably against the shop shutters. Two spotted hens wandered unhurriedly up and down at my feet, chirping as they searched for food. In front of me was the noisy clamor of the peasant market: the old man selling salted meat beating on the cauldron with a spoon; the puffed-rice bellows wheezing and whistling; the hoarse little voice of the beancurd-sheet seller crying out endlessly; plus the old sow squealing as if her throat was being cut; really, it was just like a play . . . miaow miaow, miaow miaow . . . where was that cat? I looked all around, turned, and peered through the crack between the door and frame, and there was the fat old cat crouching on the counter. Huh, my God.

"Hey!" said someone. I looked around to see a chick dangling a bunch of keys in her fingers sizing me up.

I pointed through the crack. "Thief!"

"Huh, you look like a thief to me. Out of the way, can't you go somewhere else, or hang yourself from a tree?" she said, at the same time pulling the shutter across. "Come on, give us a hand."

"Hmph, what can I do? It was the year the Indian reactionaries were sent packing." I limped over and gave her a hand. "Haven't even been able to get myself a wife."

"You're lame?" She considered me, not sure whether to believe me.

"Ah, especially here," I pointed to a knife scar on my head. "A knife got me, and it doesn't work too well now."

"You still look pretty lively to me." She opened the door. "What work do you do now?"

"Gatekeeper."

"Can you make a living?"

"Just about. Thieves are pretty scared of me and go the long way round."

"You've got a wicked look." She went behind the counter and mixed some cornmeal in a broken bowl. The cat miaowed even more vigorously, weaving round and round her. "What's your hurry, Huanghuang . . . how much do you earn a month?"

"Nothing fixed, but enough to spend when it's all added up."

"Our neighbors have a daughter, not bad-looking, born in the year of the Dragon, only she's got one problem. She's mute. What would you say to that?"

I was looking up, studying the skylight. "Are you talking to me?"

"Huh, you're a bit thick, but anyway, it's the fashion now for a girl to look for someone like that."

I tugged on a length of rope hanging from the skylight, and a shower of dust from above came flying down.

"Are you so interested in our skylight?" she asked.

"Oh, it's just right for a hanging."

"Bah! Don't be so gruesome!" She sprang to her feet, flicked her plaits, and said huffily, "What do you want to buy, hurry up!"

I broke into a grin, pulled out a ten-yuan note and drummed on the glass cabinet with my fingers. "A packet of Gongzi.[8] Can you change this?"

"So you still think you're the God of Wealth. Let me tell you, we can change bigger notes than that."

I limped out of the shop and turned into the little lane on the left. Manzi was leaning against the earthen wall smoking, spitting on the ground over and over again.

"Anything there?" he asked excitedly.

"Full of stuff."

"Will we start moving as soon as the market's over?"

"What's the rush? There's a sister in there, don't give her a hard time . . ."

Manzi chuckled. "Taken a fancy to her, Boss?"

I knocked the cigarette out of his mouth. "Don't look for trouble. Beat it, go find a strong rope, then pick a good, windy, rainy day. If you rush it you'll only get your fingers burned."

I left the laneway and ran straight into Yuanyuan. She was toting a straw basket, her eyes fixed on the toes of her shoes and looking very down-in-the-mouth.

"Halt!" I said.

She looked up, startled. "You?"

"Is your name Yuanyuan?"

"What about it?"

"It's a lovely name."

"That's enough nonsense, I'm not afraid of you."

"What are you talking about." I folded my arms across my chest. "I stirred up your birthday party. Do you hate me?"

"Yes, I hate you!"

"Is it class hatred?"

"It's because you're not a good person."

"How much is this chicken a catty?" someone nearby was asking.

[8] A brand of very cheap cigars.

"One seventy."

"A good person?" I burst out laughing. "You show me, who's a good person in this world? Now, if we take people like your father, people are like dogs . . ."

"I forbid you to talk about my father!"

"Auntie, maybe this chicken is diseased?"

"You city people quack on and on, but she still laid an egg yesterday."

"Now thieves are divided into big ones and little ones, but their methods aren't the same. The big thieves want everything, they'll even steal people's minds. But we sell our own goddamn minds for some of their leftovers . . ."

"Rubbish! Don't try to glorify yourself."

"All right, let me ask you, have you ever been hungry?"

She looked blank and shook her head.

"Ever begged for food? Slept in the street? Been beaten half to death? Eh?" I gave a low growl and took a step forward.

Her pigtails swung backward and forward like a drum roll.

"Why isn't she eating?"

"Because she had so much millet this morning."

"Come out and get some sun, then see how white and plump your warm little nest has made you."

"What's the idea, lecturing me?" Yuanyuan's cheeks swelled with vexation, tears glistening in her eyes.

"All right then," I brushed the dust from my cuffs, "it's my old trouble from when I was political commissar in '38."

Yuanyuan snorted contemptuously, then smiled. "What a weird person you are."

"Take off two yuan, Auntie."

"If you call me Great Aunt the price'll still be the same."

"Hey, look who's coming," I said.

Yuanyuan followed the direction in which I was pointing, frowned, then turned and walked away.

"Hold on—" I shouted.

Yuanyuan pressed into the crowd.

(Yang Xun)

Bai Hua pushed his way over. He pinched the crumpled khaki cap on his head. "Hey, pals, come to buy pots and pans or bedclothes?"

"We're buying stars," Xiao Ling said.

"Stars again," Bai Hua sneered, "do you want mourning stars?"

Xiao Ling smiled. "Seeing you, I feel happy."

"I'm not happy," Bai Hua said.

"Why?" I asked.

"None of your damned pretense, Yang." Bai Hua shoved his cap sideways, and the sunlight fell on his gloomy face. "As the saying goes, two mountains can never meet as one, but when two people meet . . ."

"I don't understand."

"If we go somewhere I'll straighten you out."

"Let's go then."

"Don't." Xiao Ling gripped me by the arm. "Bai Hua . . ."

"Go on, cross my heart, I'd really like to hear how you plead."

I pushed Xiao Ling away. "Bai Hua, don't be so arrogant. Just say what has to be done, and I'll see you through to the finish!"

"Hey, well said. I always took your sort for spineless cowards; good, let's first be civilized, have a little talk here. Xiao Ling, push off and keep quiet for a bit, he won't get lost."

"Go on," I say.

Xiao Ling looked at me, then at him, then turned and walked away toward the second-hand stalls by the side of the road.

Bai Hua took a box of Gongzi cigars from his pocket, peeled back the wrapping, and tapped on the box to jerk out two. I reached out and pressed down the first one, pulled out the second, took out my lighter, and lit up.

"Hey, you're not green. You've slugged out this track in Beijing too?" he asked.

"You could say so."

"But we dropped into different nests so we're not on the same track."

"I think you must have seen a lot of hardship . . ."

"Huh, don't you damned well pity me."

"None of us deserves pity."

"That's enough gush. Sooner or later you'd better understand this: I can get rid of you easily."

"And you'd better understand that threats don't scare me. Even when they put me on death row I didn't crawl to anyone."

"You've been inside too? Hey, now that's something new. For stealing or playing around with women?"

"For opposing the grain tax."

He let out a whistle. "A political criminal."

We smoked in silence. I could see from his eyes that I'd gone up in his estimation, although he might not be willing to admit it to himself.

"Do you love Xiao Ling?" I asked suddenly.

"It's not your place to ask that," he snarled. "I'll be honest with you, you do know your way around."

"You don't understand her; she's not the kind of person you imagine."

"And you're not a worm in my belly . . . all right, we poor beggars had better be sensible, eh?" He ground his teeth with a crunching sound, the flesh of his cheeks drawn tightly. "I hate you bastards with money and power, you get hold of everything . . ."

"First, I've got no money, and second, I've got no power."

"You think you and she are the same kind? Huh, I saw through that early on. You're just in it for the novelty, you could never live your whole life with her. When the fun's over you'll just swap her for another . . ."

"I find it strange to hear those words coming out of your mouth."

"You don't understand love, you don't understand . . ."

"Perhaps. But if each of us understood love a little better, the world wouldn't be like this."

"I see you're a gold-edged chamber pot, all your effort's in your mouth." Bai Hua crushed his cigar butt and tossed it onto the ground. "This business can't be dropped, it's not that cheap."

"That's up to you."

We walked over to the second-hand stalls. A line of old clothes, in all sorts of colors, hung on a bamboo pole, fluttering above Xiao Ling's head. She was gazing up at a sheer white dress amongst them, touching it with her hand. The dress and the surrounding atmosphere, with the dust, the hectic clamor, and the pedlars sitting cross-legged on the ground, did not seem to harmonize at all.

"My God, where did that come from?" said Bai Hua. "I'll take a bet it's been worn by the Heavenly Empress."

"It's too expensive, he wants thirty," Xiao Ling said.

"Twenty-five," rumbled the pedlar, half-closing his eyes. A fly kept buzzing round his bald head.

"Have a smoke, brother." Bai Hua squatted down and handed the pedlar a cigar, and continued in the local accent, "Where are you from?"

"Dingxiang."

"That's why your accent's familiar, I'm from Beixinbao, a mile away. Brother, I hear there've been more floods at home, hard to get a living in any trade . . ."

"That's right." The pedlar exhaled a mouthful of smoke expressionlessly. "Nothing we can do about it, except risk a bit of hard-earned money. Since you're from the same place, you can have this dress for fifteen, and it'll be worth selling as remnants."

"Sure." Bai Hua patted the pedlar on the shoulder, and lowered his voice. "Got any dope, brother?"

The pedlar gave a shiver, staring sideways, wide-eyed, at Bai Hua, assuming a shocked expression. "What table have you been eating at, brother?"

"There's sorghum planted behind the beancurd shop."

The pedlar blinked his crafty little eyes, and started to chat to Bai Hua in a low voice. Xiao Ling secretly pressed my hand, smiling.

"Cash on the nail, five yuan," Bai Hua said.

"If you'll do me the honor, brother, take your pick."

Bai Hua pulled out five yuan. "Hey, just a little drinking money."

The pedlar accepted the money, held it up toward the sun, and stowed it inside his clothes with great care. Bai Hua took down the dress, gave it a shake, and handed it to Xiao Ling.

"Oh, Bai Hua," Xiao Ling said.

"Take it and try it on, consider it a gift from me. Yang, brighten yourself up. If you don't behave properly toward her, don't blame me if I act like an animal, you won't find any friendly face from me then. See you."

The setting sun had lost its heat and hung below the eaves of the little mud-brick cottages like a lantern that had been lit too soon. Peaceful smoke rose from the kitchen chimneys of the distant village. The production brigade loudspeaker was broadcasting a local opera. The occasional bark of a dog drifted across. Xiao Ling walked to the edge of the canal. "Come on, let's sit here for a while, I don't feel like going back to the house straightaway."

"The evening is so beautiful here."

"Human beings build walls, not only to defend themselves against others, but also against themselves. Who can resist the lure of Nature?"

"Perhaps only I can."

"How?"

"Nothing else can tempt me now that I've fallen under your spell."

Xiao Ling gave a strange smile. "See if you can tell me, how did I tempt you?"

"You have a heart of gold."

"Well, that's quite frightening. It has the odor of a museum or a businessman. I'm just an ordinary person. Anyone who lightly makes an idol can also lightly break it."

"Impossible."

"So you don't want to make an idol."

"I want to make walls."

We sat down on the canal bank, leaning shoulder to shoulder, silently watching the rosy evening clouds flowing in the distance. The mingled scents of the early summer fields seemed even stronger as it grew darker.

"A rabbit!" Xiao Ling's shoulder moved.

I followed her pointing finger, and sure enough, not far away on the low bank between the fields, a wild gray rabbit was sniffing the air. "By the look of him he's very contented," I said.

"Why?"

"He's just stolen a turnip."

"But I stole you, and still I'm not a bit contented." She smiled, but the smile quickly vanished from her lips. As if lost in thought she shook her head and plucked a few blades of grass. "Really, at times I have the feeling that I'm a kind of thief, as if all of this has been stolen . . ."

"All of what?"

"The sunset, the evening breeze, odd smiles and happiness . . ."

I took her in my arms, cupped her chin in my hand, and gazed intently into her eyes. "All of these belong to you."

"No, the sunset and the evening breeze belong to Nature, smiles to an instant, and happiness," she paused and her eyelids dropped. "It only belongs to the imagination." She pushed me away and leaned over the canal bank, putting the shredded blades of grass bit by bit into the water and watching them swirl away. Then she twined the tip of her plait around a wildflower and slowly unwound it again. "Yang Xun, I'm worried," she said suddenly.

"What are you worried about?"

"The difference between us is too great. Difference isn't a bad thing in itself, but in a monolithic society it's often illegal."

"I can't see any difference."

"That may be because happiness has put a blindfold on you. First of all, let me ask you, do your parents know of my existence?"

"I've mentioned you in letters. There's no need to worry

about that: they're a bit confused, but they're genuine 'democrats.'"

"I suspect that what you say is too much colored by emotion. But, for the time being, I trust its reliability. Let me ask you something else. Do you understand me?"

"How else do you want me to understand?"

"For instance, do you understand my past?"

"I imagine our pasts are about the same."

"This 'I imagine' is pretty wide of the mark. Why don't you ask?"

"Haven't I run into enough snags?"

"Maybe I'm to blame, but that happened long ago. And another thing, do you understand my frame of mind?"

"You seem very happy to me."

"You're wrong. Until the day I die I can never again be truly happy. One can see that you're very happy, but I, I'm both happy and sad. This is precisely the difference between us."

I dispiritedly picked up a stone, and began tracing lines in the dust.

She grasped my hand, threw away the stone, and pressed my palm against her face. "Don't lose heart, please? I really don't mean to dampen your spirits, it's you who changed my life. I'm also willing to believe that happiness belongs to us." She jumped up and brushed herself off. "Fine. As to the question of the right to happiness, who else has an opinion? Let's have a show of hands." She raised her hand, then pulled up mine. "Add this little poplar, and that's three votes altogether, carried unanimously. Wait, I'll go and get some drinks to celebrate."

Xiao Ling went into the house and turned on the light, the window lattice fragmenting her slender figure. As she changed her clothes her movements were like a film in slow motion. In a little while the light went out and she stood in the doorway, wearing the snow-white dress, and walked over. The vast night behind her threw her into relief. Amidst the black ocean she was a glistening wave, and the stars countless drops of flying foam. She set the bottle and cups to one side, came up close to me, and looked at me, smiling.

"Come, hold me tight," she said.

I continued to gaze at her abstractedly.

"Come." She held out two shining arms.

I stood up, and drew her tightly to me till her joints creaked.

"Gently, Yang Xun," she said, gasping for breath.

Countless fragments of silver settled into a bright moon at the bottom of the cup. I raised my head. "Xiao Ling, I have something to tell you."

"Go on, then."

"My transfer's been arranged. My mother's sent a letter urging me to go back."

She watched me calmly, her face expressionless. A cold silver-gray light rose slowly behind her. The darkness seemed to tremble a little in the cold gleam. "Why didn't you mention it earlier?"

"I wasn't going to tell you anything. I don't plan to go back at all."

She turned the cup round and round in her hands. "Because of me?"

"Also because of myself."

"Go back, your mother needs you."

"No."

"You don't understand a mother's heart."

"Do you?"

She smiled desolately. "Of course I do."

"Unless arrangements are made for you to go back too, I refuse to leave."

"That's impossible, I have no family."

"It doesn't matter; nowadays the more impossible a thing is, the more possible it is that it can be achieved."

"No, no, I don't want to go back."

"So let's live here together, then."

"Yang Xun," she said fervently, catching hold of my hand, "I've never asked anything of you before, but this time you must do as I say. Go back. Although we'll be apart, our hearts will still be together, that'll be good, won't it?"

"Don't try to persuade me, it's no use."

"You, you're too stubborn." Suddenly her shoulders began to tremble.

I was alarmed. "What is it, Xiao Ling?"

"Oh, you're so foolish you should be thrashed." She smiled through her tears, brushing them away from the corners of her eyes. "I'm happy you're so stubborn."

"It's the first time my stubbornness has been a virtue."

"Perhaps I'm too selfish . . . let's talk about something else."

"Shall we discuss your past?"

"Let's have a drink first."

We clinked cups and drained them at one go.

"Um—where shall I begin?" She made a pillow of her hands behind her, gazing up at the stars. "This evening's so beautiful, isn't it?"

"Yes."

She sighed. "I don't feel like talking about it, we still have tomorrow."

In the distance the rumble of a motor started up, and a shaft of bright light leaped out, lighting up the grove of trees and piles of firewood. Countless shadows revolved in the fields, like a massive mounted army. All at once the light swept toward us, so dazzling we could not open our eyes. Xiao Ling leaned close to me, clasping my arm tightly.

The tractor drove away.

(Xiao Ling)

Mid-Autumn Festival night. The smoke billows about in the girl students' squat little hut. Most of them are crowded together on the brick-bed drinking and gossiping. Someone is playing a mournful tune on a mouth-organ, someone else is standing by the window declaiming Gorky's "The Stormy Petrel" in an affected voice, and a girl student dashes into the yard rolling drunk and dances under the moonlight, inviting peals of laughter and applause from peasants and children. I cast a glance round, shrug my shoulders, and move closer under the oil-lamp with my book.

Suddenly someone bumps into me. It's Xie Liming. "Why aren't you celebrating with the others?" he asks.

"You call that celebrating? It looks worse than crying to me."

"You should try to understand other people's moods."

"I'm studying veterinary science, I'm not interested in people."

"Why are you always nettling people?"

"Excuse me, you're interrupting my reading."

He walks off in a huff.

The last flame of the kerosene lamp splutters, flashes, and finally goes out. A moment of dead silence in the room. Suddenly, the boy who has just been declaiming "The Stormy Petrel" starts howling wildly.

I awaken from a coma. The wind is still wailing and snow flakes patter against the window paper with a rustling sound. Parched! It's as if my lungs are full of red-hot charcoal. I lick my dry, cracked lips and stretch out my hand to the cup. Not a single drop of water: the cup is sealed in a thick block of ice. With a clatter it falls to the ground, and I lose consciousness again.

The next time I open my eyes, there's a face floating in the mist, slowly becoming distinct. It's Xie Liming sitting by my bed.

"Awake at last." He rubs his brow excitedly. "The doctor's just been, he said it was acute pneumonia. He gave you an injection . . ."

"Doctor?" I murmur uncertainly.

"I couldn't get through on the phone, so I went to the commune."

Ten miles of mountain road, wind and rain; I shudder all over. "Thank you . . ."

"Oh, there's no need to mention it."

"Why didn't you go home too?"

He smiles ironically, turns round, and carries over a bowl of steaming hot noodle soup. "My mother died under the treatment ages ago, my old man's still locked up, and my relatives in Beijing are scared of getting mixed up too . . . I wanted to borrow a book from you. I saw the door was unbolted, and nothing stirred however much I knocked . . . drink, drink while it's hot. It's good for you to sweat a lot . . ."

A faint knock at the door.

"Who is it?"

"It's me, I've come to borrow a book."

I hesitate a moment, then open the door. Xie Liming stands stiffly in the doorway. A sudden gust of wind blows out the kerosene lamp.

"Xiao Ling, is it too late?"

"Come in."

I close the door and strike a match to light the lamp. Suddenly my hand is seized tightly. The match falls to the floor and goes out.

"Xiao Ling." There's a catch in his throat.

"Let go!"

"Xiao Ling, listen, listen to me . . ." He clutches my hand, speaking in a low murmur. "I, I like you a lot . . ."

"That is to say you need me?" I say with a grim smile, fiercely withdrawing my hand.

"Surely you're not saying there can't be some feelings between people?"

"What you really mean is that I should repay you."

"You're too cold and unfeeling."

"I like to be cold and unfeeling, I like being cold-shouldered by other people, I like death! Why did you go and save me?"

"Neither of us has a home." He mumbles this one sentence, turns and stumbles to the door.

"Come back!" I say.

He stops.

"What did you just say?"

"Neither of us has a home."

The long-distance bus station.

"... Papa says we'll help you move back as soon as I've graduated from university. Then we can get properly married," Xie Liming says in a strained voice, swallowing.

"I hope to hear you say it yourself."

"I, of course, that's what I mean." He looks hurriedly at his watch. "As for the child, I still think get rid of it, don't be too stubborn."

"Don't worry about it, that's my own business."

He pulls a coin from his pocket. "Let's toss and see what our luck will be in the future."

"This is how much your luck's worth." I snatch the coin from him and fling it into the gutter by the side of the road.

He climbs onto the bus step, breathing a sigh of relief. I watch him with no expression at all.

"Wait for me!" he says, raising his hand.

I am silent.

The bus roars, blows up a cloud of dust, and disappears down the road.

9

(Lin Dongping)

"How old's the child?" I asked, closing the file and rubbing my temples with my fingers.

"Two." Miss Zhang's leather shoes shuffled at the foot of the desk.

"Where is it now?"

"Floodvalley Village, where she was sent to the countryside; it's being brought up by a local peasant family there."

"Why wasn't this discovered when she was recruited for work?"

"The production brigade chief helped."

"You mean the factory knows nothing at all about this matter?"

"I've already told them."

I don't know why, but those elegant, fashionable shoes made me feel quite uneasy, probably because they were polished so brightly you could see a person's reflection in their shine. "How does the factory propose to deal with it?" I asked.

"They're waiting for your suggestion."

I drummed on the desktop with my knuckles. "Miss Zhang, have you got a boyfriend?"

"You're embarrassing me, asking me that . . ."

"Why should it be embarrassing? When a woman grows up she should get married."

"Er . . . you could say I have one."

"Where does he work?"

"In the army."

"How old is he?"

"Just over forty."

I noticed there was a tiny cigarette burn on her left sock. "Are you fond of each other?"

"Feelings are no substitute for food."

"All right, you can go now."

"Oh, I almost forgot. This is the Investigation Section's report. The relevant invoices and photocopies of the masses' letters are inside too." The leather shoes clicked out of my sight, and the door closed.

I opened the report and read it page by page. Wang Defa squinted, sneering; Wang Defa stretched out his hand, muttering a threat; Wang Defa knelt on the ground, imploring bitterly; Wang Defa . . . I shut my eyes. What was I doing? Protesting my innocence? Testifying to the inspirational power of Party principles? Testifying to the existence in the world of the self-evident truth, that evil will be punished and good rewarded? But wasn't it a little too late? After all, I was no longer sixteen. In other words, could my strength, the strength of one person, change the universal corruption of these years?

A stream of nameless agitations assaulted my mind. I pushed aside the report, took off my glasses and paced to the window. Life: already it was no longer in the room, no longer beside me. I had turned into an observer of life, there was no passion that could touch me. How frightening it was. Perhaps the meaning of life lay merely in its making you lose everything you once had: illusion, love, confidence, courage . . . the last was life. The security guard at the gate was driving away a ragged peasant with a barefoot lad in tow, who was begging for something, even kneeling on the ground kowtowing. The big French plane trees rustled. I turned away. One cannot always see everything. Life is meant to teach one what to see and what not to see.

I went back to the desk, opened the drawer, then closed it again. I lit a cigarette, and through the tangled wisps of smoke my gaze fell upon the file on the desk: Xiao Ling, female, twenty-three years old, R.I. No. 0394. At last I had found that disturbing name: Xiao Ling. Ah, it was as if this yellow file had been concealing everything that I once had. What kind of a girl was she? How could she have so many secrets at such an age? The frightening thing was that these secrets and young Xun's fate were pressed together in here.

Miss Zhang appeared in the doorway. "Chief Lin, there's a phone call from the factory, asking how to handle things."

"Handle the matter according to principle, I'm not going to offer any suggestions." I spoke rapidly, for fear of being interrupted by another idea. "And give Yang Xun a ring. Arrange for him to wait for me at home this afternoon."

"Very well."

"Wait a moment. Have you met Xiao Ling?"

"Once."

"What was your impression?"

"How shall I put it?" She smiled primly. "Very pretty."

Huh, this was perhaps the most important evaluation one woman could make of another.

I opened the investigation report again and was about to start reading when the door opened. Wang Defa stood there. I shut the report, hastily covering it with a newspaper.

"Old Lin, you've got much thinner lately." He sat down in front of the desk unhurriedly, picked up a glass paperweight and rolled it around in his hand.

I lit a cigarette and leaned back in my chair. "Got a problem, Chief Wang?"

"A problem? Well, there is one thing," he said, sighing.

"What is it?"

"I'd like to offer an apology and admit my mistake."

"And what's that supposed to mean?"

He stretched out a yellow-stained finger and tapped on the newspaper covering the report. "What criminal charge can you lay, based on this thing?"

I did not answer.

"Let's shut the door and talk, there's no need to beat about the bush. I happen to have a copy of it on hand . . ."

"That's impossible."

"I've been over everything, and the information's basically true, but there're also some tiny mistakes which I want to account for and avoid troubling you."

"Say what you really mean."

He took a small notebook from his pocket and with a wet finger rustled through a few pages. "Concerning my embezzlement of 276,000 yuan of national treasures, you should share the responsibility for 35,000 yuan, because that Ming landscape entrusted to the municipal CPPCC is hanging in your drawing room, although it's entered in my accounts . . ."

"That's a loan."

"Oh, that's a more civilized word; sounds much better than 'embezzlement.'" Wang Defa cleared his throat, gave me a swift wink, and turned another page with a rustle. "As for my diverting 2,500,000 of the flood relief funds to build the chemical fertilizer factory, there's also some discrepancy. In fact the greatest beneficiary is you. Look here, you introduced thirteen people into the factory altogether, there was even a criminal in custody with a fifteen-year sentence, but he was released after less than a year . . ."

"Rubbish!"

"There's no need to blow your top, here's the county public security bureau chief's certificate. He signed it, there's no mistake."

"That was a wrong verdict." As soon as the words were out I sensed how weak such a defense was.

"I see there's no need for you and me to worry about this matter. It can be turned over to the provincial authorities for a decision." Wang Defa turned another page. "And also . . ."

"That's enough!"

Wang Defa closed the notebook and took a cigarette from the tin on the desk in a leisurely fashion, loosening it with his fingers. "Things being what they are, there's no more to be said. For me, it's dismissal, investigation, and off I go, the usual pattern. But for you, of course it's easy; just return the painting, lock up the leopard that's escaped from his cage again . . ."

"What do you mean?"

"That criminal. A nibble of corn bread, another fourteen years, and everything'll be just fine."

There was a buzzing in my head.

Wang Defa blew out a stream of thick smoke and stretched. "For a start, what we've got to say is for behind closed doors; not entirely official. You pick on a humble citizen like me to make an example of, isn't that killing the chicken to show the monkey? If you take a look at the top, no one's completely clean. Chief Lin, think of it from my point of view. Although we both have a chief's rank, you get over two hundred a month, while I limp along on inside of a hundred with the wife and all those kids, then there are the old people at home eyeing it as well. We're only human. Since I left the army, I haven't got round this bend . . . as the saying goes, you only see the fish drinking water, you don't see the gills leaking. It's like the good old business phrase, 'normal wastage.' I've got an old comrade-in-arms who's fond of that phrase. Not long ago, I introduced him to your Miss Zhang . . ."

(Yang Xun)

As I walked up the steps, I ran into Auntie Chen, coming out to dry the clothes. "Is Uncle Lin home?"

"Go right in, the old man's waiting for you in the study."

"And Yuanyuan?"

"She seems very restless these days, out from morning till night."

I opened the study door. Uncle Lin, his arms folded on his chest, was resting on the sofa with his eyes closed.

"Sit down," he said, remaining as he was.

I sat down in a cane chair opposite him.

"Is it hot outside?"

"It's rather close."

"Turn on the fan."

I turned on the console fan in the corner and returned to my place. Silence. It was as if we both found a pretext for silence in the fan's even whir.

"Do you like that painting in the drawing room?" he asked suddenly.

"I don't know anything about painting."

"During the War to Resist U.S. Imperialism and Aid Korea, a local capitalist donated it. It's worth 35,000 yuan."

"How did it come into your hands?"

"Xun, tell me about your life in prison."

"There's nothing to tell, it was very dull."

"Were there many like you?"

"There was a bunch of political criminals from Beijing. Most were cadres and intellectuals, and some young people too."

"What were the charges?"

"There were all kinds. Some were there for just one word."

"How many years were they sentenced for?"

"They were sentenced to death."

He said nothing.

"Prison is society in a nutshell."

"Don't lump them together, they're two different things. All right, let's not talk about that." He sat up, turning his gaze out the window. "Xun, are you in love with someone?"

"You knew that long ago."

"What's her name?"

"Xiao Ling."

"What's she like?"

"First-rate."

"What does this 'first-rate' include? Family, thinking, appearance . . ."

"You asked what she's like, not whether she conforms to the standards of a Party member."

"It's not an abstract question."

"Yes, I agree. Did you ask me to come just for this?"

"For a chat." He got up and went to the little table between the bookcases, grasped the neck of the decanter, and poured a glass of cold water. "Young people are liable to act on impulse . . ."

"We've known each other for a year."

"But you have several decades of life ahead of you." He put down the glass and paced a few steps, his hands behind his back. "Xun, do you really know what she's like?"

"Of course I do."

"What do you know?"

"Her intrinsic value."

He made a mocking gesture. "It's the first time I've heard that."

"Yes, it's only those clichés about family conditions that can be duplicated by people millions of times."

"I'm opposed to making family background the major consideration."

"Only in words?"

"It seems that in today's world it's almost impossible for one person to convince another."

"Perhaps."

Standing by the window, he stretched his fingers out and ran them over the dust on the windowsill, then sighed. "Very well, take a look at the papers on the desk."

I sat down at the desk and opened the papers laid out there. The fan whirred. I felt my whole body go cold, as if the air in the room was slowly freezing.

"Is that all?" I asked, closing the file.

"What more do you want?"

I leaped to my feet and turned to face him. "It's not I who wants something, it's you."

"Calm down, Xun."

"Let me ask you, what right have you to do this?"

He continued pacing up and down.

"Your curiosity really makes me laugh . . ."

He stood still. "This is not curiosity."

"What is it?"

"Duty."

"Duty?" I laughed grimly. "An emperor's duty to the people, or a father's duty to a son?"

For a moment his right hand groped nervously for something behind him, until at last he clutched the arm of the cane chair and sat down. His gaze was dull, as if all of a sudden he'd grown old. "Xun," he called out, his voice weak.

"What's wrong?" I poured a glass of water and handed it to him. With one hand he grasped the glass, while the other tightly clutched my sleeve.

"I'm old, perhaps I shouldn't take secrets to the grave?" He seemed to be talking to himself.

"What secrets?"

"She wouldn't allow it, she wouldn't . . ."

"Who?"

His whole body trembled violently, and the water spilled. He put down the glass and gently patted my hand. "Child . . ."

"Yes?"

"Time doesn't spare people, it's too late . . ."

"What do you mean . . ."

"Nothing." He pulled out his handkerchief, wiped his hands and brow, and gradually recovered his normal composure. "Go on. I'm rather tired. Think this matter over. I've already booked you a ticket for tomorrow afternoon. Whether you go or not is up to you."

(Xiao Ling)

Yang Xun stood in the doorway, his expression gloomy, his eyes averted. I put down the little sweater and walked over to him, meaning to brush the dust from his shoulders. He dodged as if he'd received an electric shock, then slowly went to the desk, picked up Jingjing's photograph, then put it down again. "I've come to say goodbye," he said.

"Where are you going?"

"Beijing."

"For how long?"

"The rest of my life."

A moment of suffocation. After a while I let out my breath very slowly. "What time's your train?"

"Tomorrow afternoon."

"All right, I'll see you off."

He crossed to the bed, picked up the little sweater and looked at it, threw it aside, then sat down on the bed holding his head in his hands. I went to him and stroked his hair. This time he didn't resist, but with each stroke gave a slight shudder.

"I'm leaving," he said.

"You will come back."

"No, men can never turn back."

"The world's round. If you just keep walking firmly you'll come back from another direction."

"I'm not Columbus."

"You're right, it's not the age of Columbus now."

"Don't get off the subject like this!" He pushed my hands away roughly and grabbed hold of the little sweater on the bed. "Who are you knitting this for?"

"The child."

"I haven't the time to joke."

"It's started."

"What?"

"The tragedy."

"I asked you, whose child?"

"Yang Xun, I beg you, don't speak to me in that tone, I can't bear it."

"Do you think I'm enjoying this?"

"Living can never be enjoyable. I'm hoping you'll calm down before you say anything more."

"I haven't got time."

"You used to have so much time . . ."

"That was in the past."

"Tomorrow will become the past too."

"Unfortunately there won't be any tomorrow."

I silently picked up a book and sat down on the stool beside him.

"Xiao Ling, why didn't you tell me before?"

I turned the pages.

"I truly don't condemn you."

I turned the pages.

"Say something."

"There's nothing to say."

"So it all ends like this?"

I shut the book with a snap. "You mean to make me repent, wash myself with tears? I'm sorry, my tears dried up long ago."

"I'm just begging you to be honest."

"Honest? The honesty we understood when we were students hasn't existed for ages. How can you beg someone you love to tear the bandage from her own wound? And another type of honesty requires silence: loving in silence, dying in silence!"

"I'm not accustomed to talking about death."

"As you like. People think custom is everything, but they don't know it's a kind of continuous death."

"You should feel you have a duty to me."

"No, I have a duty only to myself."

"Xiao Ling—" he cried out desperately, clutching his head tightly in his hands.

I went over to him, released his hands and pressed his head tightly to my breast. "Xun, I understand your pain . . ."

"Forgive me." He raised eyes full of tears, staring at me dully.

We held each other tightly, kissing. My lips were moistened with his salty tears, and a kind of maternal love welled up in me. I should help him, protect him.

"Xiao Ling, what are you thinking?"

"Do you remember the toasts we drank in the little temple? I'm afraid there can never be any escape for us from those guns."

"Whom do you mean?"

"No one in particular. This gun consists of many parts. What's more dreadful is the mind of the hunter behind the sights, and that mind is made up of the thoughts of many people . . ."

"Do you mean traditional ideas?"

"They won't let go of us."

"Don't think this way, Xiao Ling."

"Mm."

Suddenly his gaze traveled past my shoulder and fell on Jingjing's photograph. "How old is she?"

"Two years and three months."

"Have someone else take care of her."

I let him go, staring at him in silence.

"Really, it would be better if someone else took care of her."

I went to the door and opened it. "Please go."

"Xiao Ling . . ."

"Please go."

"Don't you love me anymore?"

"You still talk so easily of love. I see you only love yourself, your shadow, your happiness and suffering, and your future! Please go."

He looked at me hesitantly, went to the doorway, paused, then strode away without looking back.

I flung myself on the bed, sobbing uncontrollably.

10

(Lin Yuanyuan)

The lower right-hand corner of the photograph was already yellowed: Mama, holding a thin little girl in her arms, standing amongst the flowers. Was this me? Diary: "Today is Yuanyuan's fifth birthday. Weight 21.5 kilos, height 1.06 meters. With the change in her moneybox she bought a block of chocolate and got it all over her face." "Yuanyuan didn't pass arithmetic, it's very worrying. Starting today I'll check her homework every day." Hairpin, fountain pen, watch, wallet, letters . . . I put back Mama's things one by one.

Suddenly, a sheet of paper floated out of a pile of letters and fluttered down on the desk.

"Dongping.

There's no need to hide the whole thing. I know about your past affair. I cannot blame you for anything in your past. But I hope that from now on you will have nothing further to do with her (when you went to the convention in Beijing last month you still maintained your relationship with her. Everyone was talking about it, I was the only person in the dark). I know you have no feelings for me, but please think of Yuanyuan, that is my only request . . ."

The blood pounded in my temples, throbbing loudly. As I read it over I remembered that whenever they quarreled they shut the door soundly, but it always seemed to be about the same thing. I went to the chest of drawers, watching the jumping gold secondhand of the little Swiss clock. Mama, poor poor Mama, why did you never divorce this sanctimonious hypocrite? Was it just for my sake, Mama?

Fafa walked in, and at once a waft of horrid perfume drifted about the room. While she wasn't paying attention, I hurriedly brushed the tears from my eyes.

"Yuanyuan, what do you think of this pleated skirt?" Fafa went up the the wardrobe mirror and twirled around.

I glanced at it. Huh, a little skirt just covering the backside. "Pretty," I said without curiosity.

"I made it myself."

"Clever."

"How about I help you make one?"

"There's no need."

She bristled. "Now what's eating you?"

I said nothing.

"Yuanyuan," Fafa walked over, meaning to put her hand on my shoulder. "Why are we always flying at each other?"

I dodged away from her hand. "I didn't ask you to come."

"Are you ordering me out?"

I turned and went to the desk.

"Ha, you are putting on airs. Don't think that just because your old man's a big official you can take advantage of it. Who doesn't know what's gone on in your family . . ."

"Get out of here!"

"Why doesn't that Yang come? His old man's an even bigger official. Can you marry into such a high family?"

I grabbed the inkstone. Fafa stepped back in fright and was out the door in a flash. I hurled the inkstone onto the ground, and it smashed into pieces. I slumped across the desk crying.

The time slipped by. I raised my head and brushed the tears from my face. What was the use of crying? You could cry yourself to death and no one would lose any sleep over you. Mama. The calendar on the wall showed a photograph of a member of a mountaineering team making an observation on a frozen mountain. Such pure ice, the air must be so fresh, you could certainly fall to your death. Huh, everyone has to die sooner or later, what's frightening about that. Really, once something has gone, there's no point yearning for it. I tore a page from the desk calendar, scribbled a few words, then opened the chest of drawers, pulled out a few clothes, and stuffed them into a bag.

The midday sun was burning hot. The pedestrians shrank into the narrow sliding shadows on either side of the street, while I strolled alone aimlessly in the sunlight. Where was I going? A full two hours had passed since I left home, and I still couldn't make up my mind. My overall feeling was still excellent, only my stomach wouldn't stop rumbling and my throat was going up in smoke.

I walked into a shop. Three or four tables were arranged in front of the counter, and a few fellows who looked like pedicab drivers twisted their heads round one after another, staring at me lecherously. How loathsome! Standing at the counter, I stuck my hand in my pocket. Oh no, I hadn't brought my purse, I only had a few loose coins. I swallowed, placed my coins on the stained and scratched counter, and counted them.

"Two pieces of cake," I said.

"No, one catty," responded a voice from behind, and at the same time a five-yuan note covered my coins.

(Bai Hua)

Yuanyuan looked round. "Hey, Bai Hua."

"What's with the shabby outfit?"

She smiled."How strange, bumping into you at the critical moment."

"What critical moment? Is the house on fire or is your mother getting married?"

"Let's talk over there." She screwed up her eyes and took the note. "How about something to drink too?"

"The money's yours."

The two of us sat down at a table. Yuanyuan gulped a mouthful of spirits, choked, turned red, and burst into a fit of coughing.

"Take it easy," I said.

"It really burns . . . I've only drunk wine before."

"That's lolly-water."

"You're right, this really has a kick." She gulped another mouthful.

"Listen, slow down a bit."

"Bai Hua, I've escaped from the nest."

I shot a quick look at her.

"Don't you believe me?" she asked.

"No."

"May I turn into a dog if I'm lying to you. I'm telling you, I never want to go back."

"Why not?"

"I'm sick of it, I can't stand that stagnant place. I like your kind of life, relaxed and free . . ."

"You make it sound so pleasant. I'll give you a piece of advice. Go back."

"Why?"

"Because there's not even the shadow of your gilt-edged life out here. Go back as fast as you can before you really have to starve."

"No, no! Don't look down on me."

"You mean you've made up your mind?"

"Of course I have."

I drummed on the cup with my fingers. "Where are you planning to go?"

"Anywhere'll do."

"How're you going to get there?"

She dipped her forefinger in the cup, drawing lines on the table. "I hadn't actually thought it out."

I picked up coins even when I pissed; it seemed I was in luck. Three days ago the thought of leaving this place hadn't even occurred to me. It was that southbound train that struck the chord, so that I end up having to sleep out in the open. . . . If a tree is moved it dies, if a man moves he lives. I mean, the good Lord had sent this precious object for me to enjoy for a while. Even if I went away, they still wouldn't be able to live in peace; the dignified chief's daughter abducted. . . . Ha ha, it was a scene from a play.

"About this business . . . I could be of some help," I said.

"Bai Hua, you're great, I knew you could help . . ."

"Listen. Wait for me at eleven o'clock tonight at the East Station gate. I've got something to do first. I'll see you tonight."

At the waiting room door of the West Station, a few pedlars squatted at the foot of the wall, listlessly crying their wares. An old blind man tapped the concrete with his stick, slowly dragging past me. Manzi, his face covered by a battered straw hat, was dozing under the wall, snoring.

I knocked his hat off. "Wake up."

"Hell, who's that? Oh, Boss." He yawned, straightened his back, collected his straw hat, and fanned himself with it. "This damned weather's suffocating."

"Wait for me at ten o'clock tonight at the shop door," I muttered under my breath.

"How come the day's been put forward?"

"Looks like it'll rain tonight; also, I'm planning to leave here tonight . . ."

"How long'll you be gone?"

"Maybe a few years, maybe a lifetime."

"I'll go with you, Boss."

"No." I paused, then went on in a leisurely manner. "When I've gone, all the family property goes to you."

"Even Number Four?"

"That's right."

Manzi's little eyeballs shone. "Thanks a lot, Boss!"

With a squeal, a green sedan drew up, the grille opened, and the car drove in.

"Whose car?" I asked.

"Lin Dongping, Chief Lin, huh!" Manzi spat in the direction of the car and made an obscene gesture. "Last time you stirred up a hornet's nest for him. He still hasn't settled that account with you."

"I have to settle with him first."

(Yang Xun)

Uncle Lin and I smoked in silence on the platform.

The wind slowly dragged the dark clouds away. Scraps of paper swirled about with the dust, fluttering down the long platform. This city had suddenly become quite unfamiliar, as if the past was being kept at a distance by this high wall. Like a traveler just passing through I would walk onto the platform, smoke a cigarette, breathe in a mouthful of fresh air, then at the urging of the whistle and the bell climb once again into the carriage.

The loudspeaker crackled with static and blared out that special soporific female broadcaster's voice. A train pulled into the station. With the puffing of the engine the stepladders at the carriage doors were let down with a bang one by one. The passengers boarding and alighting clamored and shouted, crowding into a single mass.

"It's too noisy here, let's sit inside the car for a while," said Uncle Lin.

I scanned the platform and nodded abstractedly.

"Who are you still waiting for?"

"No one." I did not know if I were answering him or myself.

We sat in the back seat of the car.

"Old Wu," said Uncle Lin, "you go, I'll drive myself back."

Fat Wu grunted a reply, took off his gloves, picked up his bag, and waddled off, carrying his tea mug and whistling a tune.

"Xun, I understand your feelings." Uncle Lin broke the silence.

"Understanding carries no obligation, it doesn't cost you anything."

"Cost."

I turned my gaze out the window.

"Did you send the family a telegram?"

"No."

"You should have let your mother know in advance."

"There's no need."

"You're too selfish."

I turned round. "That's right, it's inherited from you people."

"We're not like that at all."

"That's even sadder."

"Why?"

"You're not qualified to be model bureaucrats."

"Xun, now you're taking liberties."

"I'm sorry. I really don't wish to quarrel with you . . ."

Suddenly, a familiar figure came dashing along the platform, peering in every window. I threw open the car door. "Xiao Ling—"

She stopped, turned round slowly, and stood there. I hesitated a moment, then rushed toward her. "I'm late," she said.

"No, Xiao Ling . . ."

She drew the blue notebook from her bag. "Take it, I promised. Wait till the train goes to read it."

I took the book without a word, clutching it tightly as if afraid the wind might blow it away.

The loudspeaker rang out: ". . . the train will depart immediately, passengers please board . . ."

"Xiao Ling, I . . ."

"Don't say anything, all right?"

We held one another's gaze silently. She frowned, and on the bridge of her nose several faint lines appeared. Whatever it was that dissolved in my mind, the process was so sudden it was far more than I could cope with.

"You'd better board," Uncle Lin said behind me.

I stepped aside. "May I introduce you; Uncle Lin, Xiao Ling . . ."

Xiao Ling unaffectedly held out her hand. "How do you do."

Uncle Lin wiped his hand awkwardly on his trousers and shook her hand. "Er, we should have met earlier."

"It's not too late now, is it?"

"No, no, it's not too late."

The bell rang.

I climbed onto the carriage steps and held out my hand to her. "I'll be seeing you."

"What did you say?"

"I'll be seeing you, Xiao Ling."

"Say it once more, please."

"I'll see you, I shall come back!"

She sorrowfully closed her eyes. "I'll see you."

A sudden clang, and the train slowly began to move off. Her chin quivered, and she turned fiercely away.

"Xiao Ling—"

She turned, her face white, her expression blank. She raised her arm, and her sleeve slid down. That slender arm floated before the crowd, floated before the receding city.

(Lin Dongping)

My vision blurred: green signal lights, dark clouds dyed red in the evening light, the dim black outlines of buildings and that ribbon of never-dispelled smog all kneaded together.

The girl lowered her arm and stood there dejectedly.

"Miss Xiao, let me give you a lift."

"Please don't worry."

"It's no trouble, I'll take you back to the factory."

"My contract's already been terminated by the factory."

"What? That's impossible," I stammered. "I'll ring them immediately . . ."

"Reverse your own decision?" She shook her head. "I know all about it. But why do you still wish to avoid reality at a time like this? Really, from your point of view, you did quite the right thing."

"Young people's emotional ups and downs are temporary,

they come and go like waves."

"Have you experienced this temporariness, Uncle Lin?"

"We've undergone many painful experiences."

"So you use these experiences to teach young people a lesson, to tell them they too are doomed to failure, isn't that so?"

"I don't want to see tragedy re-enacted."

"Tragedy can never be re-enacted. Only some of the players in the tragedy repeat themselves. They believe in the legitimacy of their role in the tragedy."

"Are you referring to me?"

"What I mean is, do you believe in this legitimacy?"

"Xiao Ling, I did it for your own good."

"When we were small and went to the pictures, adults always told us the difference between good and bad. But I don't know what meaning such words have today."

I looked at my watch.

"I'm sorry, I've delayed you," she said.

"Not at all, I like to chat like this. And now, what do you plan to do?"

"Go back to the village."

"I can arrange other work for you."

"That kind of charity is the last thing I'd accept."

"You're too obstinate."

"We must act out our own roles to the end."

"You believe in your own legitimacy too?"

"Yes, I believe the world won't go on like this forever. Perhaps that's the difference between us."

"You're still young."

She gave a little smile. "So this world seems too old. Goodbye, Uncle Lin."

"Goodbye."

She walked toward the exit, the wind wrapping her clothes tightly round her and blowing her hair about. She vanished into the twilight haze.

What had I gone and done? So the girl had been sacked from the factory; how would she manage now, I wondered? But why should I be held responsible? I was only responsible for my son; surely that was right. And even if someone could be held responsible, it was a matter of the factory, Miss Zhang, or the power of convention. I had said nothing. I hadn't even dropped a hint. No, it was not my responsibility. Where was she going now, I wondered? She wouldn't be contemplating suicide, would she? Perhaps I should run after her and comfort her. No, it was not my responsibility. This generation, it was so hard to know what was in their minds, what they were thinking, what direction they were going in . . .

I started the engine and leaned my head against the steering wheel, listening to the regular beat of the engine. After a long time, I stepped on the accelerator, and the car turned into the main street. Darkness fell. The wind blew grit against the car window. The dim shadows of people and trees flashed past. A green light . . . someone stretched out a hand to block the car. I stepped on the brake—it was Su Yumei.

"Oh, this wind's terrible." She pressed down a corner of her pink blouse. "Can you give me a lift?"

I opened the front door. "Where are you going?"

"Anywhere's fine." She got in, brushing off the dust. Then

she winked at me and wiped the dashboard with her finger. "What's upsetting you?"

I let out the clutch fiercely and the car shot forward. She fell back against the seat, was startled for a moment, then burst into a cackling laugh. "I like you this way, like a bandit . . ."

The steering wheel spun in a circle. The car made a turn in the square and sped toward the city gate. Lightning streaked across the car, and raindrops came slanting down like splinters. The scene before my eyes went gray and dim, so I switched on the wind-shield wipers.

Before that thin weak girl I appeared so hypocritical and immoral; how had all this begun? And in the instant she disappeared, why did I feel she was so like Ruohong, Ruohong when she was young, especially that reproachful gaze. These waves of emotion may only be temporary, but their aftermath was too ghastly to contemplate. That line of scratch marks on Chen Zijian's livid cheek. Our underground Party district secretary; why did I always think of him in this way? There was something unforgettable about his appearance; yet it wasn't his appearance, but his words that drove like nails into my mind: "How dare you have such an improper relationship with Comrade Ruohong, her husband is a leading comrade in one of the liberated areas . . . the Party has decided to put you on good behavior, you are to leave here immediately . . ." One's memories were sometimes frighteningly clear. In the clump of trees by the riverside a boy appeared suddenly, carrying a tattered sack, a branch in his hand, his surprised face betraying a sly smile. From behind, the moonlight shone on a patch on his shoulder, covered all over with stitches. In fact I hadn't seen his face clearly; it was only from the flash of his white teeth that I felt he smiled, the smile of a child who has spied out a secret for the first time. He guessed what we were doing in this quiet, secluded place. By that time, Ruohong had already got dressed and was leaning very close to me, sobbing silently. Yes, that was our last parting. Although seven years later we met again in Beijing, it wasn't the old Ruohong at all, and Xun had grown tall too . . .

"Stop! Stop!" cried a voice.

With a whoosh, a little tree scraped against the body of the car and flew past. Only then did I realize that the car had just left the road and was bumping violently along a ditch in the fields, the speedometer needle jumping back and forth. I slammed on the brake; the car shuddered and came to a halt. What a narrow escape! There was a deep canal in front of us.

"Have you gone mad!" Su Yumei, her eyes wide and her fists clenched, looked as if she might pounce on me at any moment. "Back the car up!"

The wheels spun in midair. At last we managed to reverse. Clods of earth were flung up and fell into the invisible canal. The car skidded round and turned onto the road.

It had stopped raining and the street was deserted. Under the dim streetlights, a few boys were playing barefoot in the water. They chased after the car for a while, shouting in queer voices.

"Take me home," said Miss Su, still full of indignation.

"Where do you live?"

"75 People's Road East."

Where did I seem to have seen that address before? The workers and staff register, the trade union register . . . I couldn't remember.

She nudged me with her elbow. "This is it, just at the little gate ahead." The car stopped. She breathed a sigh of relief and smoothed her hair. "Do come in for a while."

"It's not too late?"

Without a word, she opened the door and jumped out of the car. I hesitated a moment, then locked the car. As I got out I stepped in a puddle and my shoe filled with water. The lights in the courtyard were out. She pulled a bunch of keys out of her handbag and walked ahead.

"Where have you been?" Suddenly a figure emerged from under the eaves.

"Oh! You gave me a fright." Miss Su took a step backward. "I thought you wouldn't come because of the rain."

"Who's that behind you?"

"Oh, I forgot to introduce you. Do get acquainted." Miss Su jumped aside, laughing shrilly.

Wang Defa loomed close to me, strands of wet hair sticking to his forehead.

I shuddered and turned back.

(Xiao Ling)

The ticket-booth window was shut. A girl with her hair in a bun was standing with her back to it, cracking melon seeds and chatting to a young fellow in a red jersey. Her shoulders shook, showing that she was laughing.

I tapped on the glass.

The boy pointed at the window, and the girl turned round, then threw open the window and pulled a face. "What is it?"

"A ticket to Floodvalley Village."

"Didn't you see the sign outside?!" She snorted indignantly, banging the window shut.

I looked at the sign: "Due to heavy rain, no buses for the next two days." At the end a squat full-stop was drawn, with a moist melon seed stuck near it.

In the waiting room, a few peasants were crowded in a knot, pulling at their pipes and gossiping amongst themselves. The rain pattered slowly down outside the door, like a flapping gray curtain. I walked down the steps and sheltered under the eaves, staring at the outlines of the rows of buses in the parking lot. A blinding light flashed behind them, lighting up the squares of each window, like a naughty child playing with a flashlight.

I drew the glass frame from my bag, and Jingjing smiled sweetly at me. Suddenly a big teardrop rolled down her face—it was only a splash of rain. I rubbed it out with my thumb. No, I must go back, go back immediately, even if I had to walk. Oh, my poor child.

All of a sudden someone dodged under the eaves and dropped a bag on the ground. There was the rattle of jangling coins. He took off his coat, wrung it out hard, and glanced at me.

"Hey, what are you gawking at? Think I'm a performing monkey?"

I said nothing.

"What's up, sister?"

"Bai Hua."

His mouth fell open in astonishment, and he moved closer, trailing his screwed-up coat on the ground like a wet stick.

"What, don't you recognize me?" I asked.

"Xiao Ling, you're a real tease. You here alone?"

"Yes, I'm alone."

"Keeping out of the rain?"

"And the wind, and the thunder."

"Huh, this filthy weather."

"You don't like it?"

"That's how it is in my business: the lights go out, it's pitch-black, the wind blows, and the rain pelts down. It's not a matter of liking it or not."

"Do you like the sunshine?"

"No, we can do without it, it gives you a headache."

"Do you like wind?"

"It's not bad, except in the middle of winter; otherwise it slides along nicely, nice and easy."

"Do you like this city?"

"You've hit the nail on the head. I'm just about to leave this rotten place that even pigs and dogs wouldn't touch."

"Where are you going?"

"Nowhere in particular. The world's a big place."

It was true, it was so large, one person's sorrow and unhappiness counted as nothing.

He pulled out his pocketwatch and tapped the face. "Time's up."

"All right, goodbye."

Bai Hua contemplated me in silence. Suddenly he caught hold of my hands tightly.

"Not so hard, Bai Hua, are you mad?"

"Let me say something."

"All right, say it."

"Xiao Ling, in this life I've met a lot of women, but I've never met one like you . . . just tell me this, do you like me?"

I thought for a while. "It's like what you said about liking the wind; not bad except in the middle of the winter . . ."

"But it's summer now."

"Don't you fell the coldness in your heart?"

He swallowed and seemed about to say something. But then he let go my hands, picked up his bag and coat, and turned and staggered away, his shadow lengthening under the lights.

A bat cried sharply, wheeling in the air. The rain had stopped. I too must be on my way.

11

(Yang Xun)

I closed the blue notebook and lit a cigarette. The trickles of rain drew fine, haphazard lines on the windowpane. Lights floated in the distance. Clumps of weeds by the roadbed were shot into reflection by lights from the window, flashed, and were gone.

I blew a thick stream of smoke onto the windowpane, opened the book again, and went on reading.

(Xiao Ling)

On the left was a drop of unfathomable depth. The trees beside it rustled in the rain, their branches rocking gently. The lights of the distant city were already hidden by the mountains.

The road, the road.

(Lin Dongping)

I walked out of the garage, following the crazy paving, and climbed the stairs. It was very quiet along the verandah, with a faint radiance cast by the wall lamp.

I paused before Yuanyuan's bedroom, listening, then knocked. "Are you asleep, Yuanyuan?"

Not a sound. I turned the knob and switched on the light—the bed was empty. The room was a mess. The drawers were half open, a pair of trousers hanging out. On the desk a teacup held a note in place: "Papa, I've gone away. I may never come back!"

(Lin Yuanyuan)

The stones crunched underfoot. The goods carriages stood on the side, like headless, tailless tin cans.

"When did you leave home?"

"I've never had a home," Bai Hua said.

"So how were you born?"

"Stop jabbering!"

"Why so fierce? Huh, I was just asking."

He stopped at an open carriage. "Get up."

I climbed up with difficulty. Hey, how warm it was. There were still piles of hay in the corners. I peeled off my plastic raincoat. "Do we sleep here?"

"Breathe another word and I'll throttle you!"

(Yang Xun)

I closed the book, picked up my bag, and walked to the compartment door. The buffers screeched loudly, and the train came to a halt at a little station. I climbed down the steps out into the cool breeze and approached the lit-up duty office. In the doorway stood a middle-aged man, all skin and bone.

"When does the next southbound train go through here?" I asked.

"In forty minutes."

(Xiao Ling)

A series of strange rumblings rolled out. I still hadn't realized what had happened when the raging mountain torrent surged over everything. I put out my hand to clutch at a sapling by the edge of the road, tumbling rocks thundered past and struck my ankle and leg. Arrows of intense pain.

Suddenly the mud under my feet gave way. My body twisted and fell . . .

(Bai Hua)

With a clank, the body of the train shuddered. A moment later, a long blast of the whistle.

"Get down!" I said.

"Me?"

"Go home, go back to your father's."

"What, what's the idea, cheating me?!" she said, biting her lip.

"Get down!" I forced her to the door.

"Bastard!" she finished, turned, and jumped down.

The train slowly started to move.

(Yang Xun)

I got out of the carriage. The hammers of the train maintenance crew rang out, all the louder on this rainy night. The mercury lamps were netted by the sheets of rain and transformed into dim halos.

The old ticket-collector yawned by the gate at the barrier, his rubber raincoat glistening.

(Xiao Ling)

I awakened, a little blade of grass lightly brushing my cheek. Dense fog floated across the steep cliffs above my head. Then the sky cleared, and the moon rose.

Suddenly, a girl the image of me drifted forward, and vanished in the tide of golden light . . .

Note on Sources

1. "Waves". The first draft of "Bodong" 波動 is dated November 1974. It was substantially revised in April-June 1976, and again in April 1979. The latter version was published in *Jintian* 今天 (Today), Nos. 4–6 (June–October 1979): 31–71; 1–13, 29–48; 21–56, and issued as a separate pamphlet; both *Jintian* versions appeared under the penname Ai Shan 艾珊. "Bodong" was reprinted with minor revisions in *Changjiang wenxue congkan* 長江文學叢刊 (Yangtze River literary compendium), No. 1 (February) 1981: 21–76, under the name Zhao Zhenkai 趙振開. The work has been slightly revised by the author for this edition. An earlier incomplete translation of "Waves" first appeared in *Renditions* 19/20, 1983.
2. "In the Ruins". "Zai feixu shang" 在廢墟上 was written in 1978 and first published in *Jintian*, No. 1 (23 December 1978): 3–10, under the penname Shi Mo 石默. It was reprinted in *Lasahe* 拉薩河 (Lhasa River), No. 2 (April) 1985, under the name Zhao Zhenkai.
3. "The Homecoming Stranger". "Guilaide moshengren" 歸來的陌生人 was written in 1979 and first published in *Jintian*, No. 2 (February 1979): 21–31, under the penname Shi Mo. A slightly revised version was published in *Huacheng zengkan* 花城增刊 (Flower City supplement), No. 1, *Xiaoshuo* 小說 (Fiction) (January 1981), under the name Zhao Zhenkai, and reprinted in Shu Dayuan 舒大沅, ed., *Liushui wanwan* 流水潺潺 (Meandering streams) (Canton: Huacheng Chubanshe 花城出版社, 1981), pp. 37–59.
4. "Melody". "Xuanlü" 旋律 was written in 1980 and first published in *Jintian*, No. 7 (1980), under the penname Ai Shan. It was reprinted in *Qingchun* 青春 (Youth), No. 1 (January) 1981: 18–23, under the same penname.
5. "Moon on the Manuscript". "Gaozhishangde yueliang" 稿紙上的月亮 was written in 1980 and first published in *Jintian*, No. 9 (1980): 29–38, under the penname Shi Mo. It was reprinted with minor revisions in *Shouhuo* 收穫 (Harvest), No. 5 (September) 1981, under the name Zhao Zhenkai. English translation first appeared in *Renditions* 19/20, 1983.
6. "Intersection". "Jiaochadian" 交叉點 was written in 1981 and first pub-

lished in *Xiaoshuo lin* 小說林 (Fiction grove), No. 2 (February) 1982: 10–12, under the name Zhao Zhenkai.

7. "13 Happiness Street". "Xingfu dajie shisan hao" 幸福大街十三號 was written in 1980 and first published in *Shanxi wenxue* 山西文學 (Shanxi literature), No. 6 (June) 1985, under the penname Bei Dao; slightly revised by the author for this edition.

FURTHER REFERENCES

Bei Dao, *Notes from the City of the Sun: Poems.* Translated and edited by Bonnie S. McDougall. Ithaca: Cornell University China-Japan Program, 1983.

Bonnie S. McDougall, "Zhao Zhenkai's Fiction: A Study in Cultural Alienation". *Modern Chinese Literature*, I.1 (September 1984).

Bonnie S. McDougall, "Bei Dao's Poetry: Revelation and Communication". *Modern Chinese Literature*, I.2 (May 1985).

Wolfgang Kubin, "A Literary Manifestation of the Peking Springtime: Shi Mo's *The Stranger's Homecoming*". In Kubin, ed., *Die Jagd nach dem Tiger. Sechs Versuche zur modernen chinesischen Literatur. The Hunt for the Tiger. Six Approaches to Modern Chinese Literature.* Bochum: Studienverlag Dr. N. Brockmeyer, 1984.

New Directions Paperbooks—A Partial Listing

Walter Abish, *How German Is It*. NDP508.
John Allman, *Curve Away from Stillness*. NDP667.
Wayne Andrews, *The Surrealist Parade*. NDP689.
Voltaire. NDP519.
David Antin, *Tuning*. NDP570.
G. Apollinaire, *Selected Writings*.† NDP310.
Jimmy S. Baca, *Martín & Meditations*.NDP648.
Black Mesa Poems. NDP676.
Djuna Barnes, *Nightwood*. NDP98.
H.E. Bates, *Elephant's Nest . . .* NDP669.
A Month by the Lake. NDP645.
A Party for the Girls, NDP653.
Charles Baudelaire, *Flowers of Evil*. †NDP684.
Paris Spleen. NDP294.
Selected Flowers of Evil. †NDP71.
Bei Dao, *The August Sleepwalker*. NDP692.
Waves. NDP693.
Gottfried Benn, *Primal Vision*. NDP322.
Carmel Bird, *Woodpecker Point*, NDP662.
R.P. Blackmur, *Studies in Henry James*, NDP552.
Wolfgang Borchert, *The Man Outside*. NDP319.
Johan Borgen, *Lillelord*. NDP531.
Jorge Luis Borges, *Labyrinths*. NDP186.
Seven Nights. NDP576.
Kay Boyle, *Life Being the Best*. NDP654.
Death of a Man. NDP670.
Buddha, *The Dhammapada*. NDP188.
M. Bulgakov, *Flight & Bliss*. NDP593.
The Life of M. de Moliere. NDP601.
Frederick Busch, *Domestic Particulars*. NDP413.
Ernesto Cardenal, *Zero Hour*. NDP502.
Joyce Cary, *Mr. Johnson*. NDP657.
Second Trilogy: *Prisoner of Grace*. NDP606; *Except The Lord*. NDP607; *Not Honour More*. NDP608.
Hayden Carruth, *Asphalt Georgics*. NDP591.
Tell Me Again. . . . NDP677.
Louis-Ferdinand Céline,
Death on the Installment Plan. NDP330.
Journey to the End of the Night. NDP542.
Jean Cocteau, *The Holy Terrors*. NDP212.
Maurice Collis, *The Land of the Great Image*. NDP612.
Cid Corman, *Sun Rock Man*. NDP318.
Gregory Corso, *Long Live Man*. NDP127.
The Happy Birthday of Death. NDP86.
Robert Creeley, *Memory Gardens*. NDP613.
Windows. NDP687.
H.D. *Collected Poems*. NDP611.
HERmione. NDP526.
Selected Poems. NDP658.
Tribute to Freud. NDP572.
Edward Dahlberg, *Because I Was Flesh*. NDP227.
Alain Daniélou, *The Way to the Labyrinth*. NDP634.
Osamu Dazai, *The Setting Sun*. NDP258.
No Longer Human. NDP357.
Mme. de Lafayette, *The Princess of Cleves*. NDP660.
Robert Duncan, *Ground Work*. NDP571.
Ground Work II: In the Dark, NDP647.
E. Dujardin, *We'll to The Woods No More*. NDP682.
Richard Eberhart, *The Long Reach*. NDP565.
Wm. Empson, *7 Types of Ambiguity*. NDP204.
Shusaku Endo, *Stained Glass Elegies*. NDP699.
Wm. Everson, *The Residual Years*. NDP263.
Gavin Ewart, *Selected Poems*. NDP655
Lawrence Ferlinghetti, *Endless Life*. NDP516.
A Coney Island of the Mind. NDP74.
European Poems & Transitions. NDP582
Starting from San Francisco. NDP220.
Wild Dreams of a New Beginning. NDP663.
Ronald Firbank, *Five Novels*. NDP581.
Three More Novels. NDP614.
F. Scott Fitzgerald, *The Crack-up*. NDP54.
Gustave Flaubert, *Dictionary*. NDP230.
Gandhi, *Gandhi on Non-Violence*. NDP197.
Gary, Romain, *Promise at Dawn*. NDP635.
The Life Before Us ("Madame Rosa"). NDP604.
Goethe, *Faust*, Part I. NDP70.
Henry Green, *Back*. NDP517
Allen Grossman, *The Bright Nails. . . .* NDP615.
Martin Grzimek, *Heartstop*. NDP583.
Guigonnat, Henri, *Daemon in Lithuania*. NDP592.
Lars Gustafsson, *The Death of a Beekeeper*. NDP523.
Sigismund. NDP584.
The Stillness of the World Before Bach: New Sel. Poems. NDP656.
John Hawkes, *Blood Oranges*. NDP338.
The Cannibal. NDP123.
Humors of Blood & Skin. NDP577.
Second Skin. NDP146.
Samuel Hazo, *To Paris*. NDP512.
William Herrick, *Love and Terror*. NDP538.
That's Life. NDP596.
Herman Hesse, *Siddhartha*. NDP65.
Paul Hoover, *The Novel*. NDP706.
Vicente Huidobro, *Selected Poetry*. NDP520.
C. Isherwood, *The Berlin Stories*. NDP134.
Ledo Ivo, *Snake's Nest*. NDP521.
Gustav Janouch, *Conversations with Kafka*. NDP313.
Alfred Jarry, *Ubu Roi*. NDP105.
Robinson Jeffers, *Cawdor and Medea*. NDP293.
B.S. Johnson, *Albert Angelo*. NDP628.
House Mother Normal. NDP617.
James Joyce, *Stephen Hero*. NDP133.
Franz Kafka, *Amerika*. NDP117.
Bob Kaufman, *The Ancient Rain*. NDP514.
H. von Kleist, *Prince Friedrich*. NDP462.
Elaine Kraf, *The Princess of 72nd Street*. NDP494.
Shimpei Kusano, *Asking Myself. . . .* NDP566.
Jules Laforgue, *Moral Tales*. NDP594.
P. Lal, *Great Sanskrit Plays*. NDP142.
Tommaso Landolfi, *Gogol's Wife*. NDP155.
"Language" Poetries: An Anthology, NDP630.
Lautréamont, *Maldoror*. NDP207.
Irving Layton, *Selected Poems*. NDP431.
Christine Lehner, *Expecting*. NDP544.
Siegfried Lenz, *The German Lesson*. NDP618.
Denise Levertov, *Breathing the Water*. NDP640.
Candles in Babylon. NDP533.
Collected Earlier. NDP475.
A Door in the Hive. NDP685.
Light Up The Cave. NDP525.
Poems 1960-1967. NDP549.
Poems 1968-1972. NDP629.
Harry Levin, *James Joyce*. NDP87.
Memories of the Moderns. NDP539.
Enrique Lihn, *The Dark Room*.† NDP542.
Clarice Lispector, *Soulstorm*. NDP671.
Near to the Wild Heart. NDP698.
Garciá Lorca, *Five Plays*. NDP232
The Public & Play Without a Title. NDP561.
Selected Poems.† NDP114
Three Tragedies. NDP52.
Francisco G. Lorca, *In The Green Morning*. NDP610.
Michael McClure, *Fragments of Perseus*. NDP554.
Selected Poems. NDP599.
Carson McCullers, *The Member of the Wedding*. (Playscript) NDP153.
Stéphane Mallarme,† *Selected Poetry and Prose*. NDP529.
Thomas Merton, *Asian Journal*. NDP394.
New Seeds of Contemplation. ND337.
Selected Poems. NDP85.
Thomas Merton in Alaska. NDP652.
The Way of Chuang Tzu. NDP276.
The Wisdom of the Desert. NDP295.
Zen and the Birds of Appetite. NDP261.
Henri Michaux, *A Barbarian in Asia*. NDP622.
Selected Writings. NDP264.
Henry Miller, *The Air-Conditioned Nightmare*. NDP302.
Big Sur & The Oranges. NDP161.
The Colossus of Maroussi. NDP75.
From Your Capricorn Friend. NDP568.
The Smile at the Foot of the Ladder. NDP386.
Stand Still Like the Hummingbird. NDP236.
The Time of the Assassins. NDP115.
Y. Mishima, *Confessions of a Mask*. NDP253.
Death in Midsummer. NDP215.

For complete listing request free catalog from New Directions, 80 Eighth Avenue, New York 10011

†Bilingual

Frédéric Mistral, *The Memoirs*. NDP632.
Eugenio Montale, *It Depends*.† NDP507.
Selected Poems.† NDP193.
Paul Morand, *Fancy Goods / Open All Night*. NDP567.
Vladimir Nabokov, *Nikolai Gogol*. NDP78.
Laughter in the Dark. NDP470.
The Real Life of Sebastian Knight. NDP432.
P. Neruda, *The Captain's Verses*.† NDP345.
Residence on Earth.† NDP340.
New Directions in Prose & Poetry (Anthology). Available from #50 forward to #54.
Robert Nichols, *Arrival*. NDP437.
Exile. NDP485. *Garh City*. NDP450.
Harditts in Sawna. NDP470.
J. F. Nims, *The Six-Cornered Snowflake*. NDP700.
Charles Olson, *Selected Writings*. NDP231.
Toby Olson, *The Life of Jesus*. NDP417.
Seaview. NDP532.
George Oppen, *Collected Poems*. NDP418.
István Örkeny, *The Flower Show / The Toth Family*. NDP536.
Wilfred Owen, *Collected Poems*. NDP210.
José Emilio Pacheco, *Battles in the Desert*. NDP637.
Selected Poems.† NDP638.
Nicanor Parra, *Antipoems: New & Selected*. NDP603.
Boris Pasternak, *Safe Conduct*. NDP77.
Kenneth Patchen, *Aflame and Afun*. NDP292.
Because It Is. NDP83.
Collected Poems. NDP284.
Selected Poems. NDP160.
Octavio Paz, *Configurations*.† NDP303.
A Draft of Shadows.† NDP489.
Eagle or Sun?† NDP422.
Selected Poems. NDP574.
A Tree Within.† NDP661.
St. John Perse, *Selected Poems*.† NDP545.
J. A. Porter, *Eelgrass*. NDP438.
Ezra Pound, *ABC of Reading*. NDP89.
Confucius. NDP285.
Confucius to Cummings. (Anth.) NDP126.
A Draft of XXX Cantos. NDP690.
Elektra. NDP683.
Gaudier Brzeska. NDP372.
Guide to Kulchur. NDP257.
Literary Essays. NDP250.
Selected Cantos. NDP304.
Selected Letters 1907-1941. NDP317.
Selected Poems. NDP66.
The Spirit of Romance. NDP266.
Translations.† (Enlarged Edition) NDP145.
Raymond Queneau, *The Blue Flowers*. NDP595.
Exercises in Style. NDP513.
The Flight of Icarus. NDP358.
Mary de Rachewiltz, *Ezra Pound*. NDP405.
Raja Rao, *Kanthapura*. NDP224.
Herbert Read, *The Green Child*. NDP208.
P. Reverdy, *Selected Poems*.† NDP346.
Kenneth Rexroth, *Classics Revisited*. NDP621.
More Classics Revisited. NDP668.
100 More Poems from the Chinese. NDP308.
100 More Poems from the Japanese.† NDP420.
100 Poems from the Chinese. NDP192.
100 Poems from the Japanese.† NDP147.
Selected Poems. NDP581.
Women Poets of China. NDP528.
Women Poets of Japan. NDP527.
World Outside the Window, Sel. Essays. NDP639.
Rainer Maria Rilke, *Poems from The Book of Hours*. NDP408.
Possibility of Being. (Poems). NDP436.
Where Silence Reigns. (Prose). NDP464.
Arthur Rimbaud, *Illuminations*.† NDP56.
Season in Hell & Drunken Boat.† NDP97.
Edouard Roditi, *Delights of Turkey*. NDP445.
Oscar Wilde. NDP624.
Jerome Rothenberg, *Khurbn*. NDP679.
New Selected Poems. NDP625.
Nayantara Sahgal, *Rich Like Us*. NDP665.
Ihara Saikaku, *The Life of an Amorous Woman*. NDP270.
St. John of the Cross, *Poems*.† NDP341.
William Saroyan, *Madness in the Family*. NDP691.
Jean-Paul Sartre, *Nausea*. NDP82.
The Wall (Intimacy). NDP272.
Peter Dale Scott, *Coming to Jakarta*. NDP672.
Delmore Schwartz, *Selected Poems*. NDP241.
The Ego Is Always at the Wheel. NDP641.
In Dreams Begin Responsibilities. NDP454.
Last & Lost Poems. NDP673.
Shattan, *Manimekhalai*. NDP674.
Stevie Smith, *Collected Poems*. NDP562.
New Selected Poems. NDP659.
Some Are More Human. . . . NDP680.
Gary Snyder, *The Back Country*. NDP249.
The Real Work. NDP499.
Regarding Wave. NDP306.
Turtle Island. NDP381.
G. Sobin, *Voyaging Portraits*. NDP651.
Enid Starkie, *Rimbaud*. NDP254.
Robert Steiner, *Bathers*. NDP495.
Antonio Tabucchi, *Letter from Casablanca*. NDP620.
Little Misunderstandings. . . . NDP681.
Dylan Thomas, *Adventures in the Skin Trade*. NDP183.
A Child's Christmas in Wales. NDP181.
Collected Poems 1934-1952. NDP316.
Collected Stories. NDP626.
Portrait of the Artist as a Young Dog. NDP51.
Quite Early One Morning. NDP90.
Under Milk Wood. NDP73.
Tian Wen: A Chinese Book of Origins. NDP624.
Uwe Timm, *The Snake Tree*. NDP686.
Niccolo Tucci, *The Rain Came Last*. NDP688.
Tu Fu, *Selected Poems*. NDP675.
Lionel Trilling, *E. M. Forster*. NDP189.
Martin Turnell, *Baudelaire*. NDP336.
Paul Valéry, *Selected Writings*.† NDP184.
Elio Vittorini, *A Vittorini Omnibus*. NDP366.
Rosmarie Waldrop, *The Reproduction of Profiles*. NDP649.
Robert Penn Warren, *At Heaven's Gate*. NDP588.
Vernon Watkins, *Selected Poems*. NDP221.
Eliot Weinberger, *Works on Paper*. NDP627.
Nathanael West, *Miss Lonelyhearts & Day of the Locust*. NDP125.
J. Wheelwright, *Collected Poems*. NDP544.
Tennessee Williams, *Camino Real*. NDP301.
Cat on a Hot Tin Roof. NDP398.
Clothes for a Summer Hotel. NDP556.
The Glass Menagerie. NDP218.
Hard Candy. NDP225.
In the Winter of Cities. NDP154.
A Lovely Sunday for Creve Coeur. NDP497.
One Arm & Other Stories. NDP237.
Red Devil Battery Sign. NDP650.
A Streetcar Named Desire. NDP501.
Sweet Bird of Youth. NDP409.
Twenty-Seven Wagons Full of Cotton. NDP217.
Vieux Carre. NDP482.
William Carlos Williams,
The Autobiography. NDP223.
The Buildup. NDP259.
The Doctor Stories. NDP585.
Imaginations. NDP329.
In the American Grain. NDP53.
In the Money. NDP240.
Paterson. Complete. NDP152.
Pictures from Brueghel. NDP118.
Selected Poems (new ed.). NDP602.
White Mule. NDP226.
Yes, Mrs. Williams. NDP534.
Yvor Winters, *E. A. Robinson*. NDP326.
Wisdom Books: *Early Buddhists*. NDP444; *Spanish Mystics*. NDP442; *St. Francis*. NDP477; *Taoists*. NDP509; *Wisdom of the Desert*. NDP295; *Zen Masters*. NDP415.

For complete listing request free catalog from New Directions, 80 Eighth Avenue, New York 10011

†Bilingual